ISBN: 978-1-7330665-8-7

LEIGH ANDERS

A CLINIC IN SECOND CHANCES

SECOND IN THE MOURNING DOVE SERIES

This book is dedicated to strong women everywhere who fight back against injustice, either in the work place or in their personal lives, while melding family and career. The results may not always be perfect—fearlessly trying is the point.

To everyone who helped bring this story to life. You know who you are and I will always be grateful for your help.

CHAPTER ONE

Fired! Kicked to the curb! Canned!

Use any term you like—Cass Jordan was still out of a job.

Had she known how things would play out this morning, she would've stayed in bed. Or maybe *under* the bed, curled into a ball, pillow over her head, preparing for a crash landing.

But loyal, dependable Cass showed up for work, duty bound to think first of her job and the people who counted on her. The crash landing turned into something more like a face-plant, with her being the only casualty—now her career was in freefall.

The chaotic turn her life had taken began early Saturday morning, spiraled downward from there, and culminated in Fitzgerald Medical Center firing her. The board callously took away the career Cass had worked so hard to build over the past six years. All ties to her orderly and predictable life were instantly severed.

"Unemployed" was now noted alongside "fraudster" on her rap sheet.

Fitzgerald Medical had made a huge mistake; she was not the guilty party in the crime.

Cass stalked along the sidewalks of northeast Philadelphia, her angry thoughts like a hazy red curtain before her eyes. How could the board do this to her? Other people got fired, other people got arrested, but not Cassandra Winslow Jordan. The golden girl from Westchester Prep Academy, the one voted Most Likely to Succeed, would never hit bottom! But sadly, here she was.

Mr. Blackwood, president of the board, tried to soften the blow with "We're going to have to let you go," but it all amounted to the same thing: she was *fired*. Cass wouldn't have been more surprised or insulted if he had yelled at her, calling her a thief and a liar or some other derogatory name.

Cass sighed heavily and shifted the cardboard box on her hip. A sign around her neck emblazoned with "Fired" wouldn't have advertised her unemployed status any more clearly than the cardboard box she carried, which was filled with personal odds and ends from her former office. Adding injury to insult, the sharp edges of the cardboard cut into her waist and ribs, tempting her to throw the detritus of the last six years into the first dumpster she passed. Her Excellence in Service award, presented just six months ago, would be the first item pitched on the trash heap.

Had she ever been this angry or humiliated? Maybe, once, when she was eleven years old and James Gardner III grabbed her Backstreet Boys backpack and dangled it out of reach, high over her head. He mocked her with what he thought was a clever nursery rhyme—"Crybaby Cassie, has a face like Lassie"— over and over in front of her classmates. Cass had been furious as well as embarrassed. As a tween, she was just becoming self-aware. She felt her body was underdeveloped, compared to her peers, and her gangly appendages were ugly. She avoided being the center of attention whenever possible.

But James pushed her too far that day. A well-placed double-fisted blow to his midsection got her backpack back and changed James's taunting voice into groans of pain. However, the suspension from Westchester Prep that followed horrified her socialite mother.

"Cassandra, properly bred young ladies don't behave in this manner," her mother had reprimanded her.

Cecilia was all about appearances. No doubt she'd be horrified once again when she learned that Cass's arrest had led to dismissal from her job.

As Cass grew through the "dreadful" tween years into the "horrible" teen years, she developed more self-confidence when dealing with people—even bullies. She never meekly accepted blame for things she didn't do, and she made that fact known—diplomatically, of course. Cass developed a penchant for one-liners and biting retorts in place of punches. Injustice of any kind raised her ire, and she still felt that way.

But now, Cass Jordan, defender of truth since childhood, was meekly slinking away like a stray dog who'd been caught rummaging in the neighbor's trash bin. Events far beyond her control had brought her fighting spirit to heel.

Cass was also practical. Mr. Blackwood's position wouldn't be changed by anything she said or did. By now, he'd probably removed her nameplate from the door. All evidence of Cass Jordan was instantly wiped away. She'd been a fool to think professional and loyal service to the clinic was enough to secure her employment.

"Ouch!" In frustration, Cass kicked at a stone on the sidewalk. She missed the stone completely and twisted her ankle in the process. The pain from the wayward kick added an exclamation point to an already painful morning.

The unraveling of Cass's professional and personal life had

started two weeks ago, when she became engulfed in a nightmare she hadn't anticipated. She could thank "Dear ole" Dad for that one.

The FBI had raided Kenneth Allen Jordan's north Philadelphia office and subsequently arrested him for running a Ponzi scheme and bilking investors out of millions of dollars. The judge denied his bail request because Kenneth was considered a flight risk. Her father was currently sitting in jail awaiting trial.

Cass wasn't part of the Ponzi scheme. She didn't even know anything about it until her father's arrest. When the news broke, she was worried about her father, not herself—until the FBI knocked on her door this past Saturday morning, and she was arrested. Two bank accounts were found under her name, each containing several million dollars. The Feds seized both accounts, along with her much-smaller personal bank account.

For hours after her arrest, Cass sat staring at the investigating agents, frozen like a mummy, nodding 'yes,' shaking her head 'no,' and answering their questions as truthfully as she could. As if repetition would make her confess, Agent Rogers, the lead agent, hammered her with the same questions over and over again, pressuring her to admit she was her father's co-conspirator and owner of the two illicit bank accounts.

The hours dragged on as the interrogation continued. The agents apparently didn't believe her—at first, anyway—because they didn't let up, kept grilling her, and threatened to lock her up for life.

"You're young. You don't want to spend the next fifty years in federal prison." Agent Rogers slammed the table with his fist. "Give us Kenneth Jordan, then maybe we can cut a deal."

"I don't know anything about a Ponzi scheme," Cass yelled back. She was tired, and her story was not going to change, no matter how long they held her. "I didn't open either of those bank accounts. I won't confess to something I didn't do. Go find someone else to harass."

"You're going to prison, Ms. Jordan. A pretty woman like you locked away for most of your life—such a tragedy! I hope you look good in orange," Agent Rogers threatened.

"Orange is the new black, Agent. Or haven't you heard?" Cass fired back. "But judging by your apparel, you don't keep up with fashion trends. Here's a tip—ill-fitting suits are out of style."

Mr. Anderson, Cass's attorney, gently nudged her into silence with his elbow. "What Ms. Jordan is trying to say is, she's employed, supports herself, and isn't involved in her father's business. Have you interviewed the bank manager yet?"

After that exchange, Agent Rogers lowered his voice to a more conciliatory tone—*wheedling*, is how Cass heard it—but he still kept up the same line of questioning.

Finally, an agent returned from questioning the bank manager and brought the security camera footage. The footage and bank manager's statement confirmed that Kenneth Jordan was the one who opened the accounts using Cass's name, but with his address. Any communication between the bank and the account holder went to Cass's father. He had entangled Cass in his crimes. Kenneth Jordan was better at scamming money than hiding it.

It was only after this revelation that Cass was freed from the clutches of federal investigators. That should have been the end of her part in the story—except the authorities still hadn't unfrozen her personal bank account. And then, the perp-walk in handcuffs from her apartment building following her arrest set off a whole new spectacle.

Kenneth Jordan's daughter's arrest was the weekend headline story on all the major TV news shows, online social media platforms, and print newspapers.

"*The apple doesn't fall far from the tree,*" screamed one headline.

"Jordan's daughter arrested! A ring of thieves, a conspiracy between father and daughter to defraud investors," TV banners proclaimed as the message scrolled across the TV screens in bright-red letters, promoting breaking news.

Cass spent Sunday, her first day of freedom, curled up on the sofa with headphones over her ears, hoping the music would drown out the screaming angry mob gathered outside her apartment building. She didn't have a place to hide or any avenue to rebut the media's portrait of her.

Yesterday morning, when she showed up for work at the clinic, hordes of bloodthirsty people—both reporters and those who never saw an angry mob they didn't want to join—filled the clinic's parking lot. The facts surrounding her arrest hadn't yet penetrated the perception that a wealthy person had criminally taken advantage of unsuspecting victims.

Cass doubted that any of her father's real victims were in the crowd, though they could have hired representatives from Harassers 'R' Us to do their dirty work for them. His real victims wouldn't bother leaving their penthouse apartments to harass her themselves.

As soon as she parked in the clinic's lot and exited her car, the mob surrounded her, yelling expletives and a wide range of angry insults.

"There's the bitch!"

"Die, rich bitch!"

"Arrest the bitch!"

Cass could still hear the taunts. Countless names were hurled at her. Some were words she'd never heard before, but with the vitriol in the speakers' voices, she could tell they definitely weren't flattering or in her defense.

Someone grabbed her briefcase and tried to wrestle it from her as she pushed her way through the mob. She managed to hang onto the shoulder strap—a small victory that saved her personal *data* while her *person* was angrily berated and pelted with acorns and any other objects, they found scattered around the parking lot. A paper cup filled with hot coffee narrowly missed hitting her in the face but left a dark stain on the front of her suit jacket. Other unknown substances were thrown as she dodged and wove her way through the crowd, finally making it to the employee entrance. A staff member held the door open, and she escaped inside. Cass quickly locked the door behind her, deadening the sounds of the mayhem outside, but the angry verbal threats still echoed in her head.

This morning, the mob was again waiting for her arrival in the parking lot. Unwilling to face them and subject herself to their threats again, Cass drove into the alley behind the clinic and parked her car. She entered the building through the delivery entrance, bypassing the angry mob at the front of the building.

Cass had barely set her briefcase down and stored her purse in her desk drawer when the president of the board, Mr. Blackwood, called, asking to see her in the conference room.

Mr. Blackwood wouldn't look at her as she walked in and took a seat. Instead, he fiddled with his wristwatch, then reshuffled a stack of papers in front of him. He cleared his throat a couple times before he spoke.

"It pains me greatly to say this, Cass, but I'm afraid we're going to have to let you go." He still wouldn't make eye contact with her.

"What? Why? I haven't done anything wrong," Cass protested. Of course, she knew what was behind this, but she couldn't believe Mr. Blackwood would blame her for any part of it. "My father is the guilty party, not me. My arrest never would have happened were it not for some overaggressive agents trying to make names for themselves. Don't hold me responsible for something I had no idea was going on. You have to know I wasn't involved."

"I do know, but all this publicity is damaging the clinic's reputation. The mob out front is interfering with our patients and intimidating the staff. They're blaming us for sheltering a criminal. They're not going to stop any time soon—as long as you work here."

"But—"

Mr. Blackwood raised a hand to silence her protest. "The full board had a meeting this morning. We all agree. This is best for the clinic and all concerned. We can't have someone who's accused of fraud in charge of our budgets. There have already been accusations on social media that you probably skimmed money from the clinic for personal benefit. That's mob hysteria, I know, but it will circulate through the media until it becomes fact."

"But… you know I'd never do that!" Where was fairness to her in the board's decision? "This is unfair! A mob that doesn't know anything about me can get me fired?"

"People are out for their pound of flesh—retribution for being scammed. You're just a convenient target, Cass. The majority of the people surrounding the clinic aren't even victims. Mob violence breeds more mob violence. They don't care whether you're actually involved or not."

"But my arrest was a mistake. The bank manager cleared me of all involvement!"

"But you're Kenneth Jordan's daughter. You're related to a criminal, and that makes you guilty in their eyes." Mr. Blackwood looked at Cass and shook his head. "This story won't die quickly, Cass. The news media will embellish and keep showing the video of you being arrested over and over again, just to keep it alive."

"But this is wrong! I've given you six years of my life. We've passed every audit every year, and there's never been a penny unaccounted for." Clearly, the directors weren't going to defend her. They were okay with throwing her overboard, sacrificing her to save the ship. The mob wanted her head, and the board was giving it to them. She was expendable.

"You've done a wonderful job here. The clinic's efficiency has only increased since you took over as director. I hate this as much as you. I'm really sorry, but we can't have the clinic's reputation ruined. My hands are tied. The board wants you gone by the end of the day."

Cass bit her lip and held back tears as she returned to her office. Not only had her father broken her heart, but now, he'd also caused her to lose her job.

The long days and extra hours she'd devoted to her job to maintain the high standards she'd set for herself and the clinic meant nothing now. She had put her job ahead of everything else in her life, including personal relationships. In hindsight, that now seemed like a bad trade-off.

She'd been fired despite being innocent. And they wanted her gone by the end of the day? They expected her to give them another eight-plus hours? To wrap up all the loose ends and tidy up for her successor? No! She wouldn't give them a minute longer than it took to pack up her things and leave. She wouldn't even say goodbye. She couldn't subject herself to looks of pity from the staff. They wanted her gone? *Now* seemed like the perfect time to meet their demands.

Stunned, Cass mechanically taped up the sides of an empty cardboard box and began filling it with pictures and odds and ends from her desk and credenza. She paused for a moment to reread the inscription on the award for her exceptional service, then tossed it into the box. The words engraved on the plaque were as worthless as the fake gold lettering on the plaque itself. The citation should have come with a caveat: *Past loyal service doesn't ensure future fealty.*

Shaking her head over the hollowness of Mr. Blackwood's speech at the award ceremony, Cass walked to the window and gazed out at the street traffic behind the clinic.

"Oh, God! No!" Cass groaned. "Can this day get any worse?" There went her car—hooked behind a tow truck, speeding down the street, obviously on its way to the impound lot.

So yeah, things could actually get worse. "The God of Misery," who was completely in charge of her life these days, wasn't done with her yet.

Sure, she'd seen the "15-Minute Parking, Violators Will be Towed" sign when she parked in the alley this morning, but in her desperation to avoid the mob at the front door, she'd taken a chance and parked there. She should have anticipated the "alley monitors" would be cruising the vicinity, on the lookout for Cass Jordan, fraudster and criminal.

Jordan had escaped justice once before, but not this time. They'd caught her red-handed, committing a second crime: illegal parking.

CHAPTER TWO

C ass sneaked out the clinic's back door, since the vultures continued to circle the front parking lot. They weren't shouting now, but their voices hummed like a swarm of bees as they waited in anticipation of sighting the infamous Cass Jordan.

Cass asked the car service to pick her up at the corner of Fitzhugh and Third Street and drive her to the impound lot to bail out her car. With her cardboard box perched on her hip, Cass plodded slowly to the pickup spot three blocks from the clinic. In addition to her sore ankle from her wayward kick, her toes were burning like hot coals squeezed into a too-small space in her high heels. And she still had almost a full block to walk. For a moment, Cass was tempted to sit down on the curb, pull her athletic shoes from the box, and slip her aching feet into them, fashion be damned. But someone could easily snap a picture of her and blast it all over social media, where it would then be picked up by other media outlets. A likely headline would be: "*Female fraudster reduced to a common streetwalker.*" More shame would be heaped onto her "properly bred" mother,

Cecilia.

Of course, Cecilia probably wouldn't see such a picture anytime soon. Not a stand-by-your-man type of woman, Cecilia had fled to the Winslow family estate near the Pocono Mountains at the first hint of scandal related to her husband's arrest. Cecilia left Philadelphia before a dogged reporter could investigate Kenneth Jordan's wife, her social connections, and any involvement she may have had in the Ponzi scheme.

Cass decided to tough it out. Changing her shoes like a homeless person who had just pulled footwear from a dumpster would be more humiliation than Cecilia could bear.

"Cassandra, I'm appalled by your coarse behavior!" Cecilia would say in her most cultured British accent. "What will people think, seeing a Winslow sitting barefoot on a street curb like a common trollop?"

Cecilia sometimes acted as though her British accent alone made her royalty and practically in the line of succession for the British throne—and that every move a Winslow made was newsworthy and reflected on the crown.

The Winslows were from England and comfortably well-off, but the closest her mother ever got to British royalty was when she forced Cass to attend the queen's birthday parade with her several years ago. Of course, that didn't keep Cecilia from hinting to her circle of friends—though never outright saying—she knew the royal family personally.

Cass's grandfather, Richard Winslow, had been part of the British ambassador's entourage assigned to the embassy in Washington, DC. It was during his detail to America that Cecilia had met and married Philadelphian Kenneth Allen Jordan. When Richard retired from the Foreign Service, he took up residence in Pennsylvania to be near his only child, Cecilia.

Thinking about her mother's pretensions to royalty and how Cass's behavior frequently appalled her only distracted Cass from her burning feet for a few minutes. Gritting her teeth and forcing mind over matter, Cass limped toward the pickup point.

Cass spotted the car service waiting for her as she turned the corner onto Third Street. She quickened her steps as much as her aching feet would allow and soon reached the car. The driver opened the back door, and Cass practically threw the heavy box on the seat and quickly climbed in, happy to give her feet a rest. She gave the driver directions to the impound lot, and they sped away.

Cass paid her parking fine, to the impound lot attendant, while holding her breath as they ran her credit card through the approval process. When the charge went through, she breathed again, relieved that the credit card company hadn't yet heard about her "crime spree" and canceled her card.

Reunited with her car, Cass drove straight home. As she neared her apartment building, she spotted satellite trucks and a throng of reporters milling around out front. Apparently, there wasn't any news in Philadelphia today other than her arrest.

Cass drove around the block unnoticed, entered the parking area through the commercial trucks' back entrance, and slipped into her parking spot. She hurried to the door of her building, but just as she inserted her key card into the door slot, a reporter walked around the corner. He spotted Cass and started running and shouting questions. Cass stepped inside and slammed the door in his face.

She didn't relax until she was safely locked behind her apartment door. Reporters and the slimy paparazzi were evil geniuses; they often found ways of circumventing security, even in a secure building like hers.

After changing clothes, Cass took a soda from the fridge and turned on the TV. The midday news should've been over, but no—there was her father's face once again filling the TV screen. "Coming up next, a special report on how a Bernie

Madoff-type individual swindled his investors. But this one is local, right here in the city of Philadelphia. And it could be a family affair!" the announcer practically shouted.

Cass flipped off the TV before they could move on to news of her arrest. By now, they'd no doubt learned that she had also been fired. She didn't need to see an amplified version or an instant replay of her life.

Now what? She was unemployed and without anyone to talk to.

Cass had spent so much time at her job that she never did the work needed to solidified close friendships. She'd like to blame Fitzgerald Medical for that, but truthfully, it was her own fault. She'd willingly devoted her life to her job. And look where that had gotten her! Without a job and basically without friends.

Cass had dated a few men since college, but she'd never grown as close to any of them as she had with Stephen Daniels, her college sweetheart. Unfortunately, that relationship had died quickly, smothered by Cecilia's interference, insulting comments, and constantly pushing Cass toward someone she saw as more fitting for her daughter.

Her mother would probably listen and sympathize with Cass over her current plight, but before long, she'd start nagging Cass to come and stay with her in the Poconos. No doubt, she had the latest hot nephew of a distant cousin twice-removed from Lady So-and-So who was visiting from London and dying to meet Cass.

At least, this was the way Cecilia had operated in the past— before her husband's and daughter's arrests made the national news. Cecilia's pool of eligible bachelors might be shrinking by now.

Cass might call her brother, Richard Allen. He preferred to be called 'Rich,' but Cass called him by his initials, 'Raj.' The

nickname annoyed him, and since annoying each other was
their purpose in life, that was reason enough to keep calling
him that. But Raj had escaped their mother's clutches and was
now backpacking through Europe, earning his way as he went.
He'd published one book about his travels to hidden nooks
around the world and was currently working on a second book.
She didn't know his exact location, and only Raj knew when
he'd return home. With the Jordan family in tatters, Raj might
decide to never come home. That was almost too sad to think
about, so Cass pushed the thought away.

But there *was* one person Cass knew she could talk to,
someone who would understand her situation—Amanda Clark.
They had met in college, still kept in touch, and tried to meet up
at least once each year. Mandy lived in Charlotte, North Carolina. They'd met for a three-day weekend at Rehoboth Beach,
Delaware, back in the spring.

Cass dialed Mandy's number. She answered on the first ring.

"Do you have a minute to talk?" Cass asked.

"Sure. I'm on break," Mandy replied. "I heard about your
dad. I'm really sorry."

"Thanks, but I doubt you've heard the latest." Cass swallowed, dreading putting her dismissal into words. "I just got
fired from my job. I wasn't involved with my dad's business, but
just being his child was enough to put the spotlight on me. And,
of course, there are the bank accounts he opened under my
name. Now, I don't know what I'm going to do."

"Oh no! I'm so sorry! I wish we had a place for you here,"
Mandy replied. "It would be great to work together. But Mr.
Fields has been the director here for a hundred years and looks
like he's good for another hundred."

"I understand. And you probably shouldn't recommend
someone who's been fired from their last job."

"I know you, and I would recommend you, regardless. But

Mr. Fields would never listen to me, even if we were desperate to hire someone. In his view, I'm just a lowly nurse practitioner."

"I don't believe that for a minute," Cass replied. "You keep that place running. I might have to look outside Philly to find a facility willing to take a chance on hiring me, considering my criminal past. I doubt there's a place anywhere in this region that hasn't heard of the Jordan crime syndicate."

"I'm really sorry you got caught up in this. But you know what? I just remembered something. My sister Sara is starting college and trying to decide what to study. I'm trying to direct her into a career in healthcare. I was looking up the training and qualifications needed for various jobs listed on Health-Pro—a site that lists open positions for healthcare professionals and related fields. I noticed there was a clinic director's job open in a small town west of Charlotte—Mason Valley, North Carolina. I think it's in the mountains. I've never been there, so I can't tell you anything about the town. But it might be worth checking out."

"The mountains of North Carolina? Is the dress code suspenders and flannel shirts? Would I have to give up my expensive shoe collection?"

"I don't think it's *that* remote or backwoodsy," Mandy laughed. "Seriously though, you should check it out. Maybe it's a good place to get away from all the noise around Philly right now. Sounds like your dad is going to be *the* news for some time."

"I was trying to inject some humor into a humorless situation. Plus, I can't be choosey. My options are very limited and shrinking with each newscast. I'd wear flannel, if necessary. I might even have a pair of shoes that would look good with flannel. That is, of course, if someone in the backwoods would even hire me, given my questionable past."

"Stop blaming yourself and don't give up hope. You haven't

done anything wrong."

Cass disconnected from the call, opened her laptop, and checked some jobsites for positions in the local area. Finding nothing that fit her qualifications, she went to the HealthPro jobsite. She found the job posting Mandy had mentioned. The Elizabeth Barrett Mental Health Clinic in Mason Valley, North Carolina, needed a clinical director. According to the description, the clinic was a small charitable operation, but it had an inspired mission statement: "No-cost mental health services for anyone seeking help from trained professionals." The qualifications were five years' experience as a clinical director or other managerial position, excellent analytical and problem-solving abilities, strong leadership and communication skills, and a strong understanding of budgets and performance evaluations. Nonprofit experience a plus.

With the exception of nonprofit experience, Cass's qualifications matched the needs of the job. However, her arrest might keep her from getting anywhere near a budget, as Mr. Blackwood had so callously pointed out.

Of course, she wouldn't know if they'd consider her unless she applied. Cass filled out the application, attached her resume, and submitted the forms.

How far and how quickly the mighty can fall, Cass grimly thought as she closed her laptop. She'd never imagined that she'd be forced to apply for a job in a small town in the North Carolina mountains, let alone be grateful if they gave her an interview.

Cass had been at the top of her class in all her studies in college. But that was the past, and her scholastic achievements hadn't kept her from getting fired. She'd move to the mountains in a heartbeat and jump at the chance to start over.

On the bright side, by submitting her application, she was being proactive rather than moping around. Something similar to her former life might not be found in Mason Valley, but her current chaotic life sucked. A job in a quiet place, away from harassing mobs, would make up for any lost salary. Peace of mind was priceless.

But if the FBI didn't unfreeze her bank account soon, her next move might be to a homeless shelter.

Cass spent the next few days as a hostage in her apartment. The crowds outside her building decreased in number, but there were still a few hangers-on hoping to break a big news story. A few paparazzi still slunk around the building in hopes of getting a photo of her when she finally emerged.

Friday morning, Cass received a phone call from the recruiter at HealthPro. She had been accepted as a candidate for the position of clinical director at the Elizabeth Barrett Mental Health Clinic in Mason Valley, North Carolina. The recruiter wanted to schedule a Monday-morning interview in Atlanta with Kelsey Barrett Wilder. They could do a video interview if Cass couldn't make it to Atlanta, but Ms. Wilder preferred to meet the candidates in person, if possible.

Cass quickly accepted and confirmed that she would be in Atlanta at the appointed time. Being chosen to fill the position still seemed like a long shot, but it gave her something to look forward to. She immediately booked a flight to Atlanta for Sunday afternoon, with a return flight on Monday after the interview was over.

Now, she just had to figure out how to get out of the apartment building without being mobbed.

CHAPTER THREE

Cass landed in Atlanta around four o'clock on Sunday afternoon.

She'd managed to escape her Philly apartment by hiding her blonde hair under a black wig purchased for a Halloween party last year. Rounding out her disguise was a pillow stuffed under a too-large man's shirt Raj had left on his last visit, ratty athletic shoes, and a worn-out knit jacket—an ensemble that would send shivers of horror through her mother. No one recognized her as she drove past the three men with *paparazzi* written all over them as they leaned nonchalantly against the side of the apartment building. Cass's first stop on the way to the airport was a service station where she shed her disguise and changed into normal clothing.

Cass arrived at her hotel in Atlanta, and once she'd finished check-in, she took a stroll along the streets of downtown Atlanta. For the first time in over a week, she didn't feel the need to constantly check behind her to see who might be following her or fear a camera—or worse—would be suddenly stuck in her face. Cass relaxed as she browsed and window-shopped, as any normal tourist would do.

The next morning, Cass took a taxi to a building on the east side of Atlanta for her interview. She arrived about fifteen minutes before her 9:30 a.m. appointment. The receptionist directed her to Ms. Wilder's personal assistant's desk.

"Hi, I'm Cassandra Jordan. I'm here for an interview. I'm a few minutes early. I hope that's alright," Cass said to the girl behind the desk.

"Hello, and welcome. I'm Tina, Kelsey's PA. You can go on in." Tina nodded toward the office located behind the glass walls directly in front of her. "Kelsey's expecting you."

Cass took a step toward the door, then stopped. A uniformed police officer was talking to Ms. Wilder.

At the sight of the policeman, Cass froze. Her first thought was that the authorities had followed her to Atlanta and were awaiting her arrival. But she was here to interview for a job, not rob the place.

Cass turned back to Tina. "There's a policeman in her office. I don't want to interrupt." *Or be arrested*, thought Cass.

"Oh." Tina waved away Cass's concerns. "That's just Jason, Kelsey's husband. He's not here on business—just hovering— and I suspect Kelsey might welcome the distraction. You're not interrupting. Go on in."

Cass crossed to the door but stopped again when she heard the conversation coming from the room.

"Jason, stop worrying," Kelsey said to her husband. "I'm fine! You're overreacting."

"I'm worried about you. You didn't eat anything for breakfast this morning."

"Tina brought me a smoothie, and I drank most of it. I think it's going to stay down. I'll eat lunch, I promise. Doctor Williams assured me that it's just morning sickness. It'll go away around the third month. I have about six more weeks of this."

"Six weeks?" Jason asked. "Sweetheart, I hate to see you this sick."

"Be strong, Jason," Kelsey laughed. "Morning sickness is natural and something I have to deal with. It's not a terminal illness, just pregnancy. We'll get through this. Now, go to Chief Dalton's retirement ceremony." Kelsey looked up and saw Cass at the door. She motioned for Cass to come in.

Kelsey came around the desk and hugged Jason, then kissed him on the cheek. "Go! Stop pestering me! I have work to do."

"It's my job to worry about you, but I'll go if you promise you'll eat lunch," Jason said as he returned Kelsey's hug. "And stop that! I know you're rolling your eyes behind my back."

"Come in, Ms. Jordan. This worrywart I call my husband is leaving, aren't you Jason?" She motioned for Cass to take a seat in front of the desk.

"Welcome, Ms. Jordan. Okay! Okay! I'll leave, but I'll still worry." He kissed Kelsey on the cheek again, smiled at Cass, and left the office.

"I apologize for that. This is our first child, and neither of us knows what we're doing," Kelsey laughed. "But Jason's concern has gone overboard."

"Congratulations! I think it's sweet that he's worried about you." Cass settled herself in a chair facing the desk. "Not everyone has that."

"Jason is one of a kind," Kelsey replied with a tender smile. "I'm extremely lucky to have found a gem like him. But let's get back to why you're here."

They spent the next several minutes going over Cass's qualifications and experience. Cass answered a variety of questions relating to how she handled staffing problems, resolved conflicts between staff or between staff and patients, managed time and unexpected crises, and tracked budgets. Cass was glad that Kelsey didn't throw in the time-honored question of where she expected to be in five years. She had no idea how to answer that, though still hiding from reporters and avoiding jail seemed like good possibilities.

"The Mental Health Clinic in Mason Valley has been so well-received that we're expanding and adding a medical wing to provide care unrelated to mental health," Kelsey explained. "Our community hospital closed earlier this year, so Mason Valley is what I refer to as a 'healthcare desert.' The few doctors who had practices in Mason Valley are retiring. Patients will soon need to drive to larger cities to find care."

"That's a problem," Cass agreed. "In such cases, people will often use the long drive as an excuse to not seek care."

"Exactly! It's human nature, but we want to fix that. So, it would be your job to get the new wing up and running; find staff, including doctors and other trained professionals; and merge the administration of the two clinics together. Is that something you think you can handle or would be interested in?"

"Yes, I'm very interested. I don't have much experience working with mental health patients beyond referring them to outside specialists, but the administration of combined clinics shouldn't require anything different from what I did in my previous job."

"Good. Glad to hear I haven't scared you away. Quality in the care we provide and the ability to smoothly get it to our patients is what I'm looking for."

"My tolerance for scariness has increased over the last few weeks, so it would take more than the idea of hard work to scare me off," Cass replied. "What is the town of Mason Valley like?"

"Mason Valley is a wonderful place with wonderful people. It's a small town but offers almost anything a person might need—on a small scale, anyway—except healthcare facilities. Jason's parents still live there."

"Is that where you met?" Cass asked.

"No…" Kelsey answered slowly. "We met while serving in the army in Afghanistan, but we didn't become a couple until we were reunited later in Mason Valley. Jason was the county sheriff in Mason Valley, and I went there on a surveillance contract he had with our firm. I'll tell you more about it another time."

"Sounds like an interesting story," Cass said. She fidgeted in her seat.

This was probably the time to bring up why she'd been fired from her last job. Kelsey hadn't asked about that. Still, Cass was in a building that housed a security firm and was sitting before a security analyst. Most likely, Kelsey knew more about Cass than she knew herself. If she didn't bring it up, it would look like she was hiding something.

"Um… I was fired from my last job at Fitzgerald Medical." Cass swallowed, still embarrassed and humiliated by the firing. She forced herself to go on. "I was arrested—unfairly—but Fitzgerald's board decided the risk and publicity were too much to keep me on."

"Yes, I know about that," Kelsey acknowledged. "But you were cleared of all wrongdoing. Thanks for bringing it up, though. It shows me that you have integrity and aren't seeking this job under false pretenses. I admire that."

Cass sighed, relieved that Kelsey believed her without having to repeat the details of the whole sordid event. "I haven't been financially dependent on my parents since I enrolled in college. A small inheritance from my Grandmother Jordan, plus working a job, is how I paid for college. I've been employed ever since."

"I appreciate you telling me. Maybe Mason Valley is just the place for you to recover. I know it helped me, and I found Jason there."

"I would be grateful for some peace and quiet, away from the mob that's been hounding me for days."

"Did Agent Rogers unfreeze your bank account?" Kelsey asked.

"How... how did you know about that?" Cass asked, shocked by how extensive the investigation into her past had been. Kelsey Wilder really did know everything about her.

"It's not as clandestine as it might seem. My father-in-law is a retired FBI agent and can't seem to give up the business completely. I think he knows someone in just about every field office across the country. He's very close to a few agents in the Philadelphia office and keeps in touch with Special Agent in Charge Wilkins. Your involvement came up as a by-product of my father-in-law's interest in an active case—your father's arrest. SAC Wilkins gave him the details after I mentioned that you had applied for the director's job. Ben's also on the board of directors for the clinic."

"Ah... I see. But no, my account was still frozen the last time I checked. Agent Rogers seems to think I deserve punishment for being Kenneth Jordan's daughter. I'm still living off my credit card," Cass replied.

"That must be tough. Well, Jason and I own a small house in Mason Valley, so that will be yours to live in if you're selected for the job and accept our offer. You won't have to worry about finding a place or paying rent, at least." Kelsey stood, signaling that the interview was over. "I have another candidate to interview this afternoon, and then, I'll run my selection by the board. I should have an answer for you by the middle of the week—no later than Friday at most."

Cass thanked Kelsey for the interview. After meeting her, Cass wanted to work for Kelsey more than ever. The clinic's location in the mountains of North Carolina only added a sense of adventure.

"Slow down," Cass cautioned herself as she packed her things for her return flight to Philadelphia. "You haven't been hired yet." Her arrest and her father's notoriety could stand in the way of the full board's approval, despite Kelsey's father-in-law knowing she was innocent.

Cass's return flight touched down in Philadelphia around 3:30 p.m. Once she retrieved her car, she retraced the route she'd taken on Sunday, stopping at the same service station to once again change to her disguise. When she arrived back at her apartment building, the scene was eerily quiet. The throngs of reporters and paparazzi were gone. Maybe they became bored when she didn't appear, or perhaps another, more exciting news story had wiped her "crime" off the front page.

♦

The reason the vultures were drawn away from her became clear when she entered her apartment and turned on the TV. Kenneth Jordan had just been released on bail. Hordes of reporters were now surrounding his apartment building, hoping for a glimpse of Philadelphia's most infamous white-collar criminal.

Cass was hurt and angry that her father had left her dangling while the FBI arrested and interrogated her. Did he selfishly abandon her to save himself? Or had he wanted to come to her defense but was silenced by his jailers?

Even after all he'd done, Cass wanted to visit her father, but she decided to put off confronting him for a few days, hoping her anger would cool and the mob around his building would disperse.

On Wednesday morning, Cass put on her disguise and reluctantly readied herself for a face-to-face meeting with her father. It was time to get answers to the painful questions that simmered inside her.

Just as she started to leave her apartment, her phone rang. The caller ID showed Kelsey Barrett Wilder's name.

"Ms. Wilder," Cass answered, nervously waiting for Kelsey to give her the news. She wanted the job in Mason Valley more than ever after learning what the job entailed—staffing and organizing a new clinic. She liked the idea of building something from the ground up. And yes, she desperately wanted to escape her current prison-like existence.

Cass steeled herself for disappointment as Kelsey began speaking.

"Good morning, Cass. I wanted to personally call you. I had two very strong candidates for the job in Mason Valley."

Cass's heart dropped. She always knew it was possible that she wouldn't be selected.

"Both of you have amazing qualifications, so it was hard to choose between two perfect candidates. But I always look for that extra quality that doesn't show up on a resume. The resilience you've shown recently while dealing with a difficult situation is the quality I'm looking for. Those skills are what's needed to set up the new medical clinic. I'd like to offer you the position of clinical director at the Barrett Medical Clinic in Mason Valley. Are you still interested?"

"Yes! Yes! I accept!" Cass replied enthusiastically. "When do you want me to start?"

"As soon as possible," Kelsey answered with a laugh. "I also like your enthusiasm. How about next Monday? Would that give you enough time to wrap things up there and get to Mason Valley? We can be flexible on the date if you need more time."

"That sounds perfect. The sooner, the better. I'll leave Philly on Friday and use the weekend to settle in. Thank you so much, Ms. Wilder."

"Call me Kelsey. We'll be working together. I look forward to having you on our team."

"Yes!" Cass yelled as she put down the phone and danced around the room. It was a fresh start and something interesting to focus on.

Cass's self-confidence emerged from under the rock where it had been hiding since its recent pummeling. She would take her big-city experience, apply it to the director's position in the small mountain town, and create a medical clinic that functioned as well as any big-city medical center.

The people of Mason Valley were giving her a second chance. They deserved nothing less.

CHAPTER FOUR

Cass had her car packed early Friday morning, ready to begin her journey to North Carolina. Now that the reporters were busy chasing her father, she was able to load her car without feeling like a running back, dodging bodies each time she left the building on the way to her car. Still, just in case a stray reporter lurked in the vicinity, Cass waited until after dark to emerge from the apartment building.

A busy two days had passed since Cass accepted Kelsey's job offer. Cass sublet her apartment to Susan Sullivan, a nurse who worked at a nearby hospital. Cass's bank account was hers again, with access to her funds, and just in time for her move. She suspected Kelsey's father-in-law had lit a fire under Agent Rogers.

Sifting through her personal belongings had been the most trying part of packing. Sorting out what to take, what to donate to charity, and what to store in a nearby rental unit took one full, exhausting day. What did one need in the way of clothing in an out-of-the way mountain town?

"You're obsessing over the trivial," Cass muttered as she dumped the contents of her dresser drawers on her bed. "It isn't as though you're joining a nomadic tribe at an outpost in the Himalayas. Mason Valley has modern conveniences. Plus, online shopping is always an option. Admit it! You're obsessing because you're nervous about trekking off into the unknown. Be more like Raj. Different can be exciting."

Cass emptied her bedroom closet and added dresses, suits, and pants to the pile on her bed. As she sifted through the mound of clothing, she decided to stop overthinking and just take her favorites—a mixture of business and casual attire, the same things she currently wore in Philly. There wasn't a single flannel shirt in the lot, and she made sure to include several pairs of her favorite designer shoes.

Cass turned over her apartment keys to Susan, said good-bye, pulled out of the parking lot, and headed toward the expressway. She hummed to herself, happy to be on her way and leaving Philly behind. Feeling like a fly trapped under a microscope and under constant scrutiny was exhausting.

Before leaving town, Cass reluctantly called her mother. She didn't want to listen to Cecilia's usual nonsense, but it was only right that her mother knew where she'd be for the foreseeable future.

"Cass," Cecilia said. "You've never been a quitter, but you've accepted a job that is beneath your education and skills. You're taking the easy way out. The first job that came along? Really? You're just hiding."

"That's rich coming from you! Who's hiding, Mom?" Cecilia was never short on criticism—when directed at someone else. She just couldn't see herself in the same light. "I'm not the one who fled to the Poconos. With a firing on my record, this might be the only job I can find."

"I don't believe that!" Cecilia said. "Your credentials are

excellent. You'll be wasting your talents hiding in some back-woods hamlet."

"Maybe I do want to hide—from my parents," Cass countered. "I guess I could join Raj in Europe. But it's done. I've accepted the job, and I'm leaving Philly."

Cecilia, who usually made age thirty-two sound as if Cass was over the hill, her biological clock ticking away its last minutes, mentioned only once that Cass should give up the idea of traipsing off to the North Carolina backwoods, find a man who could take care of her, get married, and stop this foolishness. Kenneth's caper may have proven to Cecilia what type of behavior actually qualified as foolishness.

The trip to Mason Valley from Philadelphia was a nine-hour drive, but Cass planned to stop in Charlotte and spend the night with Mandy. The miles passed quickly, and she reached Charlotte in what felt like record time. Running on adrenaline and excited by her new adventure, Cass wasn't even tired when she pulled into the driveway at Mandy's home.

Throughout dinner and afterward, Cass and Mandy reminisced about their college days and current love lives—the same subjects they'd discussed a few months ago at the beach. The discussion of their love lives didn't take long. Neither one had a significant other to talk about.

♦

Cass left Mandy's house on Saturday morning, anxious to reach her destination and settle into her new residence. As she merged with traffic on the interstate, Cass tapped the steering wheel and hummed along with a favorite James Taylor song that blasted from her music app. She joined in on one line in particular: "In my mind, I'm going to Carolina."

She was physically *in* Carolina, and it had never been in her mind at all until now.

Traffic was light, and by late morning, Cass exited the highway and soon entered the city limits of Mason Valley. A road sign at the edge of town welcomed visitors to "Small-town life with twenty-five thousand big-hearted residents." A positive message to visitors, no doubt created by a friendly city council.

The day was bright and sunny. The persistent morning sun had removed the chill in the air and slowly burned off the thick fog around the mountaintops. A flock of birds soared across the front of Cass's car, then swept upward into a bright blue sky. Immediately they dive-bombed back to earth. Tirelessly, the flock repeated the maneuver over and over as if playing a game of avian tag.

Love Vine Mountain, the wildest part of the mountain range surrounding Mason Valley—at least, according to her research—was easy to identify. It loomed in the distance, tall and stately, high above the other mountains. It was early September, but the highest peaks already displayed streaks of emerging fall color—a signal that the cooler weather of autumn was approaching.

As Cass drove through town, morning shoppers filled the sidewalks and strolled leisurely along Main Street. Mason Valley, a typical small town tucked away in the mountains, was picturesque, inviting, and slow-moving. Such slow movers would be trampled in Philadelphia's business district, but there was a lot to admire about taking things slow and easy.

The scenic beauty of the valley and the town with its unhurried residents renewed Cass's optimism. Losing her job at Fitzgerald Medical had made her question whether her skills as a director were as good as she thought they were. Maybe she should have worked harder. But her self-analysis always circled back to one central point: job performance was not the reason she'd been fired.

Cecilia had accused her of hiding or taking the easy way out. That sentiment didn't describe Cass's work ethic. She had never shortchanged any employer, in any circumstance. She never gave less than her best. Kelsey had taken a chance by hiring her, and the "big-hearted" residents of Mason Valley would get her total commitment as the clinic's director.

Before long, Cass's GPS took her to the complex that housed the county and city government offices. Kelsey had instructed that the keys and directions to the house and clinic would be waiting for her at the county sheriff's office.

Cass parked, got out of the car, stretched, then walked toward the complex. A man exited the office building and walked toward her.

"Excuse me," Cass said as the man approached. "Can you tell me which office belongs to the county sheriff?"

"It's the one that has 'County Sheriff' written on the door." The man stopped and looked at her with flinty blue eyes. He frowned as if to question why anyone with a brain would ask for the location when it was so obvious to him. He didn't elaborate on his answer, nor did he smile. The comment was meant to be rude, not humorous. Cass felt like an idiot—which was his intent.

"Oh! Yes, I see it now. By the way, I'm—" Cass's introduction was cut off.

"Sorry, I don't have time to chitchat." The man rudely ignored Cass's outstretched hand, walked around her, and left her gaping at his back. Tall, dark-haired, blue eyes—whoever designed people had wasted all those good looks on this obnoxious man.

Shaking her head over the man's incivility, Cass walked to the door marked "County Sheriff.

A man in a tan sheriff's uniform looked up from his desk as

Cass walked through the door.

"Sheriff Ferguson?" Cass turned at the sound of a truck driving by the office window. It was the man she'd just met, pulling out of the parking lot. "That man who just left, what's his problem? Did you arrest him—for bad manners, maybe? Give him a ticket for rude behavior in public? He's got a large chip on his shoulder."

"Oh, yeah, that's Ryan. More like a log than a chip. He's definitely not on our welcoming committee. Not a bad guy though, once you get to know him."

"*If* you get to know him, maybe. Anyway, I'm Cass Jordan. I'm here to pick up the keys Kelsey Wilder left for me."

"Welcome, Ms. Jordan. I've been expecting you." Sheriff Ferguson stood, shook her hand, and then pointed to a chair. "Have a seat. We're very glad you're here. Are you ready to tackle the job at the clinic?"

"I am. I'm looking forward to the challenge to see what we can create." Cass took the seat offered by the sheriff. "Kelsey told me that a Dr. Phillips has been the director since the original clinic opened."

"That's correct. But he says running the original clinic, plus organizing the new wing, is more than he wants to tackle. He's ready to get back to golfing and fishing. He volunteered at first just to help Kelsey get the original clinic up and running. That was two years ago. I hear he's agreed to stay on a part-time basis until you get your feet wet and up to speed."

"Well, I'm ready to jump in with both feet. With his help, maybe I won't drown. I don't plan on making too many changes at first. A newcomer is always regarded with some suspicion as it is."

"That's a smart strategy! But I don't expect you'll have any problems with the staff. Speaking of creating something new, construction of the new wing isn't quite finished. The outside is mostly done, but the crews are still working on the interior. We had a very rainy spring and summer, and that slowed construction."

"I see. That will give me additional time to get acclimated and fine-tune plans for a smooth opening. I'm certain I'll find plenty to do while the construction crews finish up."

"No doubt." The sheriff reached into a drawer, pulled out two sets of keys, and handed one to Cass. "That's the keys to the house on Willow Street. Carolyn Wilder went over there this morning. When she brought back the keys, she said everything has been cleaned and all is in order, just waiting for your arrival."

"That's very nice of her!" Cass had wondered about her reception from the town. Some people resented outsiders moving in and taking over. But she hoped not to be viewed as an outsider for very long.

"Well, that's the thing about Mason Valley," Sheriff Ferguson said. "Our attitude is more than just the roadside slogan at the edge of town. We're a small town, but our people are friendly and are mostly what we call 'good people.' But even good people can get stung by welcoming the wrong people. I guess you heard about our trouble sometime back—the cult leader and his followers who set up camp on Love Vine Mountain?"

"I read about it after I was offered the job. I was researching to get a feel for the town. That was a very brave thing that Kelsey and her partner Ron did—along with Sheriff Wilder."

Cass had been shocked by the news stories that popped up when she googled Mason Valley, North Carolina. She'd expected to find a sleepy little hamlet in the mountains, where life floated along easily, peacefully, and quietly. What she'd found instead was the harrowing tale of two local teen girls who were kidnapped and held hostage on the mountain by a human trafficking cult. Kelsey, her partner Ron, Sheriff Wilder, and the FBI had rescued them, along with several other girls who were also held to be sold to the highest bidder.

Kelsey had fled through the mountains with the two local girls, evaded the men who tracked them, and ultimately led them to safety. The encampment was shut down, and several people were arrested, prosecuted, and sentenced to long prison terms.

"That scumbag Coeburn came into our valley and brought his filth with him!" Sheriff Ferguson abruptly stopped speaking. "Sorry. I still get angry when I talk about that incident."

"I can understand why you feel that way. How are the two local girls doing?"

"Maddie and Allie? From all appearances, they're doing well. They were two of the first patients to get help when the mental health clinic opened. The therapy they received there helped them with the trauma they experienced. Both girls attend college now. Just this past summer, they worked as interns at the clinic."

"That's wonderful! It sounds as if Kelsey recognized just how badly the clinic was needed."

"Kelsey is a jewel. Jason's a good man, too. We're all excited about the baby that's on the way. Imagine my former boss and buddy Jason being a dad! I can't wait to rib him about diaper changes, feeding schedules, and of course, the lack of sleep. My wife and I have a son, so it's payback time for Jason ragging on me."

"They're off on a whole new adventure." Cass nodded in agreement.

"Do you have kids?" Sheriff Ferguson asked.

"I'm just guessing about their new adventure since I don't have any firsthand experience with babies. I've never been married. I guess I never found the 'spark' that's so obvious between Kelsey and Jason. I only saw them together for a few minutes when I interviewed for the director's job, but the spark was obvious."

"Ah, the spark of love! It's elusive, but when you know, you know. It's definitely visible between Kelsey and Jason. But you're right. Having kids *is* a new adventure."

"One of my goals as director is to relieve Kelsey of worry and stress over the clinic," Cass said.

"One less thing to worry about will help, for sure. But that's enough about my views on love and marriage. Melinda would be the first to tell you I'm no expert." Sheriff Ferguson chuckled as he slid another set of keys across the desk. "Here's the key to the clinic. It's located just outside town. Very easy to find. Also, here's a brochure the Chamber of Commerce puts out with a map, scheduled events in town and the surrounding area, and a brief history of the town. I've annotated the route to the house on the map. My phone number is on the back. If you need anything at all, just give me a call."

"Thank you." Cass took the keys and the brochure and stood to leave. "I don't officially begin my job until Monday, but would it be alright if I visit the clinic tomorrow, after I get settled at the house? I'd like to look around and familiarize myself with the setup."

"I don't see why not. You're in charge now," Sheriff Ferguson replied. "My uncle's construction company is the general contractor for the building. Since they're behind schedule, some workers might be there tomorrow trying to catch up."

"I definitely won't get in the way of construction. I know less about that than love and babies."

Cass thanked the sheriff, left the building, and found Willow Street on the map. Following the sheriff's instructions—easier than her GPS—Cass drove to the house, which would be her home for the foreseeable future.

Cass pulled into the driveway of a single-story white clapboard house trimmed in grayish blue and set amidst what she guessed was an acre, maybe more, of land. A piece of land this large would be considered a park in her old Philly neighborhood. Brown patches brought on by the cooler September days were sprinkled across the expansive, well-trimmed lawn.

Cass began emptying the cargo area of her SUV. It didn't take her long to unload the car. The Wilders' house was fully furnished, so Cass had brought only clothes and some personal items. She unlocked the door, picked up her luggage, and entered the house. Leaving the luggage in the entryway, she walked into the living room and looked around.

On the counter that separated the kitchen from the living area was a vase filled with a bright bouquet of wildflowers. A note was propped against the vase. Signed by Carolyn Wilder, it welcomed Cass to the area, adding, "The kitchen is fully stocked with groceries, including breakfast pastries. There's a lasagna in the refrigerator that only needs heating, a green salad, and a loaf of freshly baked bread." She also left her phone number in case Cass needed anything else.

No, Cass thought. *I don't need anything more right now than a kind friend like you, Carolyn Wilder.* She sniffed back tears and sagged into a chair at the kitchen table, overwhelmed by the thoughtfulness of an unknown woman.

Cass's life had turned into a nightmare. The disintegration of her family was a blow she hadn't expected nor knew exactly how to handle. She was justified in being angry at her parents, but still felt guilt over feeling that way. She'd spent many nights tossing and turning, wrestling with guilt while also worrying about her career—wondering if she would ever work again. Stoic and strong worked for her until someone showed her empathy. Now, an act of kindness from a stranger broke through the stoicism and brought her to tears.

Cass wiped her eyes and straightened her shoulders, gearing

herself up for her new life. Setting up a new clinic might not be the easiest thing she had ever done, but it was something to concentrate on other than her family that would never be the same again.

CHAPTER FIVE

Cass filled a travel mug with coffee, grabbed a bagel from the kitchen counter, and drove to the outskirts of the city. The town proper wasn't very large, so it didn't take her long to reach the Elizabeth Barrett Mental Health Clinic.

Last night, when she climbed into bed, Cass had expected to lie awake, her mind on the same roller coaster it had been on in recent days. Or maybe the strange silence—no traffic noise, honking horns, or sirens disturbing the night—would keep her awake. But shortly after she pulled the covers over her, she fell into a peaceful sleep. A night of rest energized her, and now, she was anxious to check out her new workplace.

A pickup truck from Scott Construction Company was parked at the building site on the far side of the new addition. The company was working on a Sunday, as the sheriff had predicted, making up lost time due to the inclement weather.

Cass inspected the building as she walked toward the front door of the original wing. From the outside, the complex appeared to be large and roomy. The new construction blended seamlessly into the original building. Once completed, both wings would look as if they were built at the same time. Now, the facility just needed someone to also seamlessly blend two diverse clinics into one smooth operation. That's where she came in. Cass was confident she could do that.

Challenges were not new to Cass. She had inherited a mess—an antiquated computer system and an inefficient staff—when she became director at Fitzgerald. The former director, Ms. Langley, was a sweet lady, but she hadn't kept up with modern technology or the changing requirements for records management. Cass had spent long days and many late nights bringing Fitzgerald into the digital age. But it had been time well spent; once this work was completed, it made them more efficient and able to expand patient services.

Cass entered the building and began a walk-through inspection of the clinic. The waiting room was spotless, with large photographs of local scenes decorating the walls. Since the clinic had only been open for two years, the furnishings showed very little wear.

She peeked into the front office through the check-in window. There were three work stations, along with the usual office equipment—modern computers, a fax machine, filing cabinets, and telephones. The office equipment was adequate, so that was a good start.

Cass left the waiting room and entered the hallway, taking inventory as she walked. There was a break room, a supply room, and three offices whose doors were closed and locked. Nameplates on the wall by the doors indicated these were the private offices of the therapists.

At the end of the hallway, she found the director's office, with Dr. Phillips's name on the placard beside the door. Cass unlocked the door and entered the room.

"Oh faff!" Cass exclaimed, using an expression she and Raj

had coined as kids to circumvent their mother's censure against using swear words. Cecilia didn't approve of cursing, especially for "properly bred ladies."

Those days were much more fun than "adulting" has been, thought Cass. She missed Raj and wished he were with her now—or at least living Stateside. Raj always made everything fun, but she doubted even Raj could find humor in what their father had done.

Cass also wished the room before her didn't look like a tornado had just blown through. This was the director's office? She backed up and checked the nameplate again. Yes, she had the right room, but the disarray looked more like a messy storage area than an office. Boxes of supplies were stacked haphazardly on a credenza, on the floor, and on an extra office chair. A printer and a fax machine teetered precariously on an old-fashioned metal typing table. The large double window was curtainless, and the desk, centered in the room, was positioned so that its back was to the window. A user would miss the beautiful view of Love Vine Mountain.

This isn't a storage room, Cass thought, *It's the office of someone who planned to be here temporarily.* Doctor Phillips had agreed to stay for only a short time. Why bother straightening up when a new director would arrive any moment and personalize the room to their taste? On the other hand, he'd been the director for two years, so perhaps he was just disorganized. How Dr. Phillips had managed to work in such clutter was a testament to his ability to focus on what was within his immediate vision. Cass didn't have that ability.

She walked around the desk to inspect the computer system. A laptop and a personal computer with a large monitor took up most of the desktop. There weren't any personal photos or knickknacks on the desk. Propped against the monitor was a note addressed to her. Obviously, the people of Mason Valley liked note writing. That was an outdated method of communication, but certainly more personal than email or text.

Cass opened the note and began to read:

Welcome, Ms. Jordan. Glad you're here. I planned to be in the office on Tuesday, Wednesday, and Thursday. But my wife has an appointment in Charlotte this Tuesday, so I will be in on Monday, Wednesday, and Thursday. I look forward to familiarizing you with the clinic staff, our procedures, budget records, etc. Call me if you need anything before tomorrow. The office is yours, so arrange it any way you like. Yours, Charles Phillips, MD.

Cass folded the note and placed it back on the desk. Doctor Phillips sounded like a man ready to return to retirement. Tomorrow, with his help, she'd get details on the daily operations of the clinic. But today, she had to straighten this office. She couldn't function in a cluttered mess like the one she was standing in.

Cass had just started opening a box of supplies to identify the contents when a loud crash came from the adjoining wing.

What was that? Did someone fall?

Cass hurried through the back door that connected the two clinics, then followed the sound to a room at the end of the hallway. She stopped in front of an open door.

A dark-haired man dressed in painter's coveralls and standing on a ladder was none other than the rude man she had met yesterday at the sheriff's office. He didn't appear any happier today. He glared down at a painting tray lying upside down on the concrete floor. A puddle of white paint oozed out from underneath. When he noticed Cass standing in the doorway, his scowl quickly vanished, replaced by a blank expression.

"What are you doing in here?" Cass asked. "It sounded like the building collapsed."

"Another silly question? I'm painting a mural on the ceiling of the Sistine Chapel." The painter's sarcasm morphed into a V-shaped frown between his eyes. Two chunks of blue ice would show more warmth than the eyes that looked down at Cass. "What does it look like I'm doing?"

"Making a mess, Michelangelo—on the floor and on your leg." Cass nodded toward the paint dripping down the leg of his coveralls.

The painter didn't respond but climbed down from the ladder and picked the painting tray up off the floor. Without acknowledging her presence further, he grabbed a piece of wood from a scrap pile nearby and began scraping the paint off the floor and into a dust pan.

"Go… go. Let me clean the floor while you remove your coveralls." Cass left the doorway and entered the room. "You're dripping on the floor and making a bigger mess by spreading the paint even farther."

The painter looked down at his footprints on the floor, then looked dubiously at Cass. "Helpful Hannah? Here to save the day!"

"Cass Jordan, to be more precise." Cass reached out and took the tray and piece of wood from him. He didn't object. "Who're you when you're not being Michelangelo and slinging paint all over the place?"

"Ryan Scott," the painter replied, still not smiling. "My friends call me Ryan, but you can call me Mr. Scott."

"Funny—not! A tired, worn-out joke. Can't you do better?" When Mr. Scott didn't answer, Cass bent forward and began scraping paint into the pan. "Helpful Hannah is going to clean up your mess, Mr. Scott."

Once the pan was full of paint, Cass walked to a nearby trash pile, found a plastic bag, and scraped the paint into the bag. Ryan moved out of her way and silently watched her for a few minutes. Then, as Cass had suggested, he unzipped his coveralls and started pushing them off his shoulders.

Cass turned to scrape more paint off the floor. But then, she froze. And stared. Ryan wasn't wearing a shirt beneath his coveralls. Only two words punctured the buzz in her head—*tanned* and *toned*. The coveralls came down over broad shoulders, exposing a muscular chest shaded lightly with dark hair.

Ryan stared back at Cass, not blinking, and pushed the coveralls lower, down over his hips.

Cass gulped, ready to bolt from the room, before she noticed Ryan wore jeans beneath the painter's coveralls. His unblinking stare turned into a smirk. He'd intended for her to believe he was stripping naked in front of her. He wanted to shock her.

Such a juvenile stunt. Try again, buddy! Cass sometimes rode SEPTA, Philly's subway line, and witnessed more shocking things than a half-dressed man once the bars closed and the drunk patrons boarded for a ride home.

Cass went back to scaping up the wet paint, hoping Ryan hadn't seen her initial reaction. True, she'd seen more skin on the subway, but nothing nearly as appealing as the painter— except for his attitude. What was his problem? Abandoned at birth and raised by wolves? No, wolves were actually friendlier.

But his tall, muscular body gave her an idea—more than one idea, actually, but back to the matter at hand.

Ryan had removed his coveralls and was straightening a t-shirt over his torso when Cass looked up again. "I wonder... Ryan." Cass ignored his instruction to call him 'Mr. Scott.' "Since I helped you, would you mind helping me? I want to move a desk in Doctor Phillips's office."

"But Helpful Hannah, I didn't ask for your help. And why are you moving the desk? The cleaning lady plans to steal the office furniture?" Ryan still hadn't smiled.

The name 'Helpful Hannah' was meant to belittle her, and now, he was insinuating that she was the cleaning lady? Was this just another insult, or did he not know who she was? Maybe her notoriety hadn't reached Mason Valley yet, and he really didn't know anything about her—and apparently, he didn't *care* to know anything about her, either.

"No, not the cleaning lady—or a thief. I'm the new clinic director. Doctor Phillips left a note saying I can rearrange his office—my office now—as I want. And I want to move the desk, but it's too heavy to move by myself."

"Clinic director? The city girl from Philly? Here to show the mountain people how things are done in the big city?"

"Not at all. Just like you, Country Boy, I'm just here to do a job." So, he *had* heard of her. The way he said "city girl" sounded like another insult, and he clearly wasn't impressed by her position as director. A city girl—an outsider! Why it mattered that she came from a big city, only Mr. Scott knew. "Even city girls need help moving heavy objects."

"Sure, I'll help. Lead the way." Ryan agreed so easily, Cass was taken aback. He pointed toward the door, his scowl in place. That frown must be permanently etched on his face.

Cass placed the painting tray on the floor near the ladder. She expected Ryan to slam and lock the door behind her once she walked out of the room, but he didn't. Maybe the locks hadn't been installed yet. He followed her down the hall, through the double doors, and into Dr. Phillips's office.

"See," Cass waved her hand at the desk. "I like to look outside from my desk when I work. Let's move the desk so it faces the window. Then, we can move the credenza over to the opposite wall."

Ryan gazed around the room, still scowling. Cass had interrupted his morning, he wasn't happy about it, and he didn't hide the fact that he wasn't eager to help her. She'd give him a break. Maybe he was having a bad day to begin with. And she did want the desk moved.

Ryan walked to the desk, bent over, and looked underneath it. "Moving the desk should be easy, but the computer and phone cables need to be disconnected first." Straightening, he showed a mild interest in the task at hand and pointed to the credenza. "But *that* will have to be unloaded before it can be moved."

Ryan squatted down, unhooked several electrical cords and cables beneath the desk, stood, picked up one end of the desk, and heaved it around in the opposite directions. He then walked to the other end and performed the same maneuver.

After a little more adjusting, he asked, "Like that?"

"That's perfect," Cass replied. "I was going to help you move it, though. You didn't need to do it all by yourself."

"Don't want you to break a nail." Ryan didn't look Cass's way as he spoke. He untangled the electrical cords, gathered them into a neat bundle, and then plugged them into a wall receptacle near the repositioned desk.

Pretending she hadn't heard Ryan's comment, Cass started lifting boxes off the credenza and placing them on the floor. Ryan finished with the electrical cords and cables, then joined Cass in clearing the top of the credenza. Obviously anxious to get the task over with, Ryan grabbed the end of the credenza as soon as it was cleared and pulled it across the room. He positioned it in the location Cass had indicated.

"Doesn't this look better?" Cass stood behind the desk with her hands on her hips, looking out the window. "I can see Love Vine Mountain from here. Beautiful view, don't you think?"

"A desk is a desk no matter the view," Ryan replied shortly, not even a hint of a smile lighting his blue eyes. If anything, they had hardened into blue stone.

"That's not a very Michelangelo way to think. Be bold and adventurous, Mr. Scott! You might discover new things!" Cass hadn't given up on getting a smile, even a tiny one, out of Ryan.

Yeah, like that would happen. Her charm offensive was wasted on this man.

"I see all I want to see. You need anything else?" Ryan asked brusquely, looking at the door as if in a hurry to escape. "I need to get back to painting."

"No, this is great! And thanks for your help. I..." Cass stopped talking. Ryan was already out the door, gone without a backward glance or even a goodbye.

Cass stared at the empty doorway, her hands fisted on her hips. Then, she shrugged off Ryan's rudeness. As he'd pointed out, she was a Philly girl, a place where brashness was an admired trait and something you learned to view as normal behavior. It passed as Philly etiquette if you attended an Eagles' football game at "The Linc." Dodging insults and elbows came with the ticket—not a new phenomenon to her.

Maybe she would submit a proposal to the city council and suggest they change their roadside welcome sign to read, "24,999 friendly people and one super-unfriendly grouch."

Cass returned to inspecting the boxes of supplies that now sat on the floor. While she worked, she couldn't help but think about her meeting with Ryan Scott. Was there something about her that brought out his rudeness, or was that his natural disposition? What bothered him the most—that she'd moved from a big city or that she was the new director? Why did either bother him? She didn't plan to try to remake Mason Valley in the image of Philadelphia. If being a Philly transplant was a deal-breaker for a friendly welcome from Mr. Scott, so be it. She couldn't do anything about that, nor did she want to.

Soon, Cass had transferred all the clutter in her office to the stock room in the form of several boxes of office supplies— reams of printer paper, Post-it notes, and pens—and a box of brochures that contained information on conditions like depression, stress, and anxiety, with contacts for community resources available to help relieve those conditions.

There were also stacks of small pamphlets promoting events around the area: trail hiking, horseback riding, fishing, and rock climbing, as well as exercise classes and entertainment options. They were all unique ways for patients to feel in control of their lives; plus, they offered comradery with others who shared similar experiences. The Elizabeth Barrett Mental Health Clinic was not just a clinic in name only. The services it offered were based on modern and up-to-date views on mental health.

Cass found an empty tiered free-standing magazine rack and filled it with the brochures and pamphlets, then carried the rack to the waiting room and placed it beside one of the end tables. The information wouldn't help anyone if it was packed away or locked in the supply room.

Cass's stomach began to rumble, a reminder that she hadn't eaten since the bagel she'd brought with her hours ago. She looked at the time. It was late afternoon and way past time for lunch. She'd been so engrossed in "the painter" and straightening her new office that she hadn't realized how long she'd been here.

Thanks to Carolyn Wilder, a readymade dinner sat in the refrigerator at home. Cass's mouth began to water at the thought. By the time she got home and reheated the lasagna, it would be dinnertime—or close enough for her.

Cass gathered her things and left the clinic. She stood on the front porch steps for a moment, just listening to the silence as she gazed up at Love Vine Mountain in the distance. The scenery and atmosphere were huge, but welcome changes from the mobs she'd faced in Philly.

Cass took a deep breath of sweet mountain air, and a pleasant sense of satisfaction filled her. She hadn't accomplished anything monumental today, but it was reassuring just to know that after the recent upheaval in her life, she'd landed on her feet, and found a place where she felt needed.

Tomorrow, she'd meet her staff. She was anxious to get to know them and hoped they would also be happy with their new boss.

As she walked to her car, Cass glanced around, looking for the construction truck. It was gone. Ryan Scott had left the premises. No doubt, his *sunny* personality was off to brighten someone else's life.

Was he married? Even as handsome as he was, would a wife put up with a grump like him? Doubtful! And Cass hadn't noticed a wedding ring.

But his hands weren't what caught your eye, Cass reminded herself with a smile as she started her car and drove out of the parking lot. Right now, though, what was upper most in her mind was the homemade lasagna that awaited her at home.

CHAPTER SIX

Cass entered the Barrett Mental Health Clinic with a bounce in her step, eager to meet and get acquaint- ed with the staff. She looked forward to taking on this new challenge. She'd been at Fitzgerald practically all her adult life—a summer intern while in college, assistant director, then clinic director. Once she'd pulled the office into the digi- tal world, the clinic functioned smoothly and efficiently. Real challenges were few, board meetings never changed, and life at Fitzgerald ticked along effortlessly. Maybe they wouldn't miss her at all.

Working at the same place for so long, she'd fallen into a rut and become bored, maybe even complacent and stale. Had she been unhappy and hadn't even realized it? She hadn't wanted to get fired, but would she have moved if not forced into it?

Cass paused just inside the door to her office. The disor- ganized mess she'd found yesterday was now neat and orderly, with everything in its proper place. Once she installed some window treatments, the office would be perfect—a nice work- space.

Judging from the quietness of the building, she had arrived first this morning. Muffled sounds from the construction crews' arrival were the only thing disturbing the morning silence.

This morning, Cass carried the same cardboard box she'd carried along the streets of Philadelphia just a few weeks ago on the day of infamy—the day of her firing. Except for a couple of family photos taken years ago, there wasn't much in the box she felt a strong attachment to. One photo, more special than others, was of her Grandmother Jordan, taken just before she became ill and passed away.

Grandma Jordan was Cass's mentor and biggest support-er. She knew how to cut through the Winslow BS and cull the importance of any situation. What she would say to her son, Kenneth, right now would probably set fire to Love Vine Mountain and half of North Carolina.

Wrestling the box through the door, sustaining bruises on her side for a second time, was a kind of exorcism for Cass. Placing the items on her desk and the credenza was more about sticking them in the face of the God of Misery. He—and it had to be a *he*—thought he'd dismantled her life forever and left her broken in the chaos. Not going to happen!

"That's a bit overly dramatic, don't you think?" Cass muttered. The universe didn't give a crap about her personal problems. Her father was responsible for all the chaos. The one person who was supposed to protect her had failed miserably in his job.

Cass blamed her father more for entangling her in his crime than for his original crime. He'd pay for his Ponzi scheme, but he'd never be able to undo the harm he'd caused her personally or professionally. She might never have faith in him again.

But the broken man she had visited before leaving Philly, the man who refused to look at her, deserved sympathy more than her anger. Cass hoped that one day, her anger would cool enough to do that. Her father had made a colossal mistake. And he was aware of just how colossal. She planned to apologize for the hurtful things she'd yelled at him. She just needed a little more time.

Cass had placed the last knickknack on the credenza—a souvenir she'd picked up in London on her forced trip to attend the queen's birthday parade—when she heard a noise at the door. A grey-haired man in a rumpled suit paused in the doorway.

"You must be Ms. Jordan. I'm Dr. Phillips," the man said with a look of surprise. "I didn't expect you to be in this early."

"Call me Cass, Dr. Phillips. So happy to meet you." Cass crossed the room and shook his hand. "I'm here and anxious to get started. I hope you don't mind that I took your suggestion and rearranged the office."

"No, not at all. And welcome to Mason Valley. I expected someone older." Dr. Phillips gave Cass a puzzled look. "You look like you just graduated college."

"I'll take that as a compliment." Cass smiled. "But I assure you, I have several years of experience. Maybe my youthful looks are just due to good genes and I should thank my parents. Come sit down." Cass pointed to the chair behind the desk.

"Maybe it's these tired old eyes that see things from a different perspective. Everyone looks young." Dr. Phillips left the doorway and walked into the room. A few steps in, he paused and looked around. "I must say the room looks much better." He took the chair behind the desk.

"Glad you approve." Cass sat down and faced the desk. "I'd like to get a couple framed photographs for the walls and some drapes, but then, I think the room will be finished. Oh, and a new table for the printer and fax machine." Cass pointed to the rickety typing table. "Where did that come from?"

"Mrs. Fletcher donated it to the clinic when we first

opened," Dr. Phillips replied. "She badly wanted to be a part of getting the clinic established. I couldn't hurt her feelings by not accepting it or by getting rid of it later. Her grandson was one of our first patients. One thing you'll come to understand about the citizens of Mason Valley is that they're very kind people and ready to help at any time, even in small ways."

"I've seen evidence of that already." Cass immediately discarded the idea of throwing the typing table into the dumpster. "Why don't we give the table a fresh coat of paint, put a potted plant on it, and place it in the waiting room where everyone can enjoy it?"

"That's a wonderful idea. I think I'm going to like you, Ms. Jordan, uh… Cass."

"Don't go out on a limb just yet. You've only just met me." Cass smiled. "So, what do we have going on around here? Give me an overview."

"Let's go meet the rest of the staff. They should all be here by now," Dr. Phillips suggested. "Then I'll explain our setup."

"Let's do it!" Cass followed Dr. Phillips out the door.

Their first stop was the office of Dr. Blankenship, the full-time therapist. She had just settled in behind her desk and was logging onto her computer and looked up as Cass and Dr. Phillips stopped by her door.

"Cass Jordan, our new director, this is Dr. Blankenship, our resident therapist. Her days are pretty much booked—some days more than others. Sometimes, she gets interrupted by a patient in crisis, so it's not uncommon for her to see a patient more than once a week."

"Welcome aboard." Dr. Blankenship stood up, crossed the room, and greeted Cass. "It's nice to meet you. Our current director is leaving us—thinks he has better things to do, like fishing and golfing."

"You've said yourself, Dr. B., that life is not all about work,"

Dr. Phillips said. "Too much work makes one dull."

"I did, but I didn't mean you should *play* seven days a week," Dr. Blankenship replied. "We're going to miss you, Charles."

"Nah, you won't. With Cass here, you won't even notice I'm gone. She's already cleaned and rearranged the office… just like you're always hinting for me to do."

"What? That rat's nest?" Dr. Blankenship quipped. "You're a brave one, Cass, for even entering that room. You'll work out well here. I can see that already."

"I have to agree with you there," Dr. Phillips chuckled. "I always planned to straighten up the office—*tomorrow.*"

Cass and Dr. Phillips said goodbye to Dr. Blankenship. She then followed Dr. Phillips toward the front office.

"So, Dr. Blankenship's days are fully booked? Does she have to turn patients away who want appointments?" Cass asked.

"She's here full-time, so she's not overloaded yet. But patients needing mental health help can't be herded in and out like cattle. Dr. Blankenship gives each patient as much attention as they need and tries to accommodate their work hours. Our services are gaining more acceptance. People here in the mountains often think they can and should handle mental health problems on their own."

"They view it as a sign of weakness?" At Dr. Phillips's nod, Cass added, "I think that's pretty common everywhere."

"But the patient load is what's so nice about working for a nonprofit. The doctors aren't under pressure to see a predetermined number of patients per day. We try our best to accommodate everyone," Dr. Phillips explained as they entered the office and check-in area. Two women were seated at computer stations, while another woman leaned on a nearby desk talking to them.

"This is Carolyn Wilder." Dr. Phillips introduced the woman who was standing. "She's a volunteer nurse, filling in when someone is out or on vacation. She helps out when and where she's needed. Today is pharmacy sales rep day, so she'll shepherd them through the process."

"Ms. Wilder, I've so wanted to meet you and thank you for the delicious dinner and bouquet of flowers you left at the house. That was very kind of you. It meant a lot."

"Call me Carolyn." Carolyn bypassed Cass's outstretched hand and hugged her. "No thanks needed. I wanted to make you feel at home so you'll stay here for a long time. And I'll confess, I have an ulterior motive. I want Kelsey to relax, knowing the clinic is well taken care of, so she can concentrate solely on giving us another grandbaby."

"That's Carolyn," Dr. Phillips laughed. "Always with a hidden agenda." Dr. Phillips then introduced Cass to the two women sitting at the computer stations.

Cass spent a few minutes taking to the two women, asking about their families and how long they had worked at the clinic. Then, she asked each one to explain their main duties.

Betsy Combs checked in patients and took care of patient files and all other administrative duties. Anna Wise, a former nurse, was the medical technician. She assisted the doctors with anything they required.

"Like Carolyn, we overlap where and when we're needed," Anna explained.

Dr. Phillips then led Cass back down the hallway and stopped in front of two more offices. "These offices are used by Doctors Tim and Pat Sullivan, a married couple living in Asheville. They come in two days each week. They see patients and coordinate the outside group services like equestrian therapy, hiking, and so on. They sometimes cover for Dr. Blankenship if she's out of the office for some reason. You'll be able to meet them later in the week."

"If our patient load increases to the point where we can't see everyone who needs services, do you think they'd be willing to work an additional day?"

"Maybe. We haven't reached that point yet. It'd be nice if they moved here, but they have grown children living in Asheville and don't want to relocate."

After a quick tour covering the same area Cass had explored on Sunday, they returned to Cass's office.

"Tell me about the board," Cass said as they sat down. "Who are they, and what are they like?"

"Ben Wilder, Carolyn's husband, is an unpaid board member. He's sharp, gets right to the heart of any matter, and a problem-solver. John Wilder, retired attorney and Ben's father, is another unpaid member and the legal counsel for the clinic. He's another one you'll want in your corner. Dr. Harper, a retired psychiatrist, is the medical expert. He's a good doctor, stays up to date in his field, and is always a champion of new innovative psychiatry methods. Then there's Clayton Thomas, he's… uh…" Dr. Phillips stopped talking, as if trying to decide what to say.

"Go on," Cass prompted. "What were you about to say?"

"Well… Kelsey was acting as chief executive officer and treasurer until she and Jason decided to start a family. She felt it would be too much for her—on top of her job in Atlanta and becoming a parent—to keep serving as CEO. She hired this hotshot guy from Atlanta, Clayton Thomas."

"And there's a problem?" Cass prompted.

"I call him a 'CEO for hire.' He's the CEO of several small nonprofit organizations. This is his first job in the healthcare field." Dr. Phillips paused and once again appeared hesitant to say what he was thinking.

"So… what *aren't* you saying?" Cass prompted again. "Spill it! I need to know what Mr. Thomas is like to work with."

"I… well, he hasn't been here very long, so I shouldn't be saying this, but he comes off as if you don't work *with* him, you work *for* him—at least, that's the way he strikes me. But my interactions with him have been limited, so I could be wrong. He's not only CEO and treasurer, but also chief financial officer. We're a small operation, so those jobs overlap. My initial impression is that he acts like this is his company. I understand that we have to watch our funds closely, but if you can't provide the services the patients need, then why be an organization at all?"

"I see. So, he's denied your requests for funding?" Cass asked.

"No. Well, I did suggest we hire another part-time worker to keep track of inventory, accept deliveries, and keep the stockroom organized. He shot that down. We don't keep a lot of medications on hand—mostly samples—and those stay locked in a safe in Dr. Blankenship's office. But someone should be in charge of tracking everything we purchase—what comes in and what goes out."

"And putting the supplies in the stock room." Cass smiled at Dr. Phillips. "That's a very good idea. Mr. Thomas didn't accept your suggestion?"

"No." Dr. Phillips shook his head. "This clinic was already established when he came on board, and as he saw it, we've managed without a stock clerk thus far. It's the new medical clinic I'm worried most about. There'll be even more supplies to keep track of."

"You don't think he'll let me decide what's needed?" Cass wanted to groan. She didn't need a micromanager looking over her shoulder, questioning every move she made.

"It's just a feeling I have. He'll knock down every request you make if it's above the bare necessities or not covered by your quarterly budget allotment. But you'll need to make your own judgements. It could be that I'm just jealous of his cocky self-confidence."

"Cocky and self-confident? Hmmm… some people have

accused me of that, too—wrongly, of course." Cass laughed. "I'm glad you warned me. I like to be aware of all potential problems. Do you think we could set up a video conference meeting for Wednesday? I need to meet this Scrooge from Atlanta."

"Yes, I'll do that before I leave today. One final piece of advice, though: keep Ben and John Wilder or Kelsey informed about anything you ask for that gets denied. They're your secret weapon. I know they'll have your back."

Cass and Dr. Phillips spent the rest of the day discussing patient records and computer files and procedures for referrals for specialized programs outside the clinic. Dr. Phillips also briefly went over the bios of current patients who came in for regular sessions.

Before he left for the day, as promised, Dr. Phillips scheduled a meeting with all members of the board of directors.

"It's at ten a.m. on Wednesday," Dr. Phillips informed Cass. "I tried for nine a.m., but you-know-who had his own ideas."

"That's fine. Enjoy your day off tomorrow," Cass said as Dr. Phillips said goodbye and left the clinic.

As Cass drafted a list of items to discuss at the board meeting, Dr. Phillips's warning about the new CEO was on her mind. Her tenure here in Mason Valley might not go as smoothly as she'd hoped. A confrontation with a micromanaging CEO was not how Cass wanted to start her job as director, but she was the experienced one and knew the proper way to run a clinic.

As Dr. Phillips had said, "If you can't provide the services the patients need, then why be an organization at all?" That precisely matched her personal view.

Cass was acutely aware that the bottom line was important, but the bottom line was not in the mission statement of a charitable medical facility like this one. Cass was prepared to teach Mr. Thomas that lesson—respectfully, of course.

CHAPTER SEVEN

C ass dressed carefully for the Wednesday morning board meeting. She chose a sophisticated navy-blue suit—one of her mother's designer-label purchases on their last trip to New York City. The color brought out the amber in her brown eyes. A frilly white blouse under the jacket softened the strict business look.

A rainstorm had pounded the valley overnight, and humidity hung heavy in the air this morning. Cass was forced to spend an extra half-hour smoothing out the natural curl in her hair. A blonde crown bun springing up on top of her head would look more like the stereotypical image of a librarian than a clinic director.

Chic and professional-looking, Cass was ready for the meeting. Shallow as it was, past experience had taught her that she'd be foolish not to consider her appearance. First impressions were important, and a first-time meeting with the board often set the tone for subsequent dealings. That was one lesson her mother had taught her that she agreed with.

Before today, Cass had used the building's front entrance.

But Bill Scott had left new keys for the back entrance of the medical wing with Betsy yesterday.

As Cass slipped her key into the lock on the back door, she was reminded of the day she used the back entrance at Fitzgerald Medical Center in Philadelphia to avoid the mob of protestors. That was the day she'd been displaced from her home, then dropped off in the mountains of North Carolina. But now, she viewed that day—horrible as it was—as a positive step toward where she was today. The old axiom of 'when one door closes—or slams—another one opens' just might be true.

Before entering the building, Cass paused a moment to listen to the silence. All was peaceful and quiet. The only sounds this morning were the soft cooing of the mourning doves in a thicket of maple trees surrounding the parking lot, interrupted only by a staccato tapping coming from inside the building.

The construction crew had arrived and were already at work finishing the interior of the new wing.

Cass pushed the door open and walked along the hallway, following the sound of the hammers and saws. She stopped in the doorway of a room that looked like it would be the waiting room for future patients. A crew of three was working together in a smooth, coordinated manner without conversation. None other than Ryan Scott was on a ladder nailing crown molding to the wall around the ceiling, while another man fastened trim around a large double window. An older man was measuring and cutting pieces of molding on a table saw and passing them to the other two men.

"Don't fall, Michelangelo! Or spill more paint! I don't want white paint on my pretty suit."

Ryan jumped and looked around at the sound of Cass's voice. His eyes widened briefly, then his surly mask fell back in place. He nodded slightly, turned his back on her, and resumed nailing the trim to the wall. Her pretty suit had failed to impress.

"Hey there!" The man at the window crossed the room and stuck out his hand to Cass. "I'm Mike Scott. That's my dad, Bill Scott, and my brother, Ryan." He identified the other men in the room. "You must be the new boss around here."

"Cass Jordan. New clinical director and someone who probably has more bosses than you can count," Cass replied, then nodded toward Ryan. "I met Ryan the other day—sort of. He doesn't talk much. But he showed me his tan. Ryan, does that make us BFFs?"

Ryan looked down from his place atop the ladder, his blue eyes running slowly over her. He started to say something but stopped. A joke? A rude comment? Whatever he intended, he didn't follow through. He turned back to the job at hand, completely ignoring her.

"My baby brother doesn't say much—mostly grunts," Mike replied, smiling. "Some people call him 'Hawk Man,' but I call him 'Cave Man.' Both names fit. He's brooding and aloof like a hawk and lacks manners like a cave dweller."

"Stop teasing your brother!" Bill Scott shook his head at his sons, turned to Cass, and added, "Nice to meet you. I apologize for my thirty-something-year-old offspring. They're worse now than when they were teenagers. Honestly, as a father, I never expected to say that. They were pretty bad back then. If they weren't arguing, it was horseplay."

"A boy's behavior predicts a future man—or so I've heard. Looks like you're making good progress," Cass said, motioning to the room. She looked up to where Ryan worked, but once again, he stayed mum, not looking her way or joining in the conversation.

"We're trimming out this room—the last one," Bill Scott replied. "After we're done in here, we'll add the cabinetry in all the rooms, install appliances in the break room, finish painting, and then touch up everything. Once the carpet is laid, the building will be ready for the decorator to furnish."

"It's looking very nice," Cass said. "I'm anxious to see it completed—and furnished."

"That shouldn't be too much longer," Bill said. "Of course, there's the final walk-through with Ms. Wilder and you. We'll make a punch list of any things you want redone, added, or changed."

"Ryan will have the trim in this room done before lunchtime today," Mike interjected as he walked over to stand by the ladder. Still ribbing his brother, Mike looked up and added, "When it comes to cutting and fitting crown molding, Cave Man has the hands of a surgeon. Right, Ryan?"

A short piece of corner molding Ryan had just accepted from his father slipped from his hand and fell, narrowly missing Mike. "Sorry." Ryan spoke for the first time. "That just slipped out of my hands." He didn't turn around. Mike picked up the piece of wood, slightly bumping the ladder in the process.

"Oops! Sorry, Bro," Mike said as he jabbed Ryan's hand with the piece of wood as he passed it up to him.

Ryan frowned at Mike but stayed quiet. He went back to nailing the piece of trim in place.

"I told their mother that we should put them both up for adoption," Bill said to Cass. "But she didn't want their sister, Lanie, to be an only child. I'm now thinking I should've been more forceful." Mr. Scott rolled his eyes, placed his hands on his hips, turned, and addressed Mike and Ryan. "What? No, 'he started it'? That's an improvement, at least."

"Speaking of surgeons or doctors, if you happen to know one who'd like to work here, I'm looking for candidates and scheduling interviews." When no one replied, Cass continued, "Well, I have a meeting to attend. Nice meeting you, Mr. Scott, Mike. Nice seeing you again, Ryan. Our conversations are always so stimulating! I can't wait until our next one. Let's broaden our discussions, okay? Like, world peace or maybe how the Eagles will defeat the Panthers this season? Easy topics."

Did one side of Ryan's mouth attempt to smile?

"Cass," Mike said as Cass turned to leave. "Why don't you come out to my establishment at the edge of town, The Eagle's Nest, some Saturday night? It's the local watering hole, and since you're new to the area, it's a good place to meet people. Ryan and Lanie sometimes sing with the band."

"Ooh, a Cave Man that sings? In grunts? That might be interesting to see. Thanks, Mike. I just might do that." Cass glanced at Ryan again. No reaction. She looked at her watch. "Gotta go."

Cass left the room. As she turned to walk down the hallway, she overheard Mike's voice: "What the hell is wrong with you, Ryan? Can't you see she's flirting with you?" Ryan's muttered response was too low for Cass to hear clearly, but she thought she heard the word "toying" or maybe "teasing."

Cass Jordan flirting? No! That was an art she had never mastered. She usually just blurted out what was on her mind. Subtlety was not her style.

Trying to hold a normal conversation with Ryan didn't meet the threshold for flirting, toying, or teasing in her mind. If flirting was what she wanted, she'd be at her grandparents' estate in the Poconos, attending one of her mother's dinner parties. She could flirt to her heart's desire there and with a plethora of eligible bachelors.

Ryan Scott's behavior was puzzling. His gregarious brother, Mike, didn't have trouble talking to her. But siblings didn't always see things the same way—except for her and her brother, Raj. They were in sync on just about everything. Of course, they didn't see each other that much, so it might be different if they worked together.

Cass entered her office to find Dr. Phillips waiting for her. She instantly forgot Ryan as she prepared for the board meeting. The meeting was via video conference, and if Dr. Phillips' warning about the CEO/CFO was accurate, she might be facing another unfriendly situation.

Cass took the seat behind the desk. Dr. Phillips pulled the extra chair up next to her. They briefly went over the topics to discuss and Cass added Dr. Phillips' suggestions to her list. As the time for the conference approached, Dr. Phillips opened the computer and logged in, then pushed the computer towards Cass.

"I've signed in, so we just have to select the meeting tab and join the group," Dr. Phillips said.

Cass nodded and clicked on the tab. Soon, there were clicking sounds, signaling that the others were joining the meeting. Their faces began to show up on the screen. Clayton Thomas was the last to join.

"Good morning!" Cass greeted them. "I'm Cass Jordan, here with Dr. Phillips, whom, of course, you all know. I scheduled this meeting so we can get to know each other, since we'll be working together. First, I'm very happy to be here and feel we all have the same goal: to establish a clinic that will serve the needs of the citizens of Mason Valley."

There were welcoming replies as the board members introduced themselves and offered a general agreement with her on the stated goal for the clinic.

"I talked to the general contractor this morning about the new wing," Cass said, "and it's nearing completion. They'll be ready to add the cabinetry soon. The space is looking great."

"That's wonderful," Ben Wilder said. "Bill Scott can always be counted on to do a good job."

"So, since the building will soon be ready to open, I've been looking over our staffing requirements," Cass said, getting to the most immediate issue. "We need two full-time doctors. But if I can only find one at first, they can start seeing patients right away while I search for a second doctor. At minimum, we'll need medical technicians, admin clerks, and stock clerks to open. We don't have a stock clerk now, and we desperately need one. They'll be responsible for ordering and keeping track of inventory and also assisting with other admin duties when needed. We need—"

"Cass… can I call you Cass?" Clayton Thomas interrupted. "I think one doctor will be enough. This isn't a big city like Philadelphia. Our clinic won't be serving a population like the clinic where you used to work."

Cass took a deep breath to calm her reaction to Clayton's rude interruption. *Hmm*, Cass thought. *Clayton… can I call you Clay?* But she held her tongue. The big dog in the kennel was marking his territory. She had dealt with big dogs before. She may be the smallest and newest dog in the kennel, but she could be like a female Bull Terrier when someone tried to diminish her role or her ideas.

One piece of advice her Grandfather Winslow had shared with her—something he learned as a member of the British diplomatic entourage while serving in various posts around the world—was, "Forget your last assignment and act like the post you have now is the best place in the world. No one wants to know how you did things at your last post." Cass wasn't about to be dragged into a discussion about the way things were done at Fitzgerald Medical Center or compare it to the Barrett Clinic. They were different facilities with different goals.

"Clay, there are many, many free clinics in Philadelphia, while Mason Valley has zero," Cass replied calmly. "It's over one hundred miles from Asheville and even farther from Charlotte, where the nearest free clinics are located. Our facility can't be a clinic in name only. If we have only one doctor and our people have to wait for weeks to get an appointment, they'll give up and won't seek treatment at all."

"Well, you know, Cass, we don't have the funding to serve everyone," Clay began before Ben Wilder interrupted.

"I think Cass is right. We're not building a clinic to let it stand empty. Two full-time doctors seem appropriate to me. And it's for the county, not just the town proper. We can always adjust our plans if more or less is needed."

"I also agree with Cass," John Wilder added. "If funds run low, we'll just ramp up our fundraising. And we can apply for grants."

Dr. Phillips scribbled on a piece of paper and pushed it in front of Cass. She glanced quickly at the note, then addressed the group again.

"Dr. Phillips and I have a plan. From what I've observed, the citizens of Mason Valley aren't looking for handouts. They're tough, self-reliant people. Dr. Phillips and I think we should still provide free services for anyone without insurance. Our proposal is that we waive insurance co-pays but still file claims for anyone who is insured. This would give the patients buy-in as participants in making the clinic a success. But I want to be clear that the ability to pay won't be a requirement for seeking medical care at our facility. Making a profit is not our mission."

"Accepting insurance from anyone covered is an arrangement that's common practice at many free clinics," Dr. Phillips added.

"I'm open to that idea," Clay grudgingly replied. "It would supplement the funds raised through our charity events. We should implement the same practice in the mental health clinic."

"Uh…" Cass said slowly. She strongly disagreed with Clay, but she needed to frame her reply so as not to appear to quash the suggestion as harshly as she felt it deserved. "Mental health services are different. People are often reluctant to seek out these services. Many have to be coaxed into even scheduling an appointment. They view their problem as a weakness and definitely don't want their treatment broadcast to the world."

"Citizens here in the valley will grit their teeth and try to power through most situations unless it's something obvious, like a broken bone," Dr. Phillips added, backing up Cass's point. "The idea that we might share their records with outsiders, such as an insurance company, will turn people off and just give them another excuse not to come to the clinic. They're very private people, Clay. I'm sure you can understand the fragile nature of patients with mental health problems."

"I… yes, I see how that might prevent the clinic from reaching those who need help. We'll keep the mental health services as-is. But we must still be cost-conscious."

"Cost-conscious, always, while still offering patients medical care of the highest quality," Cass replied. Dr. Phillips bumped her arm with his elbow in approval.

The meeting continued for a few more minutes with a discussion of the latest fundraising numbers. Clay was in his element and monopolized the conversation.

"I think our clinic is in good hands, Cass," Ben said during a lull in the conversation. "Kelsey and all of us are happy to have you onboard. Don't hesitate to reach out if you need anything. Nice talking to all of you." Ben closed his connection, leaving the meeting, and the others soon followed.

"That went well, don't you think?" Cass turned to Dr. Phillips.

"Because you stood up to the bully," Dr. Phillips replied. "Well played! You did it diplomatically."

"My grandfather worked in the diplomatic service for the British government. Maybe I inherited some of his skills."

"He'll be back, though. Clayton, I mean. Obstruction is how

he operates."

"I didn't say I could be diplomatic *all* the time," Cass laughed. "I grew up in Philly. Kid gloves were never part of my wardrobe."

CHAPTER EIGHT

Cass looked up from her desk and through the window, surprised that daylight had faded and darkness covered the area. The parking lot was black. A golden glow from the rising moon shimmered behind the tree line on the highest peaks of Love Vine Mountain.

Cass looked at the time; it was after 8:30 p.m. The staff had gone home over two hours ago. She vaguely remembered hearing the construction vehicles drive out of the parking lot soon after. But she had kept working and lost track of time. It had been a long day.

Inspired by the board's support for her ideas for the clinic and their siding with her in the jousting match with Clay, Cass had decided to brush up on the guidelines that covered the operation of nonprofit medical clinics. She had opened the website of the National Association of Free and Charitable Clinics, concentrating mostly on the sections about funding and grant requirements from the federal government. Reading that page was like falling down a rabbit hole because it soon led her to the Internal Revenue Service's site and qualifications for tax-exemption status. Concluding that she had a good understanding of her responsibilities as director as far as government oversight was concerned, Cass turned next to drafting job descriptions for the positions she needed to fill.

She was engrossed in her tasks, and the time ticked away without her notice until her stomach began to grumble. It had been a long time since lunch.

Cass stretched her arms over her head, removing the kinks from sitting too long. Then, she logged out of her computer, straightened her desk, and gathered her things. She was tired and ready to get home, eat dinner, and crash on the sofa. Maybe she'd relax by watching a movie—a chick flick or anything that wasn't about real life.

Cass locked up the building and walked toward her car. The parking lot was creepy dark. She had parked on the other end of the lot, in the farthest spot from the lone light pole.

"Great move, Cassandra," she muttered. "Choose the darkest spot possible!"

As Cass approached her car and started to open the door, she looked down and groaned in frustration. "Oh, faff! Great! Just great!"

Two flat tires on the driver's side, their rims resting on the ground, had just ruined her very productive day.

"Never get complacent when things are going well," Cass muttered to the darkness. "The wheels can come off at any time." In her case, the wheels went flat at the wrong time.

What happened? Had she picked up nails from the construction site? But she purposely avoided that area—which is why she chose this parking spot far away from the construction at the other end of the building.

Cass pulled out her phone. How it happened wasn't her biggest worry at the moment. Finding someone to come out and repair the flats was what she needed. Cass began scrolling and searching for a tire-repair shop.

She found Tyler's Auto Repair, located just off Main Street in town. They were a full-service auto-repair shop. As she dialed their number, Cass hoped full-service included changing flat tires off-site. But her situation didn't improve as she talked to the man who answered the phone. She had two flat tires and only one spare.

"It would be best," Mr. Tyler informed her, "if I tow your car to the shop and see what I can do for you here."

Jack Tyler arrived shortly, as promised, and hooked her car to his tow truck. Cass climbed into the wrecker's cab, and they pulled out of the parking lot on the way to his repair shop.

"You just caught me," Jack said. "I was in the process of closing up for the night. I'm Jack Tyler, by the way."

"Cass Jordan. Glad I caught you. I wouldn't want to spend the night in the clinic. I can't imagine what happened. I bought new tires before I left on the drive to come here. I think I must've picked up a nail from the construction site."

"Bill Scott is usually very careful about that sort of thing. I've worked for him at times. He has a magnet device he runs over the whole site to pick up nails and other metal debris in order to avoid causing flat tires. We'll check it out when we get to the shop."

"You know the Scotts?" Cass asked. "I met them recently."

"Ryan and I have been best friends since grade school. He and I, along with Mike and their cousin Denny Ferguson, the sheriff, played on the varsity basketball team together in high school. Ryan was the star. His quickness and smooth moves made him the best of the four of us."

"Smooth moves? The man I met didn't have any moves, smooth or otherwise."

"Ryan wasn't always the grump he is now," Jack laughed. "I'm talking about his moves on the basketball court, though he never lacked for girlfriends, either. There's something about his aloofness even now that intrigues women."

"Maybe they're just trying to figure out how anyone can be that rude and unpleasant?" Cass replied grumpily. A long, stressful day, topped off by two flat tires hadn't left her in a pleasant frame of mind, especially where Cave Man was concerned.

"Maybe." Jack continued his narrative on the Scotts. "Ryan could've gotten a basketball scholarship, but he didn't. When we graduated from high school, Ryan and Mike went off to college, and I went to auto mechanic school. I was better at using my hands than my brain."

"Well, I for one am glad you chose to open an auto-repair shop," Cass said. "I'm sure it takes brains to repair cars, especially with all the electronics and computerized equipment in newer models."

"I mostly fell into it. The shop belonged to my father, and I followed around after him for most of my life. The shop was like a second home to me. My dad was happy when I wanted to take over when he retired."

"Not everyone finds their perfect niche," Cass said. "Sounds like you found yours."

"I'm satisfied with my career choice. Not everyone gets to help pretty ladies in distress." Jack pulled into the lot in front of the auto-repair shop, found a lit area, jumped out, and unhooked the car from the wrecker. Cass trailed along behind him. "You can go inside and wait, if you like," Jack suggested.

"I'll watch, if that's okay. I'm curious to know what happened."

Jack raised the rear end of the car, removed the tire, carried it to a bench inside the garage, and placed it on a table. He began to inspect the tire. "Well, I'll be damned… er… excuse me," Jack said. "This is *not* what I expected."

"Why? What's wrong?" Cass leaned closer to take a look at the tire.

"This tire has been slashed and slashed good. I imagine the same thing happened to the front one, too."

"Slashed? I don't understand. Why would someone slash my tires?"

"I don't know. Did you piss off a Philly mob boss, and he followed you here?" Jack joked.

"I've never met a mob boss in my life. Do you have mob bosses in Mason Valley?" Jack's joking comment came too close to the truth and planted a scary thought. Maybe it wasn't an angry mob boss who'd found her, but a *mob* of angry investors.

"No, we just have cults and a few marijuana growers hiding out in the mountains. But your tire slashers are most likely vandals. We have a few of those." Jack added, "Usually, just fairly minor stuff, like writing graffiti on buildings downtown or toilet-papering someone's house. Or ringing doorbells, then hiding. Silly teenage stuff."

"Well, who did it is immaterial right now. I need it fixed," Cass said.

"Well… that's another problem. They're slashed—destroyed—and can't be repaired. I don't have replacements for these tires, either. I can get them for you tomorrow at a place in Granger, but not tonight."

"I need my car to get to work," Cass protested. "What am I going to do?"

"Well… why don't we do this? I'll drive you home tonight, and I'll ask Mike or Ryan to swing by and pick you up tomorrow morning. They'll be going to work at the same place as you. Say about 6:30 a.m.?"

"I wouldn't want to inconvenience them," Cass replied.

"It won't bother them and won't really be out of their way. After I replace the tires tomorrow, I'll bring your car out to the clinic."

"I guess I don't have a choice." Cass handed her car keys to Jack. "And thank you."

Jack closed up the shop, then assisted Cass into his personal pickup truck. He drove her home and parked in the driveway.

"I'll wait until you get inside. And you need to file a report with Sheriff Ferguson," Jack advised, "to document the incident. He'd know if it's happened to anyone else."

"I'd hate to start off my tenure here by getting some kids in trouble."

"If they're out slashing tires, they're already in trouble. You'd be doing their parents a favor."

"I'll think about it," Cass replied. "Thanks, Jack. I'll be ready by 6:30 a.m. tomorrow morning for that ride you promised."

Cass walked up the steps, unlocked the door, and entered the house. She turned on the lights in the kitchen and living area. Finding nothing amiss, she returned to the door and waved goodbye to Jack.

Cass ate dinner, changed into her pajamas, and stretched out on the sofa to watch a TV sitcom, but her mind kept wandering back to her vandalized car. Who had slashed her tires? And why? She was new here and hadn't made any enemies yet—at least, that she knew of.

Thanks to Jack's joking comment, she now had a new scenario to wonder about. Was someone local one of her father's victims, and they were now after her? Or had one of her father's victims followed her to North Carolina? The angry mobs that chased her around Philadelphia and called for her head weren't just vandals. They were vicious, and based on their threats, they wanted someone to pay. They wouldn't hesitate to make her that *someone*. But coming all the way from Philadelphia to Mason Valley just to slash her tires? That seemed unlikely and too scary to contemplate further. She discarded that scenario in the name of her sanity.

Jack suggested she file a police report, but that sounded a bit extreme if it were just a childish prank. Still, it was an expensive prank for her. She would just wait, think it over, and maybe file a report later.

Cass's mind was not on the TV show she was trying to watch, so she shut off the TV and went to bed. She was exhausted, and sleep quickly overtook the question of who had vandalized her vehicle and why.

♦

Cass was dressed and sitting on the front porch steps awaiting her ride the next morning when a white pickup truck pulled into the driveway. Ryan Scott was behind the wheel.

"I guess you drew the short straw," Cass called out as Ryan got out of the truck and walked toward her. "Out to rescue Helpful Hannah?"

Cave Man or Hawk Man, Ryan Scott was a very good-looking man. A shock of thick black hair and blue eyes—a rare and pleasant combination—sat well on his tall, muscular body. If he would only smile, he'd be what Hollywood called a "lady-killer," à la a young Paul Newman.

But smiling wasn't on today's agenda. Ryan wore his closed, blank expression—the exact same expression he'd had every other time she'd seen him.

"Just a ride. Not a rescue," Ryan replied shortly. "You ready to go?"

"With that warm greeting, I bet you volunteered for the job, didn't you?"

"I haven't said I wouldn't leave you on the side of the road."

"Oh great!" Cass wouldn't put his threat past him. But she

stood up, brushed off the seat of her pants, and picked up her purse, briefcase, and two Styrofoam cups of coffee. "I made you a cup of coffee. I added cream, no sugar—just guessing you're not the sweet, sugary type."

"Thanks. Just cream is good," Ryan replied as he accepted the cup of coffee and took a drink.

"I guessed right! No sugar wanted in your life!"

The same slight movement she'd seen before tugged at the corner of Ryan's mouth. But if that was his attempt at a smile, it was feeble and faded quickly. More likely, it was just a grimace from the taste of her coffee.

Ryan opened the door to the pickup and assisted her into the passenger seat. One thing she was learning about the men of Mason Valley was that they were gentlemen and courtly, always opening doors and pulling out chairs for the ladies. Even a cave man did that. In Philly, it was, "I got mine. Now, you get yours."

As they drove, Cass chatted about the scenes she saw along the route. Ryan's answers were brief and minimal, with very little expansion.

"So, you and Jack are friends? Went to school together?" Cass attempted to draw Ryan into a conversation.

"Yes. Friends since first grade." Ryan's eyes focused on the road as he took the turn leading out of the main part of town and toward the clinic.

"He seems like a very nice guy," Cass said. "I'm glad he was still open when I called last night. Finding two flat tires threw me for a loop. Not exactly how you want to end a long work-day."

"Have you reported the incident to the sheriff?" Ryan asked, showing more interest in the subject of her slashed tires than his friendship with Jack or any desire to get acquainted with *her*.

"No, and I don't know if I should report it. It's just one incident. I don't want to start off in my new home seen as a troublemaker."

"*You* aren't the troublemaker," Ryan snorted in response. "Whoever slashed your tires is the troublemaker. You're not worried it'll happen again? That whoever did it will get away with it and try something else?" It was the longest speech she'd heard from Ryan since she met him.

"No, it was probably kids playing a prank on the new person in town. I doubt they'll do it again."

"A prank? You've got to be kidding," Ryan said. "That was no prank."

Cass didn't have an answer for Ryan. She would be lying if she said she wasn't afraid or curious as to why someone would pick her car to vandalize. She had awakened early this morning and lay in bed wondering who would do that to her.

"Jack said you played basketball in high school—the star of the team." Cass tried to get the conversation onto another topic before she slipped and divulged that there were people in Philadelphia who had threatened to do more than slash her tires.

"You and Jack didn't have anything else to talk about but me?" Ryan asked—and not in a way that sounded pleased.

"Yep! Just you! I haven't been here very long, so I haven't met any other grouches in town, so you're it—how a grouch gets created is my favorite topic. Is the process similar to the resurrection of Zombies?" Cass laughed at her joke, but Ryan's expression didn't change. She tried again. "I played on my high school basketball team, too."

"I find that hard to believe." Ryan glanced over at Cass and looked her up and down. "You weren't afraid of chipping a nail or breaking your neck in your designer shoes?"

"No, we wore high-heeled sneakers, and a manicure was part of our after-game debriefing sessions." Cass's sarcasm didn't hide a hint of anger.

"Huh! You look more like the cheerleader type to me," Ryan

said without taking his eyes off the road. He turned into the parking lot in front of the clinic.

Ryan's comment hurt. He saw her as a spoiled rich girl. As a vacuous airhead who would never play basketball. As someone who would be content just cheering on the male team. She did go to a wealthy private school, but the girls' basketball team was awesome. No prima donnas on that squad.

Cass knew the truth, just as she also knew that she only went to that school because her mother insisted. She shrugged off Ryan's insult—his latest insult. She'd shed her thin skin long ago. But Cave Man was testing her patience, and her fuse was known to burn hot and short.

Yes, she liked pretty, well-made clothes, but unlike Ryan's insinuation, they didn't have to be designer labels. Her clothes didn't define her. Again, that was her mother's thing. And shopping was about the only thing she and her mother did together—one trip each year to New York City, where her mother dragged her to all the fashion houses open to the public. The time Cass spent with her mother was more important than the clothes Cecilia bought her.

"You can let me out here," Cass said as he neared the clinic's front door. She picked up her purse and briefcase.

Ryan ignored her and drove on until he pulled into a spot near where Cass had parked the day before. "You were parked about here?"

"One spot over, but close. Why?"

"I want to look around." Without further explanation, Ryan opened the pickup door and climbed out. He walked to the edge of the parking lot, then down the embankment into a stand of trees that separated the parking lot from the roadway.

"What are you looking for? The person's name scrawled on the pavement?" Cass asked as she followed him to the edge of the asphalt.

Ryan didn't answer but continued to look around the embankment before climbing back up to where she stood. "Let's go," he said as he turned and began to walk quickly toward the clinic entrance.

"You don't have to escort me in," Cass objected. "I can let myself in."

"I work here, too, remember?" Ryan's long legs strode quickly toward the door, leaving Cass to trail behind. She might have to rethink her conclusion about gentlemanly Tarheels.

Cass caught up with Ryan and unlocked the door, and they entered the building together. She started walking toward the hallway that led to her office, but Ryan veered to the right.

"Where are you going?"

"In here," Ryan replied as he walked into the front office. "To look at the security footage. I'll need your security code."

"Alright, but I'll key it in. It's on a need-to-know basis, and we don't share our secret codes with just *anyone*." Cass stepped forward to enter the code for the security camera covering the parking lot. She elbowed Ryan out of her way with added force—payback for his earlier rude cheerleader comment.

"What the…?" Ryan gave her a puzzled look, shrugged, then sat down at the desk. He opened the security program and began scrolling through the footage, searching until he found yesterday's recordings.

"Here it is. Look." Ryan moved over to give Cass space alongside him to view the security footage.

Cass leaned in, then took a step closer, drawn in by his clean, fresh, masculine smell. It was pure Ryan, not a cologne or an after-shave scent. She breathed in deeply, then forced her concentration to where he pointed.

"See?" Ryan pointed to a shadowy image on the driver's side of Cass's car. It disappeared quickly below the window. "Someone's head. It's not a teenage prankster."

"Teenagers have heads. How do you know it's not a teenager?" Cass asked. "All you can see is a shadowy image that *might* be a head."

"Teenage boys out to do mischief travel in packs," Ryan replied. Before Cass could formulate her next question, he added, "I was a teen once. They need their support group and don't have the courage to do their pranks alone."

"A teenage bad boy? *You* had a pack? I picture you more as a lone wolf."

Ryan looked as if he was going to snap back at her, but then, his expression cleared.

"Never mind. Not my business," Cass said. Ryan didn't do humor, apparently. Cass failed to find humor in most of the comments he directed her way, too.

"Exactly—not your business," Ryan replied as he shut down the security display. "From what I saw, it looked like only one person had climbed up the embankment to your car. A group of teens would have left more destruction—a wider trail of broken limbs and brush."

"I guess it could be something other than teen mischief," Cass agreed reluctantly. "But why?"

"I don't know. Road rage? Maybe you ran someone off the road or flipped them off when they cut in front of you. Doesn't take much to bring out the crazy in some people."

"I did *not* do any of that!" Cass answered in a huff. "I drive responsibly. I haven't had any altercations since I arrived."

"Since you arrived? Meaning you have in the past?" Ryan got up from the desk and closely peered into Cass's face. His blue eyes looked as if he were going to smile, but he quickly suppressed the urge and frowned instead. Was Ryan about to show some real emotion? Maybe there was an actual human in there after all.

"No, I didn't mean that."

"Well, I gotta go. Make that report to the sheriff!" Ryan quickly left the office and strode down the hallway.

Cass hurried behind, practically running to keep up with him. "I will, and thanks for the ride." She reached her office door, paused, then turned to thank Ryan again, but he was already at the end of the hallway.

With a backward wave over his shoulder, he reached the connecting door between the clinics and immediately disappeared.

"Don't run! You might fall and hurt yourself," Cass called out as the heavy door closed and the automatic lock clicked behind him.

Ryan's abrupt departure didn't surprise her. Him taking the time to review the security footage did. "As he stated previously, no time for chitchat," Cass mumbled as she inserted her key and opened the office door.

Soon, Cass was settled behind her desk to begin another busy day. Her promise to Ryan to call the sheriff was immediately pushed to the side. Despite Ryan's insistence that it wasn't a teenager, she wasn't completely convinced. Who else would pull a prank like that? Besides, she didn't have time to worry about something that probably wouldn't happen again. Plus, she didn't want to be questioned by the sheriff. His first question would probably be, "Is there anyone you can think of that might want to harass you or harm you?" *Yes, Sheriff—about half of Pennsylvania and a good part of New Jersey. Maybe New York, too.*

Cass desperately wanted to forget about the threatening mobs in Philly, to put it all behind her and let that episode die. Mason Valley was her home now, and her job as director was what she wanted to think about.

Cass logged onto the HealthPro website and posted job openings for the five positions discussed in the board meeting. She didn't post the positions for doctors—not yet. She'd rather fill those positions via referral from someone who had personal knowledge of the candidates. The background checks she planned to run were hard enough to sift through without overloading her schedule with candidates that were not suited for her vision for the clinic.

As promised, Jack Tyler delivered her car with two new tires around mid-afternoon. They chatted awhile, then Jack left to say hello to the Scotts at the other end of the building.

Cass finished up her workday, tidied her desk, and left the office while it was light outside. Still, she walked hesitantly toward her car, dreading that the vandal might have returned even in daylight. "Once bitten, twice shy," she muttered as she approached her car. She sighed in relief that all four tires were fully inflated.

Cass stopped at Rita's Café and picked up an order to take home for dinner. Unlike yesterday, maybe tonight she could relax and watch the movie she hadn't watched last night. *A New Kind of Love*, an old movie starring Paul Newman and Joanne Woodward, was streaming on the Classic Movie channel.

Cass loved old romantic movies—movies from a time when handsome, manly men like Newman, Gable, and Grant fought bravely to overcome heartbreaking obstacles to tenderly love and adore sassy women like Bacall, Hepburn, and Woodward. Cass usually cried through most of these movies. She probably ought to ask her streaming service to include a supply of tissues with her subscription.

A well-prepared dinner—she didn't have to cook—soft jammies, a box of tissues, and a romantic movie would be the perfect way to end the day.

Cass stretched out on the sofa, lost herself in bright blue eyes, and marveled over how Ryan Scott might be even bet-ter-looking than Paul Newman—if only he would drop the scowl and smile.

CHAPTER NINE

Cass's workdays fell into a predictable routine. She was the first to arrive each morning and the last one to leave at night. Her first order of business had been to establish a relationship with the staff. She made daily visits to the front office to chat with them, inquire about their families, and discuss any needs or any problems they were encountering in their job. She checked in frequently with Dr. Blankenship and the Sullivans for updates on issues they wanted addressed. That the staff all knew they could come to her with any problems they might have was Leadership 101 in Cass's book.

The new wing of the clinic moved closer to completion. There was a hiccup with some specialized equipment for the exam rooms, but the supplier promised the problem would be resolved and delivery could be expected soon.

Everyone seemed receptive to Cass's management style. The mental health clinic continued to function with little disruption, and the new wing was coming together smoothly. As director, her days usually moved along with few problems or fires to put out. Today was not one of those days.

Cass folded her arms across her chest and stared out the window at the mountains surrounding Mason Valley, willing the peaceful sight to calm her frayed nerves. A curtain of fog blurred the peaks, but an autumn sun was valiantly trying to break through with the promise of a warm, sunny day ahead. Love Vine Mountain, in the center of Cass's vision, added more fall finery in heart-stopping color every day. Large swaths of red, orange, and gold were broken here and there by bands of Douglas fir. It was a beautiful view, but it only managed to distract Cass for a minute.

Tension coiled along her shoulders and up her neck. Cass pursed her lips and breathed slowly in and then out in an attempt to expel the pent-up steam that was poised to blow off the top of her head and out both her ears.

Cass had just disconnected from another video call with the board of directors. The conversation with Clayton Thomas today had felt, as always, like she was engaged in an MMA fight.

Once again, the fight centered around a request for funding. Cass had initially thought a radiologic technician and a phlebotomy tech could be added later, once the clinic was fully open. But given the slow pace of responses to the job postings for the current positions, she decided to start the search now.

When she brought up the plan to the board members, Clayton exploded. "My God, Cass! Where is this all coming from? I thought we had decided on the staff positions—which, by the way, you haven't filled yet."

"I'm working on filling the positions. It's not as though they grow on trees. Radiology and phlebotomy are two critical diagnostic tools, and unfortunately, these services are not available in Mason Valley. To be a full-service clinic, we need techs."

"And just who'll read and analyze the data? You want to add labs for that, too?" Clay snarled in his big dog voice.

"No. Doctors are trained to read basic radiology films, but

my plan is to contract for the services we can't do in-house with companies in Asheville." Cass had already talked with two companies, and they had agreed with the plan. All she needed now was John's legal help with the contracts and the board's approval for funding. "This way, we'll relieve patients from having to drive to Asheville for lab work and X-rays—which many won't do if it's left up to them."

"We'll need contracts for specialists, too." Dr. Harper usually stayed out of funding disputes, but as the medical expert on the board, this was his area of expertise. "But we can do that when the need arrives. The professional building near the Asheville hospital is a good place to find specialists."

"I think you're getting in way over your head, Cass," Clay stated as though he hadn't heard Dr. Harper's comment. All Clay's ire was targeted at her. "This is going too far. I—"

"Clay, surely, you don't think we should diagnose someone with a disease and then leave them hanging, do you?" Dr. Harper asked. "We can't shortchange our patients."

"I think it's a good plan," John said. "We can do 'fee paid for service' contracts, which will control costs. Just let me know who and when, Cass. I'll draw up the contracts."

"Thanks, John," Cass replied. "I'll let you know.

Ben was the next one to concur. Cass had scored another victory, but Clay's constant criticism was pushing her close to the limit of civility.

Cass plowed on, boldly bringing up her next topic: a need for additional lighting in the parking lot.

Having lost the first battle didn't deter Clay. He immediately shot down that request, too. "The lighting has been that way since the clinic opened," Clay said, only somewhat subdued by Dr. Harper's not-so-gentle reprimand. "I don't see the need to change it now. We can't fund every whim you come up with."

"It's unsafe for the staff and patients," Cass explained, holding back a retort equally as condescending as his had been. "It gets dark early at this time of the year in the mountains, and on the backside of the new wing, it's even darker. Quite frankly, *Clay*, one light in such a large space is ridiculous." Cass tried but didn't keep all the snideness out of her reply. She was fed up with being treated like a teenager who was forced to ask her father for money after blowing her allowance.

Another intervention by Ben and John Wilder convinced Clay that it was a necessary expense.

"I don't know why this wasn't done originally," Ben said. "Better lighting will discourage vandals, and it's needed for safety reasons." Ben then went even further and suggested that extra security cameras be installed as well. "Upgraded lighting and security can be installed at the same time as the installation for the new wing."

Cass hadn't mentioned her slashed tires, but from Ben's comment, he and John must have heard about the incident.

Cass bit back another angry retort when Clay rudely pointed out that she hadn't yet filled any positions. "Clearly, this isn't your niche," Clayton said. "Maybe we should hire a consultant. I know someone who could fill the positions in no time."

"The clinic isn't even finished yet," Cass responded, barely restraining herself from shouting. "I'll handle it, Clay. We don't want unnecessary expenses, remember? Consultants are expensive, and doing it my way won't cost anything."

Clayton Thomas wasn't the first person she'd had to tiptoe around, be on guard against, and moderate what she was thinking. Being in the profession for six years, she'd effectively been told on more than one occasion, "Sit down, little lady, and let the experts handle this." Not only was she an experienced professional in healthcare administration, but she was also experienced in working with men like Clayton. If he was waiting for the "hysterical female" to snap and prove that she wasn't tough enough for the job, he'd be waiting a long time.

As much as it went against her nature to soft-pedal her comments to Clayton, she knew it was necessary to get what she wanted in the end. Another quote from her grandfather, the diplomat, seemed appropriate now: "Good diplomacy often is *not* saying what you're really thinking." In other words, "Keep your eyes on the prize."

Dr. Phillips seemed confident in her management skills. After a few days spent showing her the routine at the clinic, he'd left her on her own except for the occasional phone call.

Cass turned from the window and returned to her desk. She opened up the HealthPro jobsite. The message section beneath the job postings was still empty, and she'd just received approval from the board to post openings for two more jobs.

Only one applicant had applied over the last two weeks— for the medical technician's job. She was a recent graduate from a medical technician program at a community college in Durham, and a brief phone call had eliminated her as a candidate. She was requesting a starting salary far above the amount the clinic was prepared to pay and above comparable pay for the job.

Maybe the North Carolina mountains wasn't an attractive place to relocate. From the outside, they wouldn't know what a wonderful place it was. "But you're only here because you were run out of Philadelphia," Cass reminded herself.

If more people didn't apply over the next few days, she'd devise a different recruitment plan. A new idea was already percolating in her mind: military veterans' organizations that placed veterans in civilian jobs upon discharge. Military installations had well-trained medics with experience serving in both clinics and hospitals. North Carolina was home to several military posts, and veterans' organizations usually sprouted up around military installations. Jason and Kelsey, as veterans themselves, were also good sources for tapping that labor pool.

Feeling restless and still wound-up from this morning's tussle with Clayton, Cass decided to check on the progress of the new clinic. She entered the hallway of the new wing and soon found the crew in one of the exam rooms. Bill Scott and Jack Tyler were installing a sink and countertops on a row of cabinets. An older woman was taking measurements by the window.

"Good morning," Bill said when he spotted Cass at the door. "What do you think?" He waved his hand around the room.

"It looks great!" Cass leaned casually against the doorframe. She nodded to Jack then gazed around the room. "I love the burgundy-and-grey color scheme. It creates a very relaxing atmosphere."

"You can thank our decorator for that—my wife, Margaret." Bill nodded toward the woman at the window.

"Nice to meet you, Cass." Margaret left the window, crossed the room, and hugged Cass. "I've heard so much about you!" Margaret's blue eyes smiled in welcome.

So, this is where Ryan got his dark hair and blue eyes, Cass thought as she returned Margaret's hug. Mike looked like his dad, but Ryan was a male version of his mother.

"Where's Ryan… and Mike, your two helpers?" Cass asked.

"We're close to finishing here, so I sent them to another job this morning after Jack agreed to give me a hand," Bill replied. "Without me there to referee, they've probably had a fistfight by now… or at least a couple arguments."

"That's not true," Margaret objected. "They only argue when they're around you. They do it just to get a rise out of you, and you always fall for it."

"She's right," Jack chimed in. "They like getting under your skin. I agree that it's immature, but you seem to enjoy the give-and-take, too. Be honest, Bill—you like getting into the mix. It reminds you of when they were kids."

"Maybe, but I wish they weren't always under my feet now as adults. They should be using those expensive college educations I paid for, not hanging around a construction site. I can hire other workers." Bill crossed his arms and leaned against the countertop he had just pushed into place.

"Mike is using his business degree," Margaret pointed out. "He has the bar and grill, and it's doing very well. He'll be ready to take over the construction company when you retire. And Ryan… well, he just needs a little more time to sort things out."

"More time? It's been almost two years," Bill exclaimed. "I wish he'd get on with his life. That snarly mood he's in all the time is getting on my last nerve. And while I'm listing my grievances this morning, I wish Mike and Karen would give us a grandbaby. They're not getting any younger."

"Did you get up on the wrong side of the bed today, Grumpy?" Margaret asked. "You can't rush some things, especially when it's none of your business."

"You mean their purpose in life isn't to please me?" Bill asked. "Hmph! It ought to be."

"Dream on, Sweetie," Margaret laughed. "They have their own plans and timeline."

"That's actually what worries me the most," Bill replied "The way I see things, Ryan doesn't have any plans."

"I know," Margaret agreed. "When he and Stephanie started dating, I hoped Ryan was on the mend, but sadly, that didn't work out."

"That was a relationship of convenience," Bill said. "Trying to rekindle an eighth-grade romance rarely works. And Stephanie probably got tired of Ryan's BS."

"Listen to you, Mr. Romance!" Margaret rose up and kissed Bill on the cheek. "You should write an advice column for the local paper."

"Hmph! I can't even control my own woman." Bill hugged Margaret. "Truth is, I don't want to."

"Right answer!" Margaret patted Bill's cheek, picked up some fabric swatches, and returned to the window, where she held them against the window casing.

As she watched Margaret and Bill's good-humored discussion, Cass wanted to ask what had happened to Ryan two years ago, but she stopped herself. That was nosey and intrusive. Theirs was a private family discussion, and it sounded like a repetitive one.

"I may be overly confident in my ability to analyze situations," Jack interjected, "but I'm hoping things will change soon. Something will come along, grab Ryan's attention, and shake him up a little. And boom! That shell of his will crack into a million pieces. I have the perfect plan—if it works."

"You do?" Margaret turned from the window and looked at Jack with interest. "From your lips to God's ear."

Cass checked the time on her smartwatch and missed Jack's pointed glance at her.

Margaret added, "Oh! You don't say?"

"Yes, ma'am! He mentioned this person—a female—by name several times the other day. Talking that much about anyone, especially a female, is new territory for our boy Ryan. Has to mean something," Jack replied with a smug look.

"That's your perfect plan?" Bill gave Jack a skeptical look. "Replace 'overly confident' with 'crazy.'"

"Hey, Cass." Jack turned toward Cass, ignoring Bill's skepticism. "Why don't you come to the Eagle's Nest on Saturday night? Lanie's home from college. She and Ryan plan to sing. It'll be fun, I promise."

"Saturday night? Let me think. Uh… well, you know what? My schedule seems to be wide open." Cass smiled at Jack. "I might just do that. I'd like to meet Lanie and of course hear

them both sing. Right now, I need to get back to work. Nice
meeting you, Margaret." Cass waved goodbye to Jack and the
Scotts and returned to her office.

Her entertainment lately had only been the people on her
TV screen. A night out with live humans, music, and dancing
might refresh her mojo. Each time she met and argued with
Clayton Thomas, her ego came away black and blue. Even if a
night out didn't insulate her ego against Clayton, mixing with
other people would be fun.

◆

"*Oh, faff!*" Just as Cass arrived home on Friday evening, she
remembered that she'd planned to stop at the supermarket on
her way home. With the kitchen cupboards bare and a freezer
containing only a couple of frozen items, her choices for dinner
were extremely limited—and unappealing. Due to her wandering mind, a trip back into town was her only option.

An email from her brother Raj had arrived just before she'd
left work and distracted her.

Hey, Sis, Raj had written. *Currently in New Zealand and
finally have internet service. I'm here to research native foods,
especially interested in traditional dishes prepared under-
ground in earthen ovens. I apologize for leaving you to take
the heat for Dad's legal problems. My schedule was fixed and
couldn't be change. Before you call me a coward... I admit, I
needed to escape all the brouhaha. Selfish of me, I know. Will
try to make it up to you. I imagine Mom's had a full-blown
meltdown by now. I plan to return Stateside soon... unless I
meet someone "interesting" to hang out with. — Will be in
touch. Love, Rich, or Raj... or whatever.*

By someone to "hang out with," Raj meant a female. He

had a knack for finding women who were just like him: in no hurry to settle down and never expecting a long-term commitment from him. True, he *had* left her to face their father's arrest alone, but having Raj delay his trip wouldn't have stopped her arrest or saved her job.

In addition to grocery shopping, Cass had also forgotten a book at the clinic. Dr. Blankenship had loaned it to her to read this weekend so she could brush up on the latest research data on the benefits of group activities outside a mental health clinical setting. The clinic wasn't far from the supermarket, so she'd swing by and pick up the book before stopping at the supermarket.

When Cass reached the turnoff leading to the clinic, she braked to make the turn. A van braked very close behind her. Since the tire-slashing incident and Ryan's warning, Cass was always aware of anyone close to her whenever she was driving or parked in a public spot. If the tire slasher wasn't a teenage vandal, as Ryan believed, then anyone could be behind the violent mischief aimed at her.

Cass made her turn, and the van turned right behind her. Just as she was becoming very nervous, the driver slowed and appeared to be looking for a side street branching off the main road.

You're becoming paranoid! Cass scolded herself. She forced herself to relax and loosen her grip on the steering wheel. *It was one incident! Not everyone is out to get you.*

The van stayed behind Cass, but at a distance, until she turned into the parking lot at the clinic. It didn't follow her, but drove on by. Her imagination had replaced rational thoughts. She'd spooked herself over nothing.

Cass entered the building, then walked toward her office. Just as she started to insert the key in her office door, she noticed a black line on the hallway's tiled flooring. And the black line was moving!

"Ants," Cass muttered as she bent down and inspected the slow-moving line. Cass followed the trail backward and soon discovered where they had entered the building: a tiny crack around the pipes in the restroom. The cooler weather was probably driving them inside.

The line of ants moved rhythmically, in sync, much like a conga line—one right after the other. They marched from the restroom and down the hallway, as though following a scent, with a destination in mind.

"Oh *faff*!" Cass suddenly realized their destination: the electrical box in the front office—the box that housed all the phone and electronic equipment connections to the electrical power source. That probably wasn't what drew them inside the building, but they wouldn't pass up a chance to munch on the electrical components, even if it killed them. Most scientists agreed that for some unknown reason, electricity and anything connected to electricity attracted ants.

Cass had firsthand experience with how destructive a large group of ants could be. In her sophomore year of college, ants had invaded the electrical system of her apartment building. The little buggers shut down the entire complex for over a day.

Cass had to do something! If left alone, the ants would destroy the electronic equipment by Monday morning. The office would be shut down, and there was no telling how long it would take to get everything back in working order.

Cass grabbed a broom from the supply closet, and like an army commander heading into battle, she marched to the head of the line and knocked the ants backward, disrupting their march to the office door.

Cass immediately realized her battle plan wasn't working. The ants kept coming; ten replaced each one she knocked out of the line. There was a maintenance shed located behind the clinic. Maybe there was some kind of pesticide or ant bait stored there—anything more effective than the broom.

Cass hurried out through the back entrance of the clinic and into swirling winds that had picked up since she entered the building. Strong gusts whipped her hair across her face as she crossed the lawn toward the shed. Lightening, followed by a roll of thunder, drew Cass's attention to the towering, roiling black clouds in the sky. The storm appeared to be moving eastward, away from Mason Valley. Good! A rain storm, in addition to the ants, would not help her already miserable day.

Cass removed the padlock from the metal rings, raised the latch, and pulled open the door. A strong gust of wind tore the door from her hand, slamming it hard against the side of the building.

Once Cass stepped inside, she paused and waited for her eyes to adjust to the dark interior. Shelves lined three sides of the shed, each one loaded with a variety of tools and gardening implements.

There! On the top shelf in the back were several containers of fertilizers and pesticides.

Cass dragged a folding ladder to the shelf, opened it, then climbed up the steps. Just as she grasped the container with ants on the label, a loud bang shook the building, and the interior turned dark, as if a light had been turned off. The wind had slammed the door closed.

Cass grabbed the container of pest-control chemicals and slowly climbed down off the ladder. She crossed to the door and pushed against it. Nothing happened. The door was stuck. Cass pushed again, harder this time. The door rattled a little but still refused to budge. She peaked through a crack in the door and groaned. The latch had fallen back into its slot, effectively locking the door to anyone inside.

But how did that happen? When she removed the padlock

from the rings and lifted the latch, she was certain she'd left the latch on the outside of the slot. Maybe, in her hurry to find a pesticide and stop the ant invasion, she'd left the latch perched over the slot. The slamming door could have caused it to fall.

As Cass stood thinking, she thought she heard a noise outside. She peered through the crack, but didn't see anyone.

"Hello! Anyone out there? I'm locked in the building." She banged on the door, but no one answered. She paused to listen again, but there was only silence. "Hello! Please help!" she called again. Still, no answer.

Nothing to do but call someone, Cass thought. She patted her blazer pockets in search of her cell phone. Except for the ring of keys and the padlock from the door, her pockets were empty. *Oh, no!* Her cell phone was in her purse, and her purse sat in the hallway outside her office door.

"Oh, *faff!*" Cass sagged down on a stack of bags filled with potting soil. "Cass Jordan, you are such an idiot!" Why hadn't she called someone to come and treat the ants instead of trying to take care of it herself?

Carlos and his lawn crew had cleaned up the leaves in the yard and flower beds today, but they left early in the afternoon. Cass didn't want to disturb Carlos at home over something as minor as ants in the hallway. But they were probably the ones who stirred up the colony of ants in the first place. And Carlos wouldn't have minded coming back.

Mostly, though, she didn't call anyone for help because independent Cass Jordan was used to doing things on her own. She solved her own problems. And how hard could it be? Taking on some little ants was a simple task. Yes, very simple—unless one locked themselves inside the shed. Once again, she found herself in a pickle and all because of her stubbornness and independent streak. She had really done it this time!

Outside the shed, the evening was becoming as dark as the

interior. Cass was on her own, and without her cell phone, she was cut off from the outside world. And that was a sad statement about her life. No one would come looking for her if she disappeared for the entire weekend.

"Think," Cass ordered herself. "You're a Philly girl. You always brag about how you don't give up, and you view roadblocks as just new challenges. Now's the time, Miss Know-It-All, to put those words into action."

Cass stood up, turned on an overhead light, and moved closer to the door. She pushed against it again. Nothing moved. She leaned in closer to inspect the latch mechanism and see how it was attached to the door frame.

The latch mechanism was simple in construction. A long piece of metal—the latch—attached to the doorframe; the slot was on the door. Once the door was closed with the latch in the slot, a padlock was slipped into two rings, keeping the latch from being lifted. Since Cass had the padlock in her pocket, the door could easily be opened from the outside just by raising the latch up and over the rings. But from the inside, the door was securely fastened with the latch out of her reach.

Cass looked around the shed for something long enough to poke through the crack and lift the latch from the slot. A bundle of wooden stakes leaned against one wall. She grabbed one and returned to the door.

Her attempt to use the stick to lift the latch went nowhere. The stake was too large to fit through the crack. Time for Plan B. Did she have a Plan B? Yes, she did!

Three long bolts came through from the outside of the metal frame, held in place by threaded hex nuts on the inside. If Cass could remove the nuts from the bolts and push the bolts outward, the latch mechanism should fall off, no longer blocking the door. And if that didn't work, she'd go to Plan C: remove the hinges and take down the door completely.

One thing was certain, though: she wasn't spending the weekend locked in the shed, even if she had to dismantle the whole building.

Cass tried twisting the hex nuts with her fingers, but they were coated with rust and refused to turn. What she needed was a wrench. Cass spotted a tool box on a lower shelf near the door.

"Oh, please! Please!" Cass begged as she lifted the lid. "Let there be a wrench in here that fits." The toolbox lid creaked open, displaying an assortment of wrenches, all in a neat row and arranged by size.

Bless you, Carlos! Cass chose the wrench she thought would fit around the hex nut and tried it, but it was too large. She chose the next smallest one. Bingo! It fit snugly around the nut. Using all her strength, Cass twisted the nut hard, and the rusty coating around the bolt broke loose. Working the wrench back and forth, she soon felt the nut loosen.

Using her fingers, Cass twisted the nut until it came off the bolt, and the top side of the latch mechanism loosened from the metal frame. Cass began working on the second bolt, and before long, the second nut was off. Then finally, the third one came free.

Cass used the wrench to hammer the bolts backward and through the metal frame to the outside. She shook the door hard, and a clink sounded as the latch mechanism hit the concrete pad outside.

Cass shoved hard at the door. It swung open. Pausing for a moment, she breathed in the fresh air of freedom.

Then, grabbing the container of pesticide, Cass pushed the door closed and walked quickly toward the clinic. In her head, she had already begun making a list of things she'd have to do to repair the damage caused by the ants—and, of course, by her. On Monday, she'd ask Carlos to repair the lock she'd just dismantled. She'd also make a call to the pest-control company to treat the inside and outside of the building, another call to a plumber to plug the hole around the pipes in the restroom, and yet another call to an electrician to check out the electrical box and clean out any ants who'd electrocuted themselves while foraging for their evening meal. What a mess!

Cass had funds in the maintenance budget to cover all the unexpected expenses. Clayton was just looking for her to screw up, so he'd never believe that ants had set off the cascading events. Still, the bill would be much less than replacing all the equipment the ants might have destroyed if she hadn't stopped them.

Cass entered the hallway and walked to the head of the line of ants, which was now in the front office. They had the electrical box surrounded. Cass doused the ants nearest the office equipment, then followed the trail down the hallway and into the restroom.

She suffered a moment of guilt. The ants were just doing what ants did. She didn't want to kill them, but she wanted them gone. And this was the only way she knew to accomplish that task. *RIP, you little devils.*

Once she had finished spraying, she watched the ants for a few minutes. Those left alive were retreating back through the holes around the pipes. Instinct warned them of danger, so they were headed back to safety outside.

Cass was suddenly exhausted. What started out as a simple trip back into town had turned into a stressful, though comical, ordeal. She grabbed her purse off the floor, no longer interested in retrieving the book on her desk. Just like the ants, she wanted to retreat to the safety of her home.

A stop at the grocery store was out, too. Suddenly, a frozen dinner from the freezer sounded good. Well, not good, but quick and requiring very little effort.

CHAPTER TEN

Cass pulled on a pair of skinny jeans, added a favorite loose, flowing, tie-front shirt, and slipped into her newest pair of wedge espadrilles. She was going to the Eagle's Nest, as Jack had suggested. Anna Wise and her husband, Joe, were planning to be there and had invited Cass to sit at their table. According to Anna, whenever Lanie was in town and she and Ryan performed, they drew a large crowd—much larger than most other nights.

Performing before an audience didn't fit Ryan, the aloof man Cass had met, but talented people often had strange personalities. Strange habits didn't diminish their talents.

Cass didn't plan to mention getting locked in the shed to anyone. In the light of a new day, it seemed surreal, almost as if she'd imagined it. As comical as it now seemed, she wasn't in the mood to be teased and would rather forget it for the weekend.

When Cass walked in the front door of the Eagle's Nest, Jack spotted her and immediately made his way toward her. The place was crowded; all the barstools and tables were full. A few people leaned against the wall, waiting for the band to begin.

"Glad you came. The entertainment is just about to start," Jack shouted over the noise of the crowd.

"This place is packed," Cass shouted back. "I'm sitting with Anna Wise. Do you know where her table is?"

Jack nodded and motioned for her to follow him. He led her to a table with a vacant chair beside Anna. Anna introduced her husband, Joe, and another couple sitting at the table.

The waitress had just delivered Cass's margarita when the band took the stage. She turned her chair around to face the musicians. The band did an opening number, and when the song ended, the crowd started chanting, "Lanie! Lanie! Lanie!"

"Okay, I hear you!" the band leader said. "Let's all welcome Lanie and Ryan to the stage."

Ryan walked onstage, pulled up a stool, and without announcing what he planned to sing, began to play the intro on his guitar. The song had a pleasant, indie folk sound, but Ryan played the guitar with a more contemporary beat, giving his performance an updated sound from the usual folk or country vibe.

In a smooth, husky voice, Ryan began to sing a number Cass hadn't heard before. Lanie joined him on the chorus. The melody set a melancholy mood. It was a song of love gone wrong and lost chances. Ryan and Lanie sang in perfect harmony. When Ryan's song ended, Lanie transitioned to a solo.

Lanie's voice was exquisite. Cass understood now why the crowd chanted for her to sing. Lanie had the stage presence of a professional, a polished voice, and a wide vocal range. As their set continued, Ryan joined Lanie as backup on some numbers. They were good, and the audience loved them and showed their appreciation with loud continuous applause when their set ended.

Ryan thanked the audience, then left the stage. He stopped and spoke briefly with some admirers in the crowd, then joined

Jack at his table. Lanie remained onstage to back up the lead singer in the band. The band began to play a soft, romantic love song.

Wanting to congratulate Ryan on his music, Cass stood up and walked to his table. She also wanted to dance, but she doubted Ryan would make the first move and ask her.

"Hi, want to dance?" Cass asked as she leaned in close to Ryan's ear.

The sound of her voice evidently startled him. "No! No, I don't dance." Ryan shifted away from her. "Ask someone else. Jack might want to."

Jack might? A brush-off? Ryan Scott got ruder each time she saw him. He must stay up at night practicing his verbal jabs. But did she expect anything different from him? Not really. Still, his abrupt dismissal embarrassed her.

It was possible that he was telling the truth and didn't dance. She'd go with that one. Cass grimaced, then turned to Jack.

"Jack?" Cass asked.

"Sure. I thought you'd never ask." Jack glared at Ryan, stood up, took Cass's hand, and led her to the dance floor.

Maybe, thought Cass, *Jack can explain the problem with his buddy, Ryan, while we dance.* But they'd danced only a couple minutes when the song ended and the band moved into a fast-paced rock number. The fast beat wasn't what Cass wanted to dance to. She turned to walk back to her table, but Jack grabbed her hand and pulled her back to him.

"I want to go back to my table," Cass shouted over the music.

"Relax! Just go for it! Have some fun!" Jack shouted back as he twirled her around and around, moving her briskly across the dance floor. She was trapped. Jack's dance style would be funny if she wasn't so mad at him for forcing her to dance. His frenetic moves were somewhere between hip-hop and bad ballroom dancing. The fact that the steps didn't match the music didn't seem to bother him.

Jack continued to twirl Cass around the dance floor, then slowed, grabbed her by the waist, and hoisted her high in the air. Like contestants on a reality TV dance show, Jack spun her around and around. Jack laughed. He was enjoying himself and didn't seem to notice that Cass was not. To him, his performance was a ten. The crowd was watching them now, shouting, clapping, and cheering them on. The attention from his audience only energized Jack. He hoisted Cass even higher, then released her, catching her on the way down.

"Put me down!" Cass shouted through gritted teeth.

Jack complied and lowered her feet to the floor. Cass's head was spinning, and only the fact that Jack was holding her up kept her from hitting the floor. But Jack's exhibition wasn't finished. As the music came to an end, he twirled Cass out one more time, then back to his chest, bending her over his arm in a dip so low her hair brushed the floor.

"No! Don't touch me!" Cass shrugged away Jack's hand as he tried to escort her back to her table. Seething at him for making a spectacle of her, Cass dizzily and unsteadily threaded her way through the crowd toward her table. She had almost reached her table when she stumbled and bumped a man's arm just as he lifted his drink to his mouth. The drink sloshed out of the glass, covering the front of his shirt.

"I'm so sorry," Cass apologized, red-faced with embarrassment. "I'm truly sorry. Can I buy you another drink?"

"No, don't worry, babe," the man replied as he wiped the liquid from his shirt and waved off her offer. "No harm done. I've had too much to drink a few times myself."

Cass had almost reached her table when the meaning of the man's words penetrated her spinning head. He thought she was drunk. Were the others in the room thinking the same thing?

That the newly hired clinic director was out clubbing and dancing like a mad woman—and getting smashed in the process?

If she could get her hands on Jack, she'd… she couldn't think of a fate bad enough at the moment short of killing him.

"I'm calling it a night and going home," Cass told Anna when she reached her table. While praying her head was clear enough to walk out without ending up in someone's lap, Cass picked up her purse, ignored the stares from the crowded room, and made her way through the crowd and out the door.

Cass climbed into her car, but before starting the motor, she leaned her head against the headrest and waited for her brain to settle back into her skull. Soothed by the quietness of the car, her head soon stopped spinning.

Just as she reached toward the start button on her car, someone opened the driver's side door.

"Come with me. I'm driving you home." Ryan bent down, facing her through the open door. He reached for her arm.

"What are you doing?" Cass pulled away from him. "I can drive myself."

"It's not safe for you to drive," Ryan replied. "Trust me on this."

"What? Why?" Was something wrong with her car? As had become her routine since the slashed tire incident, Cass always checked the tires before she climbed in. She hadn't spotted anything wrong, but the head trauma from Jack's dancing might have left her eyesight a little blurry.

"Come," Ryan ordered again. "Leave the keys." As Cass hesitated, Ryan added, "Do you want me to call the sheriff?"

"Your cousin, the sheriff? No, I don't. I know whose side he'd be on. What's this about?" Cass grabbed her purse, took the keys out, and laid them on the console. She slowly exited the car, still wondering what was wrong with her vehicle.

Ryan held her arm firmly, as if he feared she'd bolt and run.

His jaw was set; he was determined to drive her home. Maybe during the drive to her house, he would explain the problem with her car—hopefully using words, not grunts.

Ryan guided her to his pickup truck, which was parked not far away. He opened the passenger-side door and assisted Cass into the seat.

"Jack, follow me in Cass's car," Ryan called out across the top of the truck cab before climbing in and starting the motor.

"If Jack can drive my car, why can't I?" Cass asked as they left the parking lot.

"Jack has experience driving under these conditions," Ryan replied.

"Is he taking it to the repair shop? Tell me! What's wrong with my car?" Cass was annoyed because Ryan wouldn't answer her questions. If her car had been vandalized again, she needed to know.

"Your car's fine. It's the driver that's the problem. It's not safe for you to be driving."

"What? I'm a very safe driver!" Cass insisted. Then, a light turned on. Ryan also thought she was drunk. "I'm not drunk, if that's what you're insinuating."

"They all say that!" Ryan looked at Cass with a smirk. "I saw you weaving like a drunken sailor coming off the dance floor, stumbling and bumping into tables."

"Oh. My. Goodness! I can't believe this!" Ryan's accusation was incredulous! "Not that I should have to explain myself to you, but I drank only half of one drink. *Half* of *one* drink!" Cass repeated angrily. "Did you also see your friend Jack toss me around like a sack of potatoes on the dance floor? My dizziness came from his *Dancing with the Stars* exhibition."

Ryan didn't look at her or answer her. He kept his eyes on the road ahead.

"You don't believe me? Then just wait until you see the scars

I plan to leave on Jack Tyler the next time I get close to him. I'm steady enough to do that!"

"I wasn't watching you dance with Jack. I saw enough after you left the dance floor. You're not getting into an accident. I'm going to make sure of that."

"Of course you weren't watching! You're too deep in your black hole to notice anyone and too busy imagining the worst about *me*—imagining things that *weren't* happening, by the way."

Ryan didn't reply. They soon reached her driveway and stopped. Jack was already there, casually leaning against the side of her car. Cass jerked open the pickup truck's door and stalked toward Jack.

"Why did you let him think I was drunk?" Cass stopped in front of Jack and kicked out, her shoe connecting hard with his shin.

"Ouch!" Jack caught Cass's hands as her nails clawed toward his face. "Slow down, tiger. I'm sorry."

Cass stopped fighting and swallowed several deep gulps of air. Her anger still boiled. "I go out for one night of fun after a very hard week, and you two jokers turn it into a humiliating spectacle. What's wrong with you?" Cass's voice shook. She was close to tears but also determined not to show it to Jack or Ryan.

"Aww, Cass. Come here." Jack pulled her into his arms and rubbed her back. "I'm sorry we ruined your night. I'm just trying to help my friend, since he won't break from his nightmare on his own. You know? Make him jealous. Maybe if I kissed you now, that would do it."

"If you want your leg broken, just try it. After dancing with you, I think you're living your own nightmare." Cass pulled away from Jack and started to walk away, then turned back. "Why would Ryan be jealous?"

"I apologize for getting carried away tonight," Jack said. "And forget I said anything about making Ryan jealous. After tonight, I'm through playing matchmaker."

"First rule of matchmaking is that you have to have two willing participants," Cass said. "As I see it, you've got *none*."

Cass looked toward Ryan, who sat silently in his truck watching her and Jack. She shouted at him, "Go home! Leave me alone! Both of you!"

Cass locked her car, then walked toward the steps leading up to the porch. She heard Ryan's truck door slam as Jack climbed in. Then, they backed out of the yard. She didn't turn around to watch them leave. She was beyond angry, and just might throw a rock—one big enough to hit both of them. But then, Ryan really would call the sheriff.

Physically, Cass felt better by the time she climbed into bed. Her head was almost back to normal size. And the anger she'd unleashed on Jack and Ryan had been cleansing. But she wouldn't forgive either of them anytime soon for tonight's humiliation.

CHAPTER ELEVEN

When Cass arrived at the clinic Monday morning, she quietly entered through the back door, trying to avoid coming face-to-face with anyone who'd witnessed or heard about Saturday night—her wild, untamed escapade at the Eagle's Nest.

Cass was mortified that Ryan thought she would get so inebriated that she couldn't drive herself home. But she was flat-out furious at Jack for making a spectacle of her on the dance floor. His behavior was the cause that led to Ryan's misconception.

When Cass got out of bed Sunday morning, the first thing she did was search the headlines of the local paper. She wouldn't have been shocked to find "*Drunk Clinic Director Seen Stumbling Around Local Watering Hole.*"

Cecilia would go absolutely bonkers if a story like that made its way to Pennsylvania.

Luckily, no such story was found. Either the local paper was slow in sniffing out the story, or her behavior wasn't an anomaly in Mason Valley. Just maybe, Cass Jordan's exploits were not as newsworthy to the local population as she thought they'd be.

As Cass inserted her key into the door of the clinic, she noticed the scratches around the lock—as if someone had tried to force the lock open. She'd first noticed them last week, but why would anyone unauthorized want to get into the clinic?

There were very few drugs kept in the clinic, and those were locked in a safe in Dr. Blankenship's office. They wouldn't be worth the trouble for a drug-addicted burglar. But that didn't mean a burglar would know that. What was of more concern were the confidential patient records and office equipment. That might interest a number of people.

But if someone was actually trying to break in by forcing this door, it would only get them into the hallway that separated the two clinics. There was also a heavy fire exit door, locked from the inside, for entry to the mental health clinic.

That someone, at some time, and for reasons only they knew, may have tried to jimmy the lock open with a sharp object was unsettling. But for all her conjecture, there might be a simple explanation. For now, she'd just point the scratches out to one of the Scotts the next time she saw them.

Just short of tiptoeing down the hall like the Pink Panther, Cass quietly entered her office, managing to sneak in without seeing anyone. Saturday night's fiasco or questions about why dead ants littered the hallway had been averted for the time being.

"Hiding things from your staff, Cassandra, is not the usual way you operate," Cass muttered. Still, before she began her workday, Cass swept up the evidence of the ant invasion, dumped the dust pan's contents into a garbage bag, tied the ends, and placed it in the main trash bin for collection.

Cass settled behind her desk, then made the calls to schedule a plumber and an electrician to inspect and repair any damage done by the ants' incursion. An email to Carlos asked him to repair the shed's door lock. She'd explain the details to everyone—later—if they asked.

Cass finished making the appointments, then opened a computer file containing the resumes of two prospective new hires. One applicant, a cousin of Betsy Combs, was scheduled for an interview this afternoon.

"Can I come in?" a voice asked from the doorway.

Cass looked up to find Lanie Scott standing just outside her door. "Of course. Come on in," Cass replied. "Have a seat."

"I hope I'm not disturbing you." Lanie took the seat facing Cass. "I'm on my way back to Durham, but Mom wanted me to stop in and invite you to Thanksgiving dinner."

"Thanksgiving?" Cass glanced at the calendar on her desk. "Oh… isn't it still October? I haven't thought that far ahead."

"Mom wants to get her invitation in before Carolyn Wilder beats her to it," Lanie laughed. "They're friends but can be very competitive."

"Well, your mom has beaten the masses," Cass said with smile. "By the way, you have a beautiful singing voice. You should go professional. Ryan, too."

"Thanks. We just sing for pleasure. The life of a starving artist doesn't appeal to either of us," Lanie said, smiling. "I know you were embarrassed Saturday night, but I don't think you need to worry. Mason Valley accepts people as they are, with very little judgement."

"Your brother's insistence on driving me home was extremely *bad* judgement. I didn't even finish my first drink." Cass didn't feel the need to explain further what happened in the parking lot. Lanie had apparently already heard the story, as had probably most of Mason Valley.

"I know. That's what Ryan does best—overreact and make an ass of himself. He didn't think beyond getting you home safely. Ryan complicates a lot of things. He wasn't always like that, and he means well."

"Everyone keeps dropping hints, but no one explains why he's so withdrawn. Being around him is like standing under a dark cloud, waiting for a drenching rainstorm."

"Ryan went through a bad experience… but he needs to be the one to tell you about it. He'd be angry at me if I even thought about sharing the details of his personal life."

"His telling me will never happen since he barely talks to me. I don't think he likes me very much."

"I'm sure that's not true. He'll be at Thanksgiving dinner. Maybe you can hit him over the head with a turkey leg or something. That might start a conversation. Jack will be there, too."

"Speaking of the extreme, Jack's on my short list marked 'Revenge.'"

"Jack's a character. He marches to his own drummer."

"Drummers have more rhythm," Cass replied. "Jack does listen, then ignores everything he hears."

"Jack's actually a good guy and about the only person who puts up with Ryan—except the immediate family, of course. So, will you join us for dinner?"

"I have a friend who'll be visiting from Charlotte. I was thinking of trying my hand at burning a turkey," Cass laughed.

"Bring your friend. We always have lots of food, and there's always room for anyone who shows up."

"Okay, then. I'd love to, and I'm sure Mandy will enjoy your mom's cooking more than my kitchen experiments."

After Lanie left, Cass considered Lanie's comments about Ryan. Saturday night, he'd felt licensed to forcibly meddle in her life without being asked. Cass's new goal was to return the favor. She'd meddle until she got a reaction out of him—hostile or friendly, it didn't matter. There must be some type of emotion other than cold indifference in that handsome body. After Saturday night's meddling, she felt entitled to some payback. Now was as good a time to start as any. Ryan's pickup had driven through the parking lot a short while ago, so he was at work in the medical clinic.

Cass found Ryan in one of the exam rooms, touching up paint scarred by the installation of the cabinets. She paused in the doorway and watched him for a few minutes without speaking.

Ryan's aloofness seemed strange for someone who seemed to have it all. He had the kind of handsomeness that would attract any living, breathing female—a tall, athletic body, with dark hair and blue eyes—a hard to resist combination.

Cass's mother's soirees were usually filled with handsome men, too, but Ryan's good looks weren't all that intrigued Cass. No one had ever ignored her with such obvious disinterest, even as a friend. And this made Cass determined to shake a smile loose, even a small one, from his cold, stone-like face.

Maybe that was it: Ryan ignored her. The men her mother found for her were fawning, obsequious, and worked hard at ingratiating themselves with her—or, more likely, with her family—and that turned her off. Ryan was different. He made it clear that he didn't care for her or care what she thought of him, either.

"I drove myself to work today and didn't run off the road even once. No ambulances or tow trucks needed," Cass said from the doorway.

The sound of her voice in the quiet room startled Ryan. He jumped slightly but didn't turn around. "Good," Ryan replied shortly, still not looking her way. He kept painting and pushing the long-handled brush up the wall.

"Who are you going to ignore when this job is finished?" Cass asked, still trying to get some kind of response. "Saturday night, you were the big, strong hero who swept in to save the poor, helpless maiden. Now, you won't even look at me."

"Saturday night was only about keeping you from wrecking your car and killing yourself. I don't have to look at you or talk to you to know what you're after." Ryan slowly turned and frowned at her. "Big-city girl, flashing her expensive clothes, on the prowl, teasing and taunting the ignorant country boy."

"Wow! You've figured me out! I can't hide anything from you, can I?" Ryan's words hurt. Just like before, he saw her as superficial and judged her by the clothes she wore. "Did a city girl break your heart, Ryan? She ditched you, and your ego hasn't recovered? You're still smarting from rejection?"

Ryan stiffened and stopped pushing the paintbrush up the wall. For a moment, he stood motionless, staring at the wall.

Cass bit down on her lip, instantly sorry that she had spouted off. She'd gone too far and obviously hit a raw nerve—just as he'd done with her. But it was too late to take back her words.

Ryan placed the paintbrush in the tray, then turned around. He didn't smile, and his blue eyes sparked angrily as he walked slowly toward her. He reached out and pulled her away from where she casually leaned against the doorframe. Before she could react, Ryan's arms closed around her like a vice.

Based on his scowl, Cass expected Ryan's touch to be rough, but his arms roved gently up and down her back, a gentle soothing caress—more like seduction than anger. Cass, caught like a deer in the headlights, didn't pull away as he bent his head and kissed her—a slow, exploring, languid kiss. Despite her desire to resist, Cass sank willingly into the kiss. She was breathless when his lips pulled away from hers.

"No, Cass," Ryan whispered, his mouth not far from hers. "*I* broke the city girl's heart. This is a warning to you. You don't control me, and you can't always put out the fires you start. Don't play games with me!" Ryan then turned her loose, and without looking her way, he picked up the paintbrush and began painting the wall once again.

An immediate response stuck in Cass's throat. Except for

the warmth Ryan's kiss left on her lips, her body was frozen in place. Incoherent and jumbled thoughts raced from *You liked it* to an angry *How dare he!* Her attempt to pry a smile out of him through teasing had created an unanticipated response, one quite different from the verbal sparring she'd expected.

Cass finally managed to engage her brain and searched for a fitting retort. Ryan wouldn't get the last word. At least, she had control of that much.

"Wow! I've never kissed a piece of stone before. Not bad! Just think how good you'd be with some practice."

"You didn't object. Are you volunteering for the job, City Girl? Be careful! Breaking hearts is my specialty." Ryan continued painting the wall, still not looking her way.

"Oh, ho! Country Boy is a braggart, too!" Cass threw back at Ryan. "I guess it's a draw, then. I've broken a few lovers' hearts myself."

Cass's voice was surprisingly steady, considering the shakiness she felt inside. Her boast was a lie. She'd dated, of course, but avoided serious relationships since college and her breakup with Stephen. And her and Stephen's broken hearts had mended quickly and completely. None of her so-called "lovers" had shaken her the way Ryan Scott had.

"See you around, Country Boy." Cass casually walked from the room. If Ryan could pretend nothing had happened, so could she.

♦

Wednesday morning, as usual, Cass arrived early at the clinic, before anyone else. She looked around for Ryan's pickup but didn't see it in the parking lot. Good! Maybe she could avoid seeing Ryan for a second day. She'd spent Tuesday on pins and needles, afraid she'd come face-to-face with him. He was sure to bring up Monday's incident, either directly or by insinuation—most likely with a disparaging and snide remark. Clearly, his aim once again was to shock her.

Cass had relived the moment many times—she should have done this, she should have said that. Finally, she'd crafted an appropriate reply and was ready to shoot back in case Ryan brought it up.

But now, Cass had a busy day ahead of her and needed all of her concentration focused on business. The impulsive kiss was just that—impulsive. But she'd readily admit that spontaneity did have its good points.

Staffing the open positions at the clinic was now falling into place. She'd gone from zero applicants to five credible candidates in a matter of days.

One job applicant was scheduled for an interview at ten o'clock. Cass expected Natalie Jackson to be well-qualified for the role. Dr. Phillips had recommended her, since she had once worked for him as a medical technician. Natalie was an empty nester now and ready to rejoin the work force.

Cass had hired Betsy's cousin on Monday for one of the administrative positions. She was experienced in filing insurance claims, a needed skill since patients with insurance would file claims for services received.

Kelsey had recommended a recently divorced and recently retired army medic with radiology experience. He had moved to Mason Valley for the fishing and hiking, so working part-time at the clinic fit perfectly with his schedule. A phlebotomist, also retired from the army, was recommended by a veterans' organization near Fort Bragg. She had lived in Mason Valley before joining the army and was anxious to move back home.

Feeling good about the direction of the clinic, Cass hummed along with a song on the radio as she parked her car.

As she walked toward the building, Cass noticed two urns, one on either side of the steps, holding recently planted winter pansies that needed watering. She walked to the side of the building, turned on the water faucet, then pulled the hose back to the steps at the front entrance. Stopping in front of the urns, she glanced up at the front door. Her breath stopped.

Words were scrawled in dripping bright-red paint across the clinic's white-painted door. "U owe me!" "U gonna die, bitch!" "I know where U live!" "Karma is here!" "Payback coming!"

"Oh… my… God!" Cass's hands flew to her mouth, muffling a scream. She threw the hose aside and sank down slowly on the top step. Doubled over, she clutched her stomach as bile filled her throat. For a minute, Cass feared she was going to throw up.

"They've found me! They've found me!" Cass buried her face in her hands and rocked back and forth. "They've found me!" Her worst nightmare had become real. "They're going to kill me!" She choked out as the full implication of the words hit home. "*They're going to kill me!*"

An arm suddenly went around her shoulders. Cass jumped, frightened by the touch and ready to fight off an attacker. She stopped struggling when she recognized Ryan sitting beside her. Weakly, Cass sagged against him.

"Hey," Ryan said. "Are you alright? What's wrong?"

"They've found me! They're going to kill me." Tearfully, Cass motioned to the door.

"What the hell?" Ryan stood up and stared at the threatening words on the door. "Who are you talking about? Who's found you?"

"It doesn't matter. I can't escape them!" Cass jumped up and turned toward the door. "I've got to clean this up. We can't let our patients or the staff see this." Cass grabbed the hose and began spraying water on the door. Droplets bounced off the door, covering her and Ryan.

"Stop! You can't wash it off." Ryan took the hose out of her hands. "I've got paint in the truck. That's the only thing that'll cover it. Wait right here."

Within minutes, Ryan had driven his pickup truck to the front of the clinic and stopped near the steps. He raised his cell phone and snapped a picture of the door, then removed brushes, a painting tray, and a gallon bucket of paint from the truck bed. Ryan handed Cass one of the paint brushes, popped open a can of paint, stirred, and poured it into the tray.

"That's gray paint, not white like the door's color." Cass's voice was still shaky as she pointed to the paint tray.

"Gray is the best color to cover the red paint. This is a primer. We'll decide on the final color later. Right now, we need to cover the graffiti."

Cass nodded, dipped the brush in the paint, and began slapping the paint on the door, concentrating on covering the blood-red words. Her only concern was hiding the threats as quickly as possible. Ryan, using a more systematic approach, started painting at the top and worked downward.

When the door and the graffiti were covered with gray paint, Ryan placed a "wet paint" sign a couple feet from the door.

"Now, what's this all about? And who's found you?" Ryan turned to Cass, his hands planted on his hips. "Who would do this to you? How do you know it's directed at you and not one of the staff?"

"Honestly, I don't know anything for sure. But first my tires were slashed, and now this. It's obviously directed at me. Someone hates me."

"And you're being straight with me—telling me everything?" At Cass's nod, Ryan continued, "Did you piss someone off unknowingly? Scratch that question. You'd do it deliberately, so 'unknowingly' would never happen!"

"Funny man." Cass smiled wryly at Ryan. Her fear had subsided. Painting the door had helped expend the initial fear and settle her nerves. Cass tipped her head to one side and assessed the new paint color. "You know, I think I like the gray paint color."

"You're dodging my questions, and that tells me a lot. Hop in, and I'll drive you around back," Ryan said as he walked to his truck and opened the door.

"Thanks, but I pulled this hose around to water the pansies, and I damn well intend to water them."

"Suit yourself, but if I don't hear you come through the back entrance in ten minutes, I'm coming to find you."

"Threats, threats, threats! All I ever get is threats." Cass smiled before realizing what she'd said. She sobered. They had just painted over threats. And she'd heard these threats before—in Philadelphia and now in Mason Valley. They didn't sound like *idle* threats either time.

Someone wanted her dead and had traveled hundreds of miles to see it through. That person's hatred was so deep, they'd traced her all the way to the mountains of North Carolina. She was guessing, of course, but she couldn't ignore what she'd already witnessed in Philly.

"I'll give a shout-out when I enter the clinic. Thanks for your help."

"Don't thank me just yet. I'm not satisfied with your answers. Getting to the bottom of obfuscation and finding out the truth is something *else* I'm good at." Ryan's eyes narrowed, conveying a message she could interpret in more than one way.

Ryan suspected that she was covering something up, but he was also reminding her of Monday's incident. At least he was now engaging in a conversation with her.

"Gottcha!" Cass replied. "A Truth-Slayer as well as a Heart-Breaker. See you around, Country Boy."

CHAPTER ELEVEN

Ryan pushed open the door and entered the sheriff's office. Ben Wilder, Mike, Jack, and Sheriff Ferguson were already seated at the conference table. Ryan had requested Ben's presence since he was on the clinic's board of directors and the vandalism had occurred there. And Jack? Despite his proclivity to pull stupid stunts, he would be as concerned as anyone for Cass's safety. Mike had left work at the same time as Ryan and insisted on tagging along.

"Ryan, why don't you start off by telling us what you witnessed at the clinic this morning," Sheriff Ferguson said.

Ryan pulled out his phone, retrieved the photo of the threats Cass found painted on the clinic's door, and passed it across to the sheriff.

"I see why you're concerned," Denny said as he passed the phone to Ben Wilder. The pictures had soon made their way around the table. "Tell us what happened."

"I saw Cass pulling the hose around to the front of the building as I drove into the parking lot. I didn't know what she was up to, so I walked toward the front to see if she needed help. That's when I heard her cry out." Ryan repeated in detail Cass's words once he reached her. "After she calmed down, I took this picture. Then, we repainted the door to cover the threats. Cass denied having any idea who vandalized the door."

"What did she mean by 'They've found me'?" Mike asked. "And how do we know the threats are aimed at her and not someone else?"

"I asked the same question. She pointed out that it was *her* tires that were slashed. That made sense to me," Ryan replied.

"Well, there's more to her story—but this doesn't leave this room." Ben paused, and the men all nodded in agreement. "Have you heard of a man in Philadelphia who was arrested recently? The one who was ripping off his investors, in similar fashion as Bernie Madoff?"

"I've heard snippets," Ryan said. "Some kind of Ponzi scheme. But what does that have to do with Cass?"

"That man is Cass's father," Ben replied.

"No kidding," Ryan said. "And she thinks his victims have followed her here? I can see why she might be concerned that someone's found her."

Ben told them the story of Cass's arrest and her face being plastered across all the news outlets. "She was completely innocent and later cleared of any wrongdoing, but angry mobs chose her for retribution anyway. She was fired from her job because of the media coverage. Cass was completely upfront with Kelsey about it all when she interviewed for the director's job."

"You're sure she didn't have any involvement?" Sheriff Ferguson asked.

"I am. I verified that with the FBI office in Philly. She's innocent," Ben replied. "But being Jordan's daughter and identified by the press… well, that was enough for the mobs and press to go after her."

Ben pulled up a video from Cass's arrest and passed it to

Ryan.

"Even after being cleared, she went through hell," Ben said. "And the threats against her were similar to those you photographed this morning."

"Wow! This *is* serious," Ryan said after viewing the video. "Cass needs protection."

"I can have someone patrol her area and drive by the house frequently at night," Sheriff Ferguson said. "But I don't have the deputies to do 'round-the-clock surveillance. She should be safe at work during the day."

"Ryan, after you called about the vandalized door, I stopped on my way here and checked the clinic's security camera footage. Whoever did this, also spray-painted the camera by the front door. The camera didn't pick them up," Ben said. "Kelsey is coming up tomorrow with a team to install an upgraded security system at the house and clinic. I just wish we'd installed it sooner. With the new system, Cass can monitor the house and the clinic from her phone at all times."

"Someone needs to tell her to stop leaving work after dark… at least until this jerk is caught." All eyes turned toward Ryan. "What?"

"You want to be the one to tell her?" Jack asked.

"Not me! Not after what happened Mon—" Ryan stopped himself.

"What did you do on Monday?" Jack asked. "Spill it! I smell a story."

"How's your shin, Jack?" Ryan scowled at his friend. "All healed up?"

"That was your fault, too." Jack added under his breath, "At least I feel *something*."

Ryan bit back an angry reply, refusing to react to Jack's dig. He'd felt much more than he expected from his *episode* with Cass. But he wasn't about to share the details with these men who were now eyeing him and waiting for further explanation.

"Nothing... nothing happened." Ryan waved off Jack's question. "Let's get back to the reason for this meeting: protecting Cass."

"Let's do that. We'll discuss the other thing later." Knowing Jack as Ryan did, his friend wouldn't forget and would try to badger an answer out of him.

"Since you don't have deputies to watch her place, I'll do it from, say, around nine or ten p.m. to five a.m.," Ryan suggested. "If this person is going to do anything at her house, it'll be during the night. I'd prefer to be gone by daylight, before the neighbors start stirring and notice me lurking in the bushes."

"You can't do this all by yourself," Mike said. "Jack and I will help. We'll set up a rotation schedule."

"Alright," Ryan agreed. "I'll take tonight. You can work out tomorrow and the next night's schedule. If you can't do it, let me know. I'll fill in for either of you."

"Are you going to share this plan with Cass?" Jack asked. The others around the table looked at Ryan, interested in his answer.

"No. I don't want to argue with her and hear how she can take care of herself and doesn't need protection. I plan to do it regardless."

"Uh huh! I see." Jack smiled. "Spending the night by the side of the road, crammed into a pickup—just an unselfish gesture for a stranger."

"I want all of you to be careful," Sheriff Ferguson interrupted Ryan's reply. "Don't try to handle this guy yourself. Call me if you see anything suspicious. My deputies will respond immediately."

The meeting broke up soon after. It was dark by the time Ryan left the sheriff's office. He drove home, changed into sweatpants and a sweatshirt, did a few outside chores, then prepared a quick dinner. Around nine o'clock, he filled a back-pack with a digital tablet and ear buds, a flashlight, snacks, and a handgun. The gun was registered, he knew how to use it, but he rarely carried it. Now, having it in his possession seemed like a good idea after the threats he'd witnessed this morning.

Ryan drove to Cass's house and parked in a clearing just off the side of the road. From his truck's windshield, he had a view of the house, but the majority of the truck was hidden by a stand of overlapping trees and bushes that grew between the road and his vehicle.

The night ticked away slowly and without incident. Alone with only his thoughts for company, Ryan replayed his reaction to Cass's taunts on Monday. He wasn't proud that he'd let her push him into the way he acted. He was more disciplined than that—usually. He'd intended to teach her a lesson, to warn her that she might stir up more than she'd bargained for. Had Cass objected, he would've quickly backed off. But rather than object to him kissing her, she had participated wholeheartedly. She'd awakened a need he hadn't felt for some time.

So, who had taught whom a lesson? But it was a one-off. He knew what to expect from her now, so he was prepared. He'd make sure it didn't happen again.

"Sure… lie to yourself." Ryan grimaced in the darkness. "One small taste of honey rarely satisfies anyone's cravings."

The sky was lightening in the east when Ryan started his truck and drove away. His father had instructed him and Mike to take some time off the day following their night on guard duty at Cass's house. But after a hot shower, breakfast, and a short nap, Ryan planned to arrive at the jobsite no later than nine a.m.

This wasn't the first time he'd pulled an all-nighter. But he'd never spent the night scrunched up in the front seat of a pickup. Neither did he recall his knees being as stiff as they were this morning when he exited the pickup.

It wasn't until Wednesday night of the following week that something odd happened and caught Ryan's attention. Around one a.m., a small white delivery van drove by. It slowed as it passed Cass's house, then picked up speed and drove on. Soon, the van circled back from the direction it had gone. Once again, the van slowed as it passed the house. *Could be someone who's lost or unfamiliar with the street*, thought Ryan.

He brushed away the van's appearance, but when it appeared again and repeated the same maneuver the following week, Ryan's instincts told him this was not someone lost or someone in the neighborhood on business at this hour.

Sheriff Ferguson had advised them to call him with anything suspicious, but Ryan wasn't exactly sure what he had seen. His instincts could be wrong.

Ryan pulled out onto the road and followed the van, staying a safe distance behind to avoid suspicion from the van's driver. The van drove to an all-night convenience store on the edge of town and pulled into the parking lot, stopping near the front door. The driver didn't exit the vehicle.

Ryan pulled up to a gas pump and began filling his gas tank. While the gas pumped, Ryan moved to the shadows near the window cleaning station, raised his cell phone, and took several photos of the van. The driver's face wasn't visible and remained hidden in the shadow of the cab. But perhaps his camera might capture some details that he couldn't see from where he stood.

Once the gas tank was full, Ryan decided to go into the store and maybe catch a glimpse of the driver as he walked by. But just as he started to walk toward the store, the van backed out of its parking space and pulled out onto the street through the side entrance.

Disappointed that he hadn't photographed the driver, Ryan climbed back into his truck and started reviewing the photos he'd just taken.

A temporary paper license plate was displayed on the van's rear end—another red flag? Ryan's suspicions increased. Counterfeit tags were sold on the black market. If the driver used this van for criminal activities—such as casing Cass's house—he probably wouldn't drive around with a license plate that identified him.

The number of small coincidences nagged at Ryan, but they could all add up to nothing. The van's driver's odd behavior indicated that legitimate business wasn't what brought it to Cass's neighborhood on two different occasions in the middle of the night. But odd behavior alone was not a crime.

Ryan sent the pictures to Sheriff Ferguson and Ben with an explanation of the van's appearances in Cass's neighborhood. He included Jason Wilder on the text. The more experienced eyes reviewing the photos, the better.

Ryan was back at his lookout station three nights later, hoping the van would make another appearance. This time, he planned to stop it and find out who the driver was and why he appeared to be casing Cass's home.

Ryan yawned, shifted his weight, and stretched his legs across and into the passenger's side of the cab. He'd just settled into a more comfortable position when a car service pulled up and stopped at the edge of Cass's driveway. Ryan looked at his watch—almost eleven p.m. Had his suspect ditched the van and switched to a car service? That seemed unlikely, but could have an accomplice.

A man exited the car, pulled a bag out behind him, slung it over his shoulder, and walked toward Cass's front porch.

Ryan jumped out of his truck and raced down the embankment toward the house, staying hidden behind a screen of trees until he came to an open section of the yard. Ryan bent low and sprinted across the open area. He stopped behind a tall bush at the corner of the porch.

Ryan peaked around the corner, but Cass hadn't turned on the porch light, so details of the man were hidden in the dark. As Ryan watched, the man sat down in a wicker chair on the porch and fumbled with his backpack. What was he looking for? A gun? A bomb? Or did he have an innocent reason for being here? A late date with Cass?

The man stood up and turned toward the door with something in his hand. Ryan made his move. He bounded up onto the porch, crossed it silently, and wrapped his arm around the man's throat. Overpowered by the surprise attack, the man didn't fight back. Ryan had both arms twisted behind the man's back before he could react.

The breath grunted out of the man as Ryan pushed him hard against the wall. "What the hell?" the man yelled. "Why are you assaulting me?"

The porch light switched on, and Cass opened the front door. She was dressed for bed, wearing loose-fitting flannel pajama bottoms, topped by a Philadelphia Eagle's t-shirt.

"Stay back, Cass," Ryan ordered. "I think this is our vandal."

"Ryan?" Cass asked, surprised. "What are you doing here?" Then, she glanced at the other man. "Raj, what are *you* doing here?"

"I came to see you, but this big oaf jumped me from behind," Raj replied.

"Do you know this guy?" Ryan asked. "He was snooping around out here on your porch and pulled a weapon from of his backpack."

"Weapon? It's my cell phone—to let Cass know I'm out here. I meant to be here earlier, but my flight had a weather delay. If you'd stop slamming me against the wall and turn my arms loose, I'd show you." Raj yanked his arms free of Ryan's hold.

"Idiots! Both of you! Come on inside." Cass rolled her eyes

at the two men as she held open the door for them to enter. She led them to the kitchen table and pointed to the chairs. "Sit down. Want some coffee?" she asked.

"None for me, thanks, and I'm sorry." Ryan stood by the chair, refusing her invitation to sit. "I should go. I interrupted your night. Obviously, you have plans."

"Ryan," Cass frowned at him, both hands on her hips, "this is my brother Raj…"

"Rich—Richard Allen Jordan." Raj stuck out his hand to Ryan. "Stay. Sit down and join us. If I were looking for a midnight booty call, it wouldn't be with my sister. And you, Big Guy, owe *me* an explanation as to why *you* were lurking outside my sister's house."

"Sorry for the rough welcome." Ryan returned Raj's handshake, then addressed Cass. "Have you noticed anything unusual happening at the clinic recently or here at the house?" Ryan walked over to the newly installed security monitor.

"Just some guys in pickup trucks hiding in the bushes out by the road," Cass deadpanned. "You didn't think I'd recognize your truck?"

"With you, I'd expect nothing less. But I thought my truck was hidden. I'm surprised you didn't run us off," Ryan responded as he punched a button on the security system. The screen lit up.

"I did consider calling the sheriff. Your truck is pretty well hidden, but just so you know—for the next time you're on a covert mission—the moonlight bounces off your windshield," Cass replied. "Also, Jack told me what you were up to."

"Jack never could keep anything to himself, especially if a woman's involved. I didn't tell you because I didn't want to frighten you even more than you were." Ryan pointed to the security monitor. "You don't even have the motion alerts on this system turned on! What are you thinking?"

"I… it's annoying to be alerted every time the wind moves a bush or a tree," Cass said.

"You can choose the 'people only' setting. It's not the trees I'm worried about."

"Oh! I didn't think about that. But you can call off the guard dogs now that Raj is here."

"What's going on? Why does Cass need a guard dog?" Raj asked.

Ryan gave Raj a brief history of the vandalism at the clinic and how he and the other men were helping the sheriff. Then, he asked, "Raj, can I talk to you privately? Over here?" Ryan stood and walked into the living room.

"Sure. What's up?" Raj followed and stopped beside Ryan in the middle of the room.

Ryan pulled out his phone to show Raj the photos of the clinic door. "Apparently, these are the same threats Cass got in Philadelphia," Ryan said. He was scrolling to the picture of the white van he'd trailed when Cass leaned against his back and peered around his arm to look at the pictures, too.

"Don't you think I should hear this conversation, too?" Cass pressed even closer to Ryan. A light scent from her body lotion filled his nostrils. Ryan stopped scrolling through the pictures, distracted by the feeling of Cass pressed against him.

"Uh… yes, of course." Ryan stepped away from her, walked back to the table, and sat down.

He was stupid to think Cass would let them have a private conversation in *her* living room. She was also right; she should know about the van.

"I saw this white van pass by on two different occasions. It appeared to be unusually interested in this house." Ryan pushed his phone over to Raj. Cass propped her elbow on Ryan's shoulder, once again pressing her upper body firmly against his back as she stretched to see the photos. Her breath brushed softly against his ear.

A crazy urge to turn around and bury his face in Cass's neck was almost overpowering. Ryan shook himself. If he was thinking like that, his head clearly wasn't in the right place. Wanting Cass in this way was just a fantasy, and in his experience romantic fantasies rarely translated into reality.

And Cass was playing a game—again—deliberately teasing him. He'd figured her out the first time they met. She was all cute and sassy and not the least bit shy about saying whatever popped into her head—anything to get under his skin. Cass's flirting at the moment wasn't serious; it was just payback for his warning that he would break her heart. She was warning him too—that she wasn't without weapons of her own. Heartbreak was a two-way street. She was pushing him, while acutely aware that with Raj present, he wouldn't call her bluff.

"Thanks for showing me," Raj said, drawing Ryan back into the conversation. "This is scary stuff. But Cass is right. I can stay indefinitely and keep a lookout for this guy—or guys. I've got nowhere else to be. I'm writing a book about my travels and just recently pitched the idea of turning it into a documentary film. I'm waiting to hear back from the producer."

"Well…" Ryan hesitated, reluctant to give up his self-appointed role as Cass's guardian. He'd never forgive himself if the stalker harmed her. His negligence had cost him one friend; he couldn't lose another one.

"Look," Raj said, "despite being subdued so easily on the porch, I'm actually an expert in a variety of self-defense skills. I have a black belt in Tae Kwon Do and learned from the masters in South Korea. A few months spent with the Congolese army taught me guerrilla warfare tactics and shooting all styles of weapons. Boomerangs and spears were the weapon of choice of the locals during my time in the outback of Australia. The tribes in the jungles of Africa favored bows and arrows."

"Hmph," Ryan snorted. "What? No bomb making?"

"That was part of the guerrilla warfare," Raj calmly answered. "I can even diffuse one, if needed. I'll guard her with my life, unless she's kidnapped and a ransom is offered, paying us to take her off their hands, of course."

"Very funny!" Cass retorted.

"I've got this, and she *is* my little sister."

"You're many years younger, maturity-wise. Don't let him fool you, Ryan. He's here hiding from our mother."

"By the way, Mom said that if I see you, I should pass along that she has a marriage arranged between you and Lord Gigolo. The title 'Lady Gigolo' has a nice ring to it, don't you think?"

"Now that you're back in the States, you'll be in her sights, not me," Cass replied. "She's given up on marrying me off. According to her, I'm past my prime."

"I think having you stay here is a great idea." Ryan interrupted Cass and Raj's playful argument. "I sent the photos of the van to the sheriff. I'm meeting with him sometime tomorrow to hear his take on them. I'll keep you posted." Ryan stood up to leave.

Cass walked him to the door. "You didn't have to take on this job as my security guard. I appreciate it, but you should get back to spending your Saturday nights wooing the ladies at the Eagle's Nest. I probably overreacted when I found the writing on the clinic door," Cass said as they stopped by the front door.

"No, you didn't overreact," Ryan replied. "And like Raj, I've got no other place to be right now."

"That's very sad, really. I get why Raj feels that way. He blows around like a leaf on the wind, never staying long enough in one place to get attached to anyone. But you?" Cass nodded and concluded, "I know your problem. You're way too serious, unfriendly, and closed off. If you smiled more, lost that frown, and became more accessible, girls would swarm to your blue eyes like bees after honey."

"Doesn't City Girl know that bees sting? And I'm as accessible as I want to be"

"So sad! I bet it's lonely perched up there on your high horse." Like a mother sending her kindergartner off to school, Cass reached up, straightened Ryan's shirt on his shoulders, patted his cheek, and rested her hand on his chest. "Stand tall and have more self-confidence! Good kissers are always in demand. I have intimate knowledge that you qualify." Cass batted her eyes seductively at Ryan.

"There's nothing wrong with my self-confidence," Ryan stated. "I'm untouchable up here on my high horse—so entrenched that the batting eyes of a pretty flirt can't unseat me."

"Oh, I like that! A challenge!"

"I'll bet you do." Ryan ran his fingertip down her cheek and neck, stopping at the neckline of her shirt. "You know what's really sad? This Eagles T-shirt you're wearing. I'm going to buy you a Carolina Panthers shirt."

With a "Goodnight," Ryan turned and walked out the door, heading back to his truck parked by the road.

With Raj staying with Cass, Ryan's guard duties were over. His time working at the medical clinic would also come to an end soon. He wouldn't be seeing Cass as much after that. This was a good thing, because his perch on his high horse teetered even more precariously with each time he was around her.

Ryan didn't turn around or acknowledge that he heard Cass's yell from the doorway: "Hey, Country Boy! Don't waste your money on that shirt! Eagles all the way!"

CHAPTER THIRTEEN

I'm sorry Dad got you mixed up in his scheme," Raj said. "He should be ashamed."

"He is ashamed—as well as scared."

Cass drove along Main Street on her way to drop Raj off at Jack's repair shop before heading to work. Jack had stopped by the house yesterday for a visit—he was still trying to make amends for his dance at the Eagle's Nest—and had offered to loan Raj a car to use while in town. Jack's hobby was buying used cars and repairing them. He currently had two on hand.

"This whole affair is hard to believe," Cass added. "That the father we grew up loving could be capable of bilking and stealing from his clients—some were his friends!"

"Did you go see him before you moved here?"

"I did—a short visit. But with my arrest and losing my job, I should've waited. I was at my breaking point. I'm ashamed that I unloaded all my anger on him."

"You shouldn't be. What he did to you is unforgiveable."

"But I argued with a beaten man who melted into a puddle before my eyes. He didn't even defend himself. That made me feel even worse. All I accomplished was to remind him of everything he must already know."

"Don't criticize yourself," Raj said. "There's nothing wrong with honestly holding him accountable, and telling him how his criminality has affected you."

"But I handled it all wrong. I'm frustrated with both our parents, and my words spewed out like a geyser. Truthfully, I'm as angry with Mom as I am with Dad. He was the one trapped in his apartment with an ankle bracelet—a convenient target—so he got the brunt off what I felt toward both of them."

"Our family is complicated, and this is a messy situation for sure," Raj said.

"Dysfunctional is more like it. Mom abandoned us—or, me and Dad, anyway. She was only concerned about herself and her image. My grievances with her have been building for years. I'm frustrated with myself, too. I let Mom drag me along on her climb up the social ladder. What I want never seems to matter to her."

"Personally, I think if it really mattered to you, you'd have rebelled."

"Maybe. I guess I didn't *let* it matter. Everything that's happened lately—through no fault of my own, I'd add—has finally shaken me out of my passivity. Quite frankly, I'm fed up with Mom treating me like I'm nothing more than a ticket to English nobility. I'm a little old for my mother to be choosing my suitors."

"I know," Raj said. "She's pretended for so long that I think she believes all that royalty crap. Dad couldn't give me a good explanation for what he did, either—just that people treated him like a big shot because he was making them tons of money. He let it go to his head and kept getting in deeper and deeper. Before long, he didn't know how to stop."

"He could've left me out of it. I can't even move out of state and get away from the harassment and threats."

"So, what's the deal with you and Jack?" Raj asked. "He seems like a nice guy. I sense that he likes you a lot."

"He's very nice. We're friends. And if you're asking if I'm attracted to Jack romantically, the answer is no." Cass put on her turn signal and moved into the left lane. The street leading to Jack's repair shop was about a block away.

"Hmm… that's what I figured," Raj said, nodding. "It's Ryan, isn't it?"

"What? No! Where did you get that idea? I'm friends with him, too, but we're not romantically involved, as you seem to be insinuating."

"Are you sure? There's something—"

"Get that nonsense out of your head," Cass cut Raj off. "I enjoy teasing Ryan. He's as dower as a grumpy old man. I can't figure him out. And I have too much on my plate as it is to deal with whatever baggage he carries around."

"I'm a writer, remember? An observer of human nature," Raj pointed out. "I'm saying you have the hots for Ryan Scott. I saw you flirt with him Saturday night."

"You don't know what you're talking about," Cass replied. "I can barely get him to acknowledge my existence. Everyone keeps hinting that he went through a traumatic experience a couple years ago. I'm guessing it involved a woman, and he's not over her yet." Of course, Ryan had said *he* was the one who broke someone's heart. Maybe he regretted that decision.

"Some people just want to be left alone, Sis. Maybe you should stop meddling, thinking you can fix things you only suspect, but don't know for sure."

"You really think that will happen?"

"No, not your style. But Ryan isn't spending his nights in a pickup by the roadside, looking out for your safety, without feeling something for you."

"Jack and Mike have also done that. Any citizen of Mason Valley might do it if asked. They're kind, caring people, even with strangers."

"As an unbiased observer, judging by what I witnessed the other night—once he was done assaulting me—Ryan is definitely aware of you," Raj said. "Maybe the iceberg is thawing. Of course, if he's been on Celibate Island for a couple years, anyone would look good."

"You want to walk the rest of the way to Jack's?" Cass, exasperated with her brother, braked and slowed the car. "Change the subject, or I'm putting you out right here."

"Subject changed," Raj acquiesced. "What does Ryan do for a living?"

"He works with his dad in construction. Their company is building the new wing of the clinic."

"Construction? Ah… I see. Women love a Toolbelt Man! The grittiness of the work, those calloused hands against your soft skin, the individualism, the can-do attitude. They're usually very muscular, too."

"Is that an outline for your next book? Fantasy genre, maybe?" Cass frowned at Raj, who smiled broadly, looking pleased over his latest jab.

"Mom would have a coronary, wouldn't she, if you married Ryan the construction worker?"

"You're ridiculous! Out of my car!" Cass pulled into the parking lot in front of Jack's shop and braked to a stop. She pushed Raj toward the door. "Go!"

"Love you, Sis," Raj laughed as he opened the car door and got out. As he walked toward the shop, he began whistling the "Wedding March."

Cass couldn't help but smile over Raj's crazy antics. He loved to joke, especially at her expense. Despite their squabbling, Cass's life would be very dull without Raj in it. And she felt better now, after sharing with Raj her guilt over her confrontation with their father. Raj always understood her situations, offered sensible advice, and rarely criticized her.

Jack waved from the doorway of the repair shop. Cass waved back, then drove onto the street that would take her to work.

Jack and Raj would get along well together. Like two peas in a pod, they could cause all kinds of mischief. Her anger at Jack for what he'd done that night at the Eagle's Nest had mellowed a bit. By voluntarily guarding her house and now loaning Raj a car, he'd shown that a kind heart lived in his prankster's body.

The utility contractor's employees were busy laying out plans for the exterior lighting project when Cass arrived at the clinic. Better lighting might keep her tires from being slashed, but if the white van belonged to the person stalking her, he had found where she lived. He might have a different plan of attack now.

Cass entered her office, and the first thing she noticed was a flashing light signaling a voice mail message on the answering machine. She hit the 'Play' button then groaned at the voice of Clayton Thomas.

"Cass, this is Clayton. I have a great idea I'd like to share with you."

Cass flinched at the word "share." Not using the word "discuss" meant Clayton had made up his mind on whatever great idea he had come up with.

Cass stored her purse in the desk drawer and reluctantly reached for the phone. She'd rather not talk to Clayton and have him put her in a bad mood. She had three interviews lined up today and no time to argue with Clayton. Cass dialed Clayton's number. He picked up so quickly, his hand must have been hovering over the phone, just waiting for her to call.

After a few minutes of friendly chat, Clayton got to his

"great idea": "I'm thinking we should merge the staff in the mental health clinic with the staff in the medical clinic. This way, we'd need only one waiting room, one stock room, and one clinical staff. We could eliminate some positions. This would save a lot of money—even on the decorating and maintenance of two different offices."

Oh, faff! thought Cass. *Penny-pinching Clayton, at it again.* If only Dr. Phillips were here or she had Ben or John Wilder on the line. But this was her job, and most likely, this wouldn't be the last time she'd have to battle Clayton.

"So… you're suggesting we use the current staff for both clinics?" Cass began slowly, stalling while she formulated her rebuttal to what she knew was an unworkable idea. "You do remember that I've hired four people already, right? And I have three interviews lined up for today."

"We could probably fit those you've hired into part-time roles," Clayton replied.

"Two are already part-time, and the others aren't looking for part-time work. But let's put the number of staff aside for a minute." Cass wanted to put the kibosh on this idea before it went any further. "As you noted, the clinics are two separate entities. We can't merge the two. And we've discussed this before. The people who come in for mental health services don't want to broadcast their situation to a crowded reception room. And definitely not to people they might know—maybe their neighbors—who would stare at them, wondering what problems they're here for."

"But it's redundant to have two waiting rooms where sometimes only one or two people will be using it at the same time. Just a waste," Clayton objected. "You haven't thought this through."

"The Barrett family started this clinic for mental health services. We aren't making a spectacle of our patients by taking away their privacy." Cass's voice rose. Clayton's proposal was ridiculous. Cass lowered her voice back to a more conversational tone so she could calmly explain why his idea wouldn't work. "We have a new building, practically finished, so it doesn't make sense to change it now and leave vacant rooms spread throughout the clinics. Besides, at this point, you don't know how many patients we might have. My analysis shows that for a town this size, plus the county, we'll have many more than one or two patients at a time."

"I can talk to the Barrett family and see what they think. I feel Ms. Wilder would see the logic in this," Clayton persisted.

"As the clinic director, I say we keep it as two separate clinics and serve our patients in a way that's best for them, just as planned," Cass stated firmly. "But I agree that the stock rooms can be run by one clerk who's responsible for both." That had been her plan all along, but presented this way, it sounded like a concession—a bone thrown to the big dog, while also reminding him that daily operation of the facility was her job. Cass hoped the big dog would grab the bone, retreat to his corner to chew on it, and stop meddling in her territory.

"I see... yes, what you're saying does make sense. Privacy concerns for certain patients had crossed my mind, too," Clayton said, backpedaling and sounding slightly cowed by Cass's firmness. "But maybe I'll run it by Ms. Wilder... just to get her opinion."

"Sure, if that's what you want to do. It wouldn't hurt to hear what she thinks," Cass agreed in an effort to smooth any ruffled feathers. She believed she knew what Kelsey's reaction would be.

After hanging up the phone with Clayton, Cass dialed Kelsey's number. An old Cass Jordan proverb came to mind: *Those who strike first usually have the advantage.*

Cass relayed Clayton's proposal to Kelsey but didn't imme-

diately say what her argument to Clayton had been. She wanted
an unbiased opinion from Kelsey on the matter.

"That's one of the dumbest ideas I've ever heard." Kelsey's
response was as expected. "Does Clayton think we're running
a mom-and-pop shop or something? The Barrett philosophy is
all about the dignity of our patients as well as providing them
the services they need. That's what's most important to me, not
whether we have one or two waiting rooms in order to save a
few bucks."

"That's basically my feelings, too, and I told him that."
Kelsey's reaction was even more heated than Cass had expected.
"It's a free clinic, but patients shouldn't feel like we're skimping
on their comfort, privacy, or care."

"Clayton came highly recommended, but I'm beginning to
wonder if I made a mistake in hiring him," Kelsey said.

"I think he's good at what he does, but he's not familiar with
what's needed in a free medical setting or what's appropriate
for Mason Valley. And because he doesn't know, he's afraid
something will get out of his control. I'll keep trying to educate
him," Cass said. Her intention wasn't to get anyone fired. "I just
wanted to run the situation by you and hope I made the right
decision. He may call you."

"Yes, you made the right decision, and I'll back you one
hundred percent," Kelsey said. "Keep up the good work."

"How are you feeling, by the way? Has the morning sickness
abated?"

"It's better. Jason's mom talked to him, and he's stopped hovering and nagging me so much. That helps. We plan to come to
Mason Valley for Thanksgiving. Would you be available to show
me around the new wing while I'm there?"

"Absolutely! Just let me know the time. I think you'll be
pleased," Cass replied.

Cass hung up the phone, gratified that Kelsey backed her

decision, though she didn't plan to keep going to Kelsey behind Clayton's back. Neither did she want to keep butting heads with him. She needed his support. But *he* needed to accept that her work experience wasn't just words on her resume.

Cass finished up her day by interviewing the last candidate—a stock person who would fill in on other administrative tasks when needed. She had hired all the interviewees today on the spot. She may have been feeling pumped after winning her latest wrestling match with Clayton, but she didn't think so. The three candidates were well-qualified, experienced in the medical field, and seemed eager to get to work as soon as the clinic opened. All that was left—and was the toughest part—was finding two doctors willing to work in a brand-new clinic in the mountains of North Carolina.

Before leaving work, Cass dialed Raj's number to see what was planned for dinner.

"I'm on my way to meet Jack and Ryan at the sheriff's office," Raj said. "I'll pick up some take-out on my way home."

"Sounds good," Cass agreed. *Hmm… a gathering at the sheriff's office? Wonder what that's about. Well, no better way to find out than to crash the meeting.*

♦

Cass walked into Sheriff Ferguson's office just as Ryan had uploaded the photos of the white van onto a video screen on the back wall. Ben Wilder, Ryan, Mike, Jack, and Raj were all gathered around the table—The Knights of the Round Table, gathered to protect the distressed fair maiden. A cloud of testosterone wafted up from the table.

All heads turned toward the door as she entered the room.

"What's going on, fellas? A meeting concerning me, and I

wasn't invited?" Cass asked as she approached the table.

"Have a seat, Cass," Ben said as he pulled out a chair beside him. "Glad you could join us."

"I didn't invite you because I thought you'd be tied up at work," Ryan said. "Glad to see you left the building before it became pitch-black outside." Despite his words, he didn't appear glad to see her at all.

"I had a secret meeting to attend." Cass was positive the meeting concerned her; otherwise, why were all the members of her protective detail here, gathered around the table with the sheriff?

"I first spotted this van a couple weeks ago on Wednesday." Ryan ignored Cass and pointed to the picture on the screen. "Did either of you guys see it?" He looked at Mike and Jack.

"I didn't," Mike said, followed by Jack shaking his head no.

"Then, last week, it was back and again cruising by Cass's house. It followed the same pattern each time: drove by, turned around, and drove back by again."

"I ran the license plate number you gave me. It's legit but belongs to a recently purchased Ram truck. The owner works the night shift at a convenience store out on the Charlotte highway," Sheriff Ferguson said. "The tag was stolen. But when I called the owner, he said the tag was on his truck this morning. He hadn't known it had been removed."

"Our guy is a real sneaky S.O.B.," Ben commented. "That's brazen to make two trips—one to steal the tag, then one to put it back on the truck."

Ryan rose from the table and wrote some dates on the whiteboard. "These are the dates of when our vandal struck and when I saw the van in the vicinity."

"Uh… this probably isn't important," Jack said slowly, "but have you noticed that these are all Wednesdays? Is this a Wednesday-only stalker? Don't you think that's odd?"

Cass, along with the men in the room, looked again at the white board. Sure enough, the nights Ryan had seen the van were Wednesdays, as was the night her tires were slashed. Plus, she had found the threats painted on the clinic's door early on a Wednesday morning.

"Jack, I think you've got something there," Sheriff Ferguson agreed.

"Could be a crime of opportunity," Ben added. "Maybe he's out and about only on Wednesdays. Or it could be that he's alone that night and can get away. Or maybe that's his night off from his job."

Cass felt chills run down her arms. Why an evolving pattern made the danger seem even more real, she wasn't sure. But the stalker was clearly organized, so maybe he spent the other days and nights during the week plotting and planning, getting ready to strike on Wednesdays.

"Good eye." Ryan nodded at Jack. "I guess there's brains in that head of yours after all. Striking only on Wednesdays, if it holds as his MO, might be the clue that helps us identify him."

"I was just showing off for the pretty lady." Jack winked at Cass.

"If you improved your dancing, that would impress the lady even more." Cass narrowed her eyes at Jack. "I haven't forgotten."

"Dancing? Can't wait to hear what that's about," Raj said.

"Let's get back on topic." Ryan pointed again at the photo.

"Right, Boss." Jack winked again at Cass and turned to give his undivided attention to Ryan.

"Look at this photo closely." Ryan enlarged the image. "Do any of you recognize something or spot anything that might help identify the van?"

"It's only a shadow," Cass offered, "but there, through the rear window, it looks like stacks of something. Delivery boxes?"

"Could be," Ben agreed. "What if it's not his night off, but his night *to* work? Too bad we can't see what he's delivering—if that's what he's doing. That would give us a lead on his job."

"Do you think someone saw my arrest in Philly, followed me, and got a job as a cover while terrorizing me?" Cass asked, then silently groaned. She had just spilled the details of the story that had sent her running to the North Carolina mountains. "I mean…"

None of the men in the room showed any reaction or asked what she meant. So, they already knew! According to Kelsey, Ben had known. He must have thought it necessary for all of them to know the extent of the danger she'd faced previously. Cass had known her arrest and firing would come out eventually, just not like this.

"We don't know, Cass," Sheriff Ferguson said. "We could sit here all night and speculate. I think our best bet is to send copies of the photos to Kelsey in Atlanta. She has access to military-grade imaging analysis. Maybe she can spot some clue on the van that we're missing."

"Good idea." Ryan shut down the video screen. "That's about all we can do at this point. Keep us posted, Denny, on what Kelsey finds out."

Cass stood up to leave as the men around the table said goodbye and began to disperse. She walked to the door with Ben and waited for Raj to finish talking with Ryan.

"We'll get him," Ben said as he stopped beside Cass. "Your brother is with you at night, and Kelsey has hired guards for the clinic. They'll be discreet, so most people won't even notice they're there."

"You mean there are security guards available for hire?" Cass asked, smiling. "I thought they were all in this room and worked for free."

"These guys are definitely a good group. We take care of our own in Mason Valley. You're one of us now. Don't worry." Ben patted Cass's arm, said goodbye, and left through the double doors.

Raj and Ryan finished their conversation and walked toward Cass.

"A conversation between friends or another discussion concerning me?" Cass asked as they approached.

"About you," Raj replied with a serious expression. "I asked Big Guy here what his intentions are with my sister."

"Raj," Cass said with a frown, "if Jack hadn't loaned you a car, I would make you walk home. Since you already have a ride home, you can sleep on the porch."

Cass glanced at Ryan. Did a tiny smile creep into those blue eyes? Most likely, it was a reflection from the overhead lights. Cave Man didn't smile.

"Actually, I was telling Raj that he should drive you to work and pick you up at night," Ryan said. "To make sure this person doesn't get braver and strike during daylight hours when you're on the road."

"What? No way! I don't need an escort to and from work," Cass objected angrily. "Besides, everything you just detailed is based only on your suspicions. You don't actually have hard evidence that I'm his target. Either way, I'm not letting him control my life."

"That's the problem," Ryan replied just as heatedly. "I don't know anything for sure, but the morning I found you on the steps scared out of your wits, *you* thought you were his target."

"That was my initial reaction upon seeing the door vandalized. I'm over that now," Cass replied.

"Huh! Well, I'm not over it," Ryan replied. "Look, I told you the night I drove you home from the Eagle's Nest that I wasn't letting anything happen to you. Different danger, same promise."

"Knock yourself out, Dick Tracy. I can drive myself wherever I need to go. Stop organizing my life without my permission! I'm going home." Cass whirled away from Ryan and Raj. Tired of Ryan's dictating what she should or shouldn't do, Cass stalked toward the door. Then, she turned and stomped back, stopping directly in front of Ryan. "Look, I appreciate your concern. I really do. But if you're so fixated on me, you might miss some other clue as to what this guy is up to." Cass reached out and placed her hand on Ryan's. "I'm grateful for your help. I'll be careful. I promise."

"Our evidence points to you, but your point is valid, City Girl," Ryan acknowledged as he rubbed the back of her hand with his thumb. "We need to consider all angles. Sorry if you feel I'm overreacting."

"Fixated? You're fixated on my sister?" Raj had remained quiet as he watched Cass and Ryan argue but now spoke up. "I knew you had designs on her!"

Cass closed her eyes and shook her head in frustration. She dropped Ryan's hand. "Go home, Raj. Sleeping on the porch, remember?" She walked to the door and out into the night.

She looked around as she approached her car but saw nothing out of place. Surely, she was safe at the sheriff's office. Still, she hurriedly got in and immediately locked the doors. Despite her bravado just now, lately when she was alone, she was tense and guarded. This meeting had only added to her anxiety.

She had promised Ryan that she'd be careful, and she would, but she was determined not to let some stranger control her life. She wouldn't live constrained by threats or be intimidated by fear. That wasn't the Cass Jordan way.

CHAPTER FOURTEEN

O nly two physicians left to hire. How hard can that be?"
Cass muttered as she reviewed the payroll information
for the new staff positions and submitted the report to
Clayton. He'd called earlier, wanting data on salaries and cost
projections for the rest of this year and the coming new year.

"Am I interrupting you?" Carolyn Wilder asked from the
doorway.

"No. Come in! I'm just talking to myself. Have a seat."

"I won't stay very long. Everyone else has left. I just wanted
to wish you a happy Thanksgiving and let you know that Kelsey
and Jason just called. They're having a baby boy!"

"That's wonderful!" Cass came around from behind her
desk and hugged Carolyn. "I can see you're over the moon with
the news."

"I didn't care. Boy or girl is fine with me. But I've been waiting to find out before I decorate and refurbish the nursery."

"I'm happy for all of you. I can't wait to meet the new addition."

"Enjoy your time off, Cass. Forget about work and enjoy

yourself. See you on Monday." Carolyn practically floated out the door.

Would Cecilia express the same excitement if she or Raj married and started a family? Of course, since there wasn't a potential husband on the horizon for her, children were out of the question for now—unless she used a donor.

Cass almost laughed out loud at the thought. Her mother would pass out at the mere mention of a sperm donor. Cecilia would clutch her chest and say, "Cassandra, the Winslow bloodline doesn't need to be tainted by the riffraff that donates… uh… for money." Cecilia wouldn't let herself say something as crude as "sperm."

Thinking about babies, sperm donors, and her mother's reaction was only entertaining speculation. Cass had several years left before her biological clock wound down to zero.

Cass straightened up her desk, locked her door, and left the clinic. Darkness had already started to descend over Mason Valley. An autumn moon was on the rise, creating a silvery glow behind the trees on Love Vine Mountain. Cass pulled her jacket tighter around her as she left the shelter of the back entrance, walked around the building, and crossed the parking lot to her car. Fallen leaves, picked up by strong gusts of wind, swirled across the pavement in front of her. The days were shorter and becoming colder and darker, but the parking lot was well-lit now, since the contractor had finished upgrading the lighting. Still, Cass steered clear of the deep shadowy pockets near the building—spaces large enough for a person to hide. Today was Wednesday, the stalker's preferred night, so Cass wasn't taking any chances.

She hurried to her car, quickly checked the exterior, then got inside and locked the doors. As she drove toward the parking lot exit and pulled onto the highway, Ryan's truck came from the construction workers' parking area and pulled in behind her. If Ryan's tailing her was his idea of a covert operation, he wasn't being very covert.

But that wasn't the point he was making. Since she'd refused his suggestion that Raj drive her to and from work, Ryan's goal was to see that she got home safely, denying the Wednesday-night stalker the chance to strike again.

How long would Ryan keep this up? Cass found it hard to believe that he didn't have someone waiting for him or at least something more interesting to do than escort her home. His comment that he didn't have any place else to be was a sad story, but then again, her own story wasn't much better.

Ryan tailed her home, but when she pulled into the driveway at her house, he kept driving and didn't follow her in. She tapped the horn in thanks, and Ryan sounded a short beep in return.

Cass entered the house to the smell of something delicious cooking in the kitchen. Raj, wearing an apron, was busily chopping and assembling a dinner salad.

"What are you doing?" Cass asked. "I thought you were picking something up from Rita's Café. Mandy should be arriving any time now."

"I'm fixing lasagna. It's a recipe I learned in Bologna. I traveled all over Italy, but the food in that city was the best."

"You can cook?" Cass asked with skepticism. "Is it edible?"

"Your offensive comment cuts me to the bone. Of course, I can cook. I rented a room from a Signora Russo for a few weeks, and she graciously taught me how to cook—a few things, anyway. She had a beautiful daughter, too, and that made my visit even more fun." Raj wiggled his eyebrows at Cass.

"You're hopeless." Cass smiled at her brother. "It had better be good! I want Mandy to enjoy her visit. She rarely takes time off, so she needs rest, good food, and entertainment. I have an ulterior motive, too. I'm trying to persuade her to move here and practice at the clinic. She's a nurse practitioner and has to work under the supervision of an MD. Finding an MD is my next challenge."

"Great idea. I won't let you down, Sis—if she likes lasagna," Raj promised. "Ryan said he couldn't join us. Needed to catch up at work."

"He tailed me on the way home but drove on by." Ryan was behind at his regular job due to the time he spent keeping watch over her. Instead of making her angry that he thought she couldn't take care of herself, the idea of Ryan vigilantly looking out for her safety gave her a warm feeling.

"He didn't stop?" Raj wagged a finger at Cass. "When are you going to admit that Ryan does interest you? He's a challenge, and you love a challenge. Plus, he's not one of those namby-pamby men that Mom loves to fix you up with. You know, the ones who trip all over themselves trying to impress you. Am I right?"

"Wrong! And you're going to lose that finger one day if you keep sticking it in my face—and my business." Cass slapped away Raj's hand.

"Liar!" Raj laughed at her threat. "Jack is coming, though. I made too much food, so I've invited other guests to help get rid of it. Signora Russo only made one size."

"Why didn't you halve the recipe?"

"Oh! Never thought of that. A group is more fun, anyway. Sadly for you, four is all I could arrange."

"With Jack coming, you have a crowd. He makes up for at least another four people."

"He *is* entertaining."

"I'll set the table." Cass carried plates, silverware, and napkins to the table. She had just finished with the place settings when the doorbell rang. "Mandy's here!"

Jack arrived close behind Mandy. After introductions, Cass

poured glasses of wine for everyone. The next few minutes were spent catching up, and then, Raj announced that dinner was ready. Raj's meal was delicious, as promised.

Jack kept them all entertained, but when he started to bring up the night at the Eagle's Nest, Cass shook her fork at him, a stern warning for him to drop the subject immediately.

"Cass still doesn't see the humor in the incident… or in my dance routine!" Jack laughed. "I understand, since she was the one who got bulldozed into letting Ryan escort her home. He can be very persuasive when he gets something in his head."

"You mean Ryan can be very bullheaded, thinks he knows everything, and didn't want to hear my side," Cass corrected Jack.

"Umm, yeah, something like that."

"Hmmm… I want to meet this Ryan guy," Mandy said.

"Ryan's great!" Raj said. "I invited him to dinner, but he couldn't make it. That's why Cass is so glum. She's smitten by our boy, Ryan."

Cass threw a piece of bread at Raj. It landed in his salad. He picked it out of his salad and threw it back at Cass, where it landed in her wine glass, spreading a greasy film over the top of the wine.

"Oh faff! Look what you've done!" Cass fished the bread out of her wine glass, popped it into her mouth, chewed, and swallowed the wine-soaked bread. "Not bad!"

Jack and Mandy looked on, their heads following the bread back and forth.

"Exactly what does *faff* mean?" Mandy asked. "I've heard you use it numerous times and always wondered."

"It's quite a funny story, really," Cass explained. "Our mother didn't approve of cursing—which is strange, considering the British penchant for using swear words. You only need to attend an Adele concert to see that. So, to keep Mom from sending us to our rooms, Raj and I created a phrase to use for times when only a curse word would do."

"*Faff* was a word our Grandfather Winslow frequently used," Raj added. "And it sounded naughty to Cass and me. We assumed it was a lesser-known version of the f-word. To make the codeword fit our purpose, we created a list of expletives that would be represented by the phrase, 'Oh, faff!'"

"We codified the agreement by signing it and making it an official document. Raj knew more curse words than I did, so his contribution was very extensive." Cass smiled at her brother.

"Much later, we learned that *faff* is actually a British expression meaning 'to goof off' or 'someone who procrastinates.' But by then, using the word had become a habit and firmly stuck in our vocabularies—plus, there was that official codified agreement."

"And it worked well for our purposes. Our mother would look at us curiously when we said it, but she never caught on."

"That sounds like a very complicated effort just to come up with a swear word," Jack commented.

"True, but we thought we were very clever. Cass was ten, and I was almost twelve," Raj finished the story. "We weren't yet the geniuses we are today."

"What you were, were troublemakers. Poor Cecilia," Mandy said. "One day, you should confess and tell her."

"Nah, she'd still try to send us to our rooms," Cass laughed. "Mom doesn't like being tricked."

"Why don't we all go to the Eagle's Nest on Saturday night? They won't censure your swear words there. Lanie's home for the Thanksgiving holiday, and she and Ryan are performing," Jack suggested.

"I think a night of dancing sounds like fun," Mandy said. "And I need to get the feel of life in Mason Valley—since someone wants me to move here."

"Fantastic," Jack replied. "You in, Cass?"

"I guess," Cass agreed reluctantly. "No stunts like you pulled last time."

Jack leaned over to Mandy and whispered, "I'll give you all the details later."

◆

Following Jack's directions, Cass easily found the Scotts' farm on Thanksgiving morning. The house, a large rambling farmhouse located a few miles east of Mason Valley, sat on several acres of land not far off the main highway to Charlotte. Bill and Margaret came out onto the porch to welcome them.

Everyone gathered in a large sunroom at the back of the house. Drinks, along with before-dinner snacks, were set up on a buffet table on one side of the room. Denny Ferguson; his wife, Melinda; their son, Corey; Mike; his wife, Karen; and Lanie were milling around the room, chatting, and catching up. Only Ryan was missing. Apparently, Cave Man really didn't have time for chitchat, even with dinner guests.

Once the newcomers were welcomed and each had a glass of wine, Karen left to assist Margaret with dinner preparations.

"Ryan's out back on an errand for Mom: getting a booster seat for Corey out of the storage building. I'll let him know you all are here," Lanie said as she left the room and headed toward the kitchen.

Ryan entered the room about fifteen minutes later and stopped at the bar to pour himself a drink. Cass tapped Mandy on the shoulder, ready to introduce her to Ryan.

"Oh my God! I don't believe this!" Mandy exclaimed as she turned and faced Ryan. Her eyes widened, and her mouth dropped open. "Dr. Scott? You're here? What… where…it really *is* you! We all wondered what happened to you. But never imagined you were living this close to Charlotte."

"Hi, Mandy. Glad you could join us." Ryan gave Mandy a hug. "How are things in Charlotte?"

"*Doctor* Scott? You... you know each other?" Cass interrupted. "How? From where?"

"We worked together at Carolina General—in the ER—before we both left," Mandy explained. She turned to Cass and added, "Everyone at Carolina General loved Dr. Scott—our very own Dr. McDreamy. We, especially the nurses, were all devastated when he left."

"You're a doctor? But you work in construction—for your father," Cass sputtered, shocked. Her brain was having trouble processing Mandy's words. "I don't understand."

"It's a long story," Ryan said. "I—"

Ryan's explanation was interrupted by his father announcing that dinner was on the table. They all filed into the large dining room and sat down. Cass had just taken the seat next to Mandy when someone tapped her on the shoulder.

"You're messing up the seating arrangement," Jack said in her ear. "You know: boy, girl, boy, girl? You're in my seat. Yours is over there." He pointed across the table to the empty chair next to Ryan.

Cass frowned at Jack. His motive was twofold: *he* wanted to sit next to Mandy, and he wanted her seated next to Ryan. She got up and walked around the table.

"Thank you," Cass mumbled stiffly as Ryan held the chair for her.

Cass refused to look at Ryan as he sat down beside her. She seethed with anger. In all the conversations they'd had, he never once mentioned that he was a doctor—a nonpracticing doctor, but still. She'd been played for a fool, because everyone in town knew but her—and Raj.

Cass had started to believe that Mason Valley-ians had accepted her as one of their own and that she belonged here. But apparently, she had miscalculated how they actually viewed her. Not one single person had shared Ryan's former occupation. Obviously, secrets weren't shared with "outsiders." Cass felt duped—by everyone.

Cass bit her lip, holding back all rude questions or comments. She was Cecilia Jordan's daughter, and any subject deeper than clichéd social chatter was considered bad manners and not tolerated around the dinner table.

Cass turned away, avoided Ryan altogether, and spent most of dinner talking to Mike across the table. Ryan's tension was obvious, too, when their hands bumped as dishes of food passed between them.

Dinner was almost over when the front doorbell rang.

"I'll get it." Mike rose from the table to answer the door. He returned quickly. "Ryan, it's Mr. Gleason. He's looking for Hawk Man," Mike said as he sat back down to finish his dinner.

Hawk Man, Cave Man, doctor—Ryan Scott answered to a long list of names. Ryan immediately laid down his napkin and went to see Mr. Gleason.

"Poor Ryan," Jack said, shaking his head. "As if his life isn't complicated enough, he can't even enjoy a holiday meal without being interrupted. Mr. Gleason comes looking for him at least once a day. Ryan always accommodates him. It's amazing he stays so calm."

Calm, Jack said? To Cass, Ryan's behavior was more indifferent than calm. Totally wrapped up in himself, he never missed a chance to disparage her with a snide comment of some kind. Even the kiss at the clinic was a power struggle to show her that he was in charge. The implosion of her life couldn't possibly compare to his problems, and a little empathy for her situation was apparently too much to expect. Ryan keeping his profession a secret was just more of the same indifference. And Jack making excuses for Ryan's behavior only encouraged him to continue the status quo.

A red haze floated before Cass's eyes. Common sense and her mother's etiquette training were forgotten as the words built inside her, then almost involuntarily came pouring out. Everything that had happened to her recently consolidated into one explosion. "Poor Ryan?" Cass looked at Jack, but her words were for everyone at the table. "Everyone coddles Ryan as if he's a fragile little flower. You tiptoe around him, while he isolates himself from everything. And apparently, he plans to remain that way for the foreseeable future. Ryan has a life most people only dream about, with a loving family and loyal friends. He's smart and good at everything he does, whether it's construction or, according to Mandy, medicine. Most people would be happy having one-tenth of what Ryan has. It might be time he…" Cass sputtered to a halt, embarrassed as her anger ran out of steam. The dinner guests were all staring at her.

What was she doing? She'd just offended the family who had kindly invited her to share their holiday dinner. What did Ryan's parents think of her outburst? Would they now ask her to leave?

Cass looked at Margaret, an apology forming on her lips. She expected disapproval, but Margaret looked steadily back at Cass. Censure wasn't evident in Margaret's eyes. Maybe there was even silent approval.

"I'm so sorry," Cass addressed Margaret. "Please forgive me." Cass's face felt hot, and color blazed across her cheeks. She'd made a major faux pas, but opinionated Cass Jordan never missed a chance to meddle in other people's business and make a fool of herself. Cecilia would disown her if she knew.

Suddenly, all eyes turned away from Cass and toward the door of the dining room. Ryan stood there, leaning casually against the doorframe with his arms crossed over his chest. He'd heard every word of Cass's outburst. A V-shaped frown formed deep creases between his eyes. Unlike his mother, approval was not in his look.

"Cass, take a walk with me." Ryan straightened, abruptly turned, and walked toward the back door, not waiting for her reply. It wasn't a request, but a demand.

"If you're not back by dark, I'll come looking for you," Jack joked as Cass pushed back her chair and stood up.

"You've done it now, Sis," Raj taunted as Cass passed his chair. "We'll send out the bloodhounds to find you."

Cass scowled at Raj, grabbed her jacket from the hallway coatrack, and followed Ryan to the back of the house. He was leaning against a post on the back porch, waiting for her. A large cage holding a hawk sat in the yard under the shade of a maple tree.

"Oh! Is he injured?" Cass asked, happy to see something that could stall the lecture she knew was coming. She approached the cage.

"One of his wings is broken, maybe from a gunshot," Ryan replied. "Mr. Gleason found him. It's a red-tailed hawk."

"He's beautiful. You're going to fix his wing?"

"I'm going to try once he settles down some. His talons are sharp as razors. He'll chill out more once he gets used to the cage."

"So, you haven't given up medicine altogether?" Cass asked, despite knowing she should hold her questions—that question, especially. And just like that, she destroyed the momentary peace between them.

"Let's walk," Ryan said as he turned and walked toward a trail that led into a wooded area behind the house.

Oh, faff! Cass thought as she followed Ryan onto the trail. *He's taking me into the woods, probably to leave me to find my way home alone.*

"Slow down!" Cass yelled at Ryan's back. His long stride had taken him several yards ahead of her, and she couldn't keep up. Her shoes weren't made for hiking or jogging. "It's a walk, not a marathon! And I'm not dressed for either!"

"Sorry." Ryan slowed and waited for her to catch up.

The trail gradually wound upward. Ryan stayed silent, withdrawn as usual. Most of their past interactions were tepid at best, but even tepid now seemed desirable compared to this awkwardness. Cass wanted to apologize again for her outburst, but Ryan's stony silence indicated that he wasn't in the mood to hear it.

Soon, they came to a break in the trees with an unobstructed view of the autumn glory of Love Vine Mountain on the other side of the valley. A bench hewed from a fallen tree was strategically placed to face the mountain. Cass suspected that the homemade bench was Ryan's handywork. Judging by its worn appearance, it was used often. Perhaps this was his secluded spot to sit and think about whatever tragedy had made him withdraw from society.

Ryan brushed the leaves and debris from the bench, then pointed for her to sit. Cass sat down, and for once, she stayed quiet, holding all questions. She had a good idea why she was here, so she would just relax and enjoy the view while she could. She waited for Ryan to speak first.

"It's funny, the misconceptions people have about birds." Cass was surprised by the topic Ryan chose to begin their conversation. She was prepared for a "stay in your lane, mind your own business" tirade, not a lesson on avian wildlife.

"Huh? How so?"

"Take the hawk." Ryan pointed up into the sky where two hawks circled, looking for prey, while a flock of mourning doves darted about beneath them. "People think that because of its size and its vast wingspan, the hawk is the most vicious and mean-spirited bird in the wild."

"That's what I've heard. You disagree?"

"No, it's true. But the hawk is real and doesn't try to hide what it is. Compare the hawk's reputation—vicious and mean—to that of the mourning dove, whose rep is that it's a small, gentle, and sweet-natured bird," Ryan said.

"What's wrong with that rep? Doves are the symbols of peace."

"No, trust me, they're not—or, at least, not all doves. That tagline doesn't apply to mourning doves."

"Maybe they have a good PR agent?" Could that be a flicker of a smile at the corner of Ryan's mouth? Not likely. Like the hawk, brooding and fierce, it would take more than a silly joke to crack his stone face.

"The doves' quickness allows them to cause all kinds of havoc. They badger, poke, prod, and dive-bomb. They're a real nuisance to other birds. They're no match against giant birds like the hawk, of course—unless they annoy them to death—but the demure little doves are actually aggressive bullies. They can use their wings to karate chop and slap down lesser opponents. They're especially aggressive when defending their territory or their feeder."

"That's a bad thing? Guarding what's yours and standing up for yourself?" Cass asked. This discussion wasn't really about birds, Cass realized. And she had a good idea where it was headed. The birds were an analogy—Ryan's way of telling her that she was annoying. She was the pesky dove, aggravating the mighty hawk—him.

"It's very annoying if you're a hawk minding your own business and a tiny bird not a third your size starts harassing you every chance she gets."

"And... that's relevant, how?"

"You remind me of the mourning dove. A real nuisance."

Ah… she was right. This lesson on the habits of birds was his way of telling her to mind her own business. Cass waited for Ryan to spell it out and give a detailed list of all the times she'd invaded his territory or irritated and annoyed him. But his next comment surprised her.

"Enough about birds." Ryan paused a moment, then said without preamble, "I had just finished my residency at Charlotte General when I met Cheryl Rhinehart. Her father was a big shot CEO from New York who transferred to Charlotte during the business boom a few years back. Ours was a whirlwind romance, and within a few months, Cheryl and I were engaged. I was very naïve—or maybe just flattered that someone as sparkly, worldly, and exciting as Cheryl would fall in love with me, a country boy from the mountains of North Carolina."

"What? You were married?" Cass asked, surprised.

"No. Things were okay until a few months after our engagement. That's when Cheryl began pushing me to move to New York and take a job with a well-known cardiologist who was a family friend. I promised that I'd think about it, but I wasn't being truthful. I didn't want to leave North Carolina and my family. Life in a big city didn't interest me."

"Did you go?"

"No. Shortly after that, I killed my fiancée." Ryan's knuckles whitened as he gripped the side of the bench.

"What? You killed her?" The calmness of Ryan's statement shocked Cass. "Why? Over a dispute on whether to move to New York? An overreaction, don't you think?"

"No, I didn't kill her directly." Ryan shook his head. "But I caused her death."

"Oh… well, that does make a difference, you know."

"We had dinner at my house one night." Ryan, caught up in his story, seemed not to hear Cass's comment. "Cheryl announced that she'd found us an apartment in New York City and had scheduled an interview for me with the cardiologist. I told her to cancel the interview, because I wasn't moving. I told her that I liked my job and wanted to remain in Charlotte. I asked her to stay."

When Ryan paused in telling his story, Cass prompted, "What did she say?"

"She wouldn't answer that specific question, and we got into a heated argument. This went on for quite some time. The more we argued, the more she drank. I begged her to spend the night or let me drive her home. She wouldn't agree to either offer. Cheryl stormed out of the house. Nothing I said or did could change her mind. She didn't want anything to do with me."

Cass picked up Ryan's hand, but he jerked it away, resisting any comfort as he reached the worst part of his story.

"She sped out of the driveway. I heard the squeal of brakes and the sound of a collision as she swerved into oncoming traffic. She hit a semitruck, ran off the road, and wrapped her car around a tree."

"I'm so sorry," Cass said.

Ryan leaned forward, rested his chin on his hands, and propped his elbows on his knees. He continued his story in a mechanical, dispassionate monotone. "When I saw the ball of fire light up the night sky, I knew Cheryl hadn't survive that crash." Ryan's pained look focused on something in the distance, seemingly unaware that Cass sat beside him. He was caught up in the horrors he had witnessed that night. "At the time, I worked in the ER and routinely treated accident victims. This was one of the worst accidents I'd ever seen."

"It wasn't your fault," Cass said, but Ryan didn't acknowledge that he'd heard her.

"Cheryl was badly burned and had extensive internal injuries. She was gone by the time the paramedics cut her from the wreckage. Still, I tried everything I knew to save her on the way to the hospital. But I failed."

"I'm so sorry!" Cass rubbed Ryan's tensed shoulders, and this time, he didn't pull away. Ryan's graphic description of the accident and imagining how painful it must have been for him brought a lump to her throat.

"I stopped practicing medicine that night. I didn't even go back to the hospital to get my personal belongings. I was done. I caused her death, and I had to get away before my mistakes caused someone else to die."

"You must have loved her very much. You gave up your career and isolated yourself here, away from all reminders of her."

"I'm not sure about 'love'—that's another thing I feel guilty about. I was infatuated, that's true. We got engaged before we really knew each other. I'd already started having second thoughts. If I'd just been honest with her, the accident never would've happened."

"You were not at fault! Horrible things happen all the time. She caused the accident, not you," Cass assured Ryan.

"No, I'm to blame!" Ryan objected. "She wasn't in love with the real me, either. I could never have made her happy. She spent more on a dinner out than I earned in a week. Expensive clothes, vacations in Paris, and dining at five-star restaurants, while nice, were never high on my list of priorities. I was a coward for not telling her this. Cheryl paid for my cowardice." Ryan's voice was filled with disgust at himself for not breaking the engagement sooner.

Cass shifted uncomfortably and pulled her expensive skirt down over her Manolo Blahnik shoes—a birthday present from her mother. She had a closet full of expensive clothes, too, and yes, they *were* nice, but that was more about who her mother was than her.

"You can't blame yourself for her accident," Cass insisted.

"Cheryl was the one driving recklessly, not you."

Ryan's overreacting the night he drove her home from the Eagle's Nest—and his snide comments about city girls with expensive tastes—suddenly made sense. But she wasn't anything like Cheryl, so putting them in the same category was wrong.

"But I do blame myself. Her parents blamed me, too. They became media darlings, appearing on TV constantly, threatening to sue me—which was ridiculous, since Cheryl was alone in the car. But I let her drink too much, they accused, and didn't drive her home. No one ever stopped Cheryl Rhinehart from doing anything she wanted to do. But her parents' accusations were the same as the ones I threw at myself."

"You're not responsible for what others do. Do you think you'll ever practice medicine again?" Cass asked.

"No. I like what I'm doing. It's slow and easy, and my mistakes don't cost people their lives. I can do my job without even thinking," Ryan said.

"That sounds like coasting. Living in limbo. Stuck in a rut. Sleepwalking through life. Avoiding anything difficult." In for a penny, in for a pound, Cass decided, so she added, "You're hiding from life and looking for an easy ride. Now *that's* cowardice."

Despite Ryan's protest, Cass didn't believe that working for his father gave him the same satisfaction as practicing medicine. The only times she'd seen Ryan fully engaged in anything was when he'd been discussing her stalker, assisting the sheriff, or protecting her. Ryan needed something more challenging than what he was doing—something that required him to think.

"Did anyone ever tell you that you're pushy *and* bossy?" Ryan's recounting the story of Cheryl's death had exhausted him emotionally. His question came out more as a statement.

"All the time, but I plow ahead anyway—when I'm right," Cass replied. "Listen, I need a doctor for the clinic. What better way to get back into medicine than by serving your friends and neighbors—the people of Mason Valley?"

"What do you know about the needs of Mason Valley? You're a city girl from a wealthy family who seems to be related to British royalty. And don't try to hide your shoes. I recognize the brand."

Ryan had researched her? Cass didn't know whether to be flattered or angry. Also, "related to British royalty"? Cecilia would be flattered that someone outside Philly had bought the hints she frequently planted in the tabloid press. Never outright lying, Cecilia didn't bother to correct the assumptions, either.

"Yes, we're the upper crust of Philly society," Cass said sarcastically, her voice hovering somewhere between anger at Ryan's remark and self-pity over the collapse of her own life. "My father is a criminal on his way to prison, and my mother is hiding out in the Poconos, managing a PR campaign as she tries to separate herself from ever having known any of us. Meanwhile, I'm desperately trying to convince an ill-tempered, ill-mannered, reclusive doctor that I need him. Yes! You're right! Cass Jordan's life is absolutely perfect!"

"It's not always about what you want or need, you know?" Ryan said curtly.

"No, it's not." Ryan's callous insinuation that she always got what she wanted and had lived an easy life annoyed her. Her voice erupted like a fireball. "I wanted to stay in Philadelphia and keep my job! I wanted my father not to be a criminal! I wanted to not be arrested, perp walked, and grilled for hours on end! I want my mother to stop pressuring me to live my life as a copy of hers! But mostly, I want whoever is trying to kill me to *stop*!"

Ryan blinked, taken aback by Cass's shouted list of difficulties she was dealing with. "I'm sorry. Forget I said that, please." He placed his arm around her and squeezed her shoulder. "I don't think I'm ready to practice medicine yet. Maybe someday, but everything about the accident is still raw. And my nightmares don't seem ready to stop reminding me, either."

"Your story is tragic, but don't expect pity from me. You've got to get back to your life. You can't wallow in guilt forever. The medical field needs compassionate people like you. You clearly love medicine. Otherwise, you wouldn't be treating injured hawks and doves."

Cass braced for another sneering comeback. He wouldn't miss the opportunity to remind her that she'd once again plowed into territory that was none of her business. It wouldn't surprise her if Ryan got up and walked away, leaving her sitting here alone.

"You could be wrong, too." Ryan surprised Cass with his flat, emotionless reply. He wasn't angry, but his mask was back in place, unsmiling and stoic. In Cass's view, this was worse than anger.

"Didn't I tell you that I'm always right?"

"Huh! Always annoying, maybe, but not always right. One thing I forgot to mention in my lesson about birds: the hawk is a bird of prey. He doesn't take sass or nonsense from any bird, especially the mourning dove. Turns out, they're his favorite meal."

"Nice thought! Exactly what I'd expect from Gloomy Gus. I'll remember your warning… maybe."

"Well, there you have it: the story everyone has been tiptoeing around, as you so brazenly accused them of doing at dinner."

"Brazenness is in my DNA, it seems. I apologize for my outburst. Everything that's happened to me recently just piled up and boom! I spouted off without thinking. I was rude—like someone else I know," Cass replied pointedly.

"I have no idea who that might be."

"Ha! At least I admit that my mouth does run away at times. But within my head, I see a truth that must be spoken aloud."

"What you call speaking truth might be considered insulting by your target." Ryan didn't look at her but focused on the birds that wheeled around overhead.

"I'll try to remember that—a lecture from a man who takes churlishness to a whole new level. When you asked me to go for a walk, I thought I was headed for the proverbial woodshed because of my comments."

"That could be interesting, but not today. Just a walk." Ryan actually smiled—a ray of hope that a smidgen of normalcy was buried somewhere in that handsome body if he could only overcome his guilt over Cheryl's death and his self-imposed penance because of it. "Come on. Let's go home. My mother should have the dessert table set up by now, and even doves are less annoying when on a sugar high." Ryan stood, took Cass's hand, and pulled her up from the bench.

"Sounds good, Hawk Man." Cass brushed off the back of her skirt. "Just don't walk so fast this time. We royals don't like to be dragged through the dirt."

◆

Margaret said goodbye to the dinner guests and invited them all to come back anytime for a visit. The house was quiet after so much laughter had filled the rooms throughout the afternoon.

Mike and Karen had gone home, and Bill left for the barn to feed the farm animals. Lanie had gone for a walk, and Ryan had disappeared immediately after he finished his dessert. He hadn't reappeared to say goodbye or to see their guests off. Margaret suspected he'd gone to treat the injured bird, but he could have spared a few minutes to say goodbye.

She'd have to find her "Manual for Polite Behavior" and give Ryan a refresher course.

Margaret found Ryan sitting on a bench in the backyard. His chin rested on his clasped hands as he watched the injured hawk in the cage. His open medicine bag sat on the ground beside him.

Wandering off alone and ignoring basic etiquette rules had been Ryan's pattern of behavior for almost two years. He hadn't always been this withdrawn. At one time, he was as much of a prankster and chatterer as Mike.

Ryan had been a fun-loving and gifted child who found joy in even the smallest things: chicken hatchlings in the barn, a frog in the pond, or a beautiful sunrise or sunset. He'd grown into a wonderful young man, always joking and laughing. He cultivated friends like a Pied Piper wherever he went. As a teenager, Ryan was a basketball star and one of Mason Valley High's most popular students. Part of his charm was that he never let his popularity go to his head. He was always down-to-earth and treated everyone equally, regardless of who they were.

To see Ryan hurting and so withdrawn following Cheryl's death broke Margaret's heart. Bill was less sympathetic and thought Ryan needed a good talking-to, not soft-pedaling. He wanted to tell his son to just shape up and get over it.

Margaret had often agreed that she should talk to Ryan and remind him—as Cass had at dinner—to stop hiding from life and enjoy all the goodness around him. But she held back. She didn't want to add to the pain Ryan was obviously feeling. She'd assumed he would eventually work through the loss and deal with the aftermath the way most people dealt with death. But thus far, that hadn't happened. Maybe Bill was right. After almost two years, it was time to point out that by submerging himself in grief, Ryan was destroying another life—his own.

And he was hurting everyone who cared about him in the process. Hurting oneself and those who love you never rewrites the past.

It took a stranger—Cass—to point out that by avoiding a confrontation with Ryan over his withdrawal, the family wasn't helping him; they were only making the situation worse.

"How's the hawk doing?" Margaret asked as she sat down on the bench beside Ryan. "I see you splinted his wing."

"He's going to be fine. He should be able to fly again as soon as he's healed. Someone probably took a potshot at him. He's calm now, so I won't move him. I'll leave him here and check on him again tomorrow morning—if that's alright."

"Of course. Glad to hear he's going to be okay. Dinner turned out well, don't you think?"

"Yes, it did, like always. You're a great cook." Ryan lapsed back into silence.

"Cass seems nice. Carolyn says she's quickly whipping everything into shape at the clinic. Dr. Phillips was nice, but he was always temporary and just marking time until he could get back to retirement. Cass is giving the staff real direction and leadership for the first time."

"Some people think she's nice, I imagine. She's bossy, I know that much—always meddling in other people's business."

Margaret wanted to reach over and bop Ryan on the back of his head for his short, indifferent comments. Mike was right when he called Ryan "Cave Man," but even a grunt from Ryan would be an improvement over most conversations with him. Engaging Ryan in dialogue was like talking to a statue—frustrating and futile.

"Well, I like her. Sometimes, it takes an outsider to point out what should be obvious to the people involved. People often get buried so deep in their problems that they lose sight of how to dig out from under them."

"Cass's just another rich female who thinks that when she speaks, everyone should jump and do her bidding. She had no right to disrupt dinner. That was rude and uncalled for!"

"Speaking of rude…" Margaret let the sentence hang unfinished, but she doubted the message penetrated Ryan's current mood. "She didn't disrupt dinner, and I like her spunk." Margret placed her arm across Ryan's shoulders and gave him a gentle hug. "Give her a break. She's dealt with a lot, between what her father did, reporters chasing after her, vicious threats, losing her job, and then moving to a new town where she knows no one. I admire her. She's a very strong young woman. That she's not cowering in fear in a basement somewhere says a lot for her character."

"I want her to stop interfering, like she did today. I don't need her to point out what I'm doing wrong. It's my life! No one likes a bossy woman." Margaret expected a pout to go with that comment, but Ryan remained stone-faced. At least a pout would be more emotion than the sullen look he wore.

"Your dad doesn't object to a bossy woman. That's what attracted him to me in the first place." Margaret chuckled. "It keeps our relationship *interesting*. Do I need to explain?"

"No, please don't! But this situation is different. I'm done listening to rich women who want to reshape me into their image of the perfect man."

"Ryan, I'm going to put this to you straight. Cass is what's different in this situation. She's very different from Cheryl and in all the best ways. Cheryl wouldn't have joined us for dinner today, much less have given us all a tongue-lashing. I applaud Cass for speaking her mind. She cares and recognizes your good qualities—things you should be happy about. If you'd come out from under your rock, you'd see that, too. She just reminded all of us that you can't go on like this."

"Hmph! Don't worry about me. I can handle my problems

by myself. I don't need interference, especially from someone who doesn't even know me."

"I don't see *any* evidence that you're handling your problems very well." Margaret felt another inclination to bop Ryan on the head. "When you returned from your walk today, I thought you and Cass had settled some things between you. You seemed more relaxed. Then, as usual, you clammed up and disappeared."

"I had to see to the hawk."

"I think you were hiding again."

"Maybe. Sometimes, I have to get away from people. Scenes from the accident come back suddenly—the sounds, then the silence, followed by the roar of the flames and the loud explosion. The fact that I caused it just won't go away."

"Cheryl caused it, not you. You can have memories of your good times with Cheryl, but the mourning period for her death has to end. I understand why this is hard for you. You've always been a caring person. It's why you became a doctor. Maybe what you need is a diversion or something new to concentrate on."

"I don't want you to worry. Give me time. I'll get there." Ryan paused, then looked over at Margaret. "But I've been thinking—about many things—lately. What eats at me the most is frustration over how I dealt with everything. I gave up my profession—something I loved. I ran away, and that was just plain cowardly of me."

"You can fix your frustrations by getting back into practicing medicine again."

"I was afraid of my reaction when faced with another life-or-death situation," Ryan continued. "If my negligence caused another death, I'm not sure I could've handled it."

"But don't you think you would've gotten beyond that?"

"I don't know, and that left too much to chance. But now, I don't want to get out of my safe rut. The status quo suits me just fine. Sure, I may be coasting through life, but making a wrong decision isn't something I have to worry about."

This is a start. A small one, but still... Margaret thought. Ryan usually clammed up at such topics; he hadn't spoken this freely since the accident. Margaret wanted to pull him into her arms and assure him that everything would be alright, just as she had when he was a child and bruised his knees by falling off his bike. But Ryan was a grown man, and now was the time for a mother's tough love.

"You're not a coward, just acting like one. But it's good that you're starting to sort things out and see them more clearly. You admit that you're in a rut, but it's up to *you* to crawl out. And thus far, you're not even trying to do that!"

"I know. It's much easier to stay in my rut—no decisions, no mistakes."

"Don't you think you've wallowed in self-pity long enough? Did you ever think the nightmares won't go away because you spend too much time alone—at your cabin and even at work? You don't have anything to look forward to or focus on. Even in a crowd, you close yourself off and don't join in the conversation. The only thing you do for entertainment is sing at the Eagle's Nest. And most of the time, you don't even look like you're enjoying that."

"Maybe I'm just putting myself into the song—a tortured artist who feels the lyrics." If Ryan was attempting to make a joke, his blank expression removed any humor from his comment.

"More like a tortured artist who can't get out of his own head. You're not the only one being tortured. Everyone who loves you is, too. You've been on a 'woe is me' binge for much too long. Punishing yourself for something that wasn't your fault is well... dumb and stupid." Margaret's voice rose, and she shook Ryan's shoulders in frustration.

"Why don't you kick me while I'm down?" Ryan snapped. Then, his voice softened as he apologized, "I'm sorry. I didn't mean that. I know you're trying to help."

"I'd kick your *ass* if I could and thought it would help," Margaret snapped back. "Listen to me! I know you blame yourself and think you could have done the impossible and saved Cheryl's life, but you couldn't. You're a great doctor, but you're only human, and you need to get that fact through your thick head. A break from medicine at the time seemed normal, but it's time to get over yourself and get back on the job."

Ryan didn't respond at first but sat quietly thinking. Then, he straightened, put his arms around Margaret, and hugged her. "I'm sorry I've caused you so much worry, and I don't doubt for a second that you *could* kick my ass if you wanted to. I see why you like Cass so much. Cut from the same cloth, two peas in a pod, as they say."

"I like Cass because she cares for people—for you. She's brave enough to speak the truth and not dance around the edges when she has a point to make."

"Cass just wants a doctor for her clinic. Women like Cass aren't above pretense to get what they want."

"Ryan," Margret said, her frustration mounting again, "Cass is nothing like Cheryl. You didn't fit into Cheryl's world. Cass is here, living in *your* world. You lost your way for a while, but it's past time to put all that behind you."

"You make it sound easy. It's not." Ryan turned to look at the hawk. "But don't think I'm happy living this way, either. I feel much like this hawk: injured and locked in a cage."

"Don't go maudlin on me! Your injury is self-inflicted, and you can do something about it." Margaret was through coddling Ryan. His pity party was becoming annoying. "I'm taking Cass's advice. I'm through tiptoeing around, waiting for you to wake up. Prepare yourself. I'll no longer hesitate to point out when

I think you're wrong. And you're wrong about a lot of things. Wise up!"

"You're right! Sorry! That was a little overly dramatic."

"A little? It's not your best line, either. Don't use it in the next song you write," Margaret laughed.

"I know someone aside from Cass who doesn't dance around the edges." Ryan hugged Margaret tightly. "I'll try to do better, I promise. I don't want to hurt you and Dad anymore."

"You're hurting yourself. But 'try' is all I ask right now." Margaret tipped Ryan's face toward her and looked into his blue eyes that were so much like hers. "I love you, my son, but just so you know, that ass-kicking is still on the table."

CHAPTER FIFTEEN

O h, man. You look rough." Ryan glanced at his image in the hallway mirror on his way to the kitchen to start a pot of coffee. His hair stood on end from a night of tossing and turning—and thinking. A day-old beard shaded his jaw. He had the look of someone coming off an extended party binge—or maybe just of a night spent wrestling with the demons from his past. Bleary-eyed, he mechanically measured the coffee into the filter and pressed the 'Brew' button.

His mother's lecture yesterday, on top of Cass's criticisms, wouldn't let his mind rest last night, forcing him to analyze what he was doing—or not doing—with his life. The thoughts that kept him awake were filled with questions, but thus far, he hadn't pinned down any answers.

Did it make sense for him to continue beating himself up over something he didn't have the power to change? Why had he taken on all the blame for Cheryl's accident? Then, he beat himself up over his cowardice and weakness in letting his life disintegrate and letting the accident dominate his life.

Concrete answers to his questions spun out of reach in the

darkness, but the bottom line was that he needed to change directions. His mother said so, and unlike Cass, she *was* always right.

Ryan had promised his mother that he'd try to make changes. That would be harder to do than to promise. But at least now he admitted he was on a fast track to nowhere if he didn't do something soon.

Ryan's plans for the day were few. It was Friday, and everyone at the construction company was off for the Thanksgiving weekend. Ryan had volunteered to give Kelsey a walk-through of the clinic today while she was in town. His only other task was to pick up the injured hawk at his parents' house and bring him to the cabin for treatment. Other than that, his schedule was wide open. And that spoke volumes about his life. He had time to fill and nothing to fill it with.

After the verbal ass-whipping from his mother yesterday, during which she'd pointed out how his solitary, monk-like existence wasn't a life at all, Ryan now wished he had something fun planned for today and someone to do it with. While the two tasks on his schedule were important, they didn't fill the longing he felt. The image of Cass's face flushed with color and her eyes snapping with anger as she yelled at him in the meadow yesterday appeared before his eyes. Cass wouldn't back down from anyone if she thought she was right.

Hmmm… what would life be like around such a spirited and stimulating person all the time? Exhausting, probably, but definitely not boring.

Ryan was pouring himself a cup of coffee when a loud knock—more like pounding, really—sounded on his door.

"What the hell?" Ryan jumped, sloshing coffee over his hand and down the front of the cabinet. He grabbed a towel, wiped up the spilled coffee, then walked to the door. Jack stood on his porch.

"I need to talk to you." Jack pushed past Ryan and into the house without waiting for him to fully open the door. Ryan stared as Jack took a cup from the cupboard and poured himself a cup of coffee.

"What's going on? What—" Ryan sputtered.

"Sit down and listen," Jack commanded as he sat down at the table, added cream and sugar to his coffee, and stirred vigorously.

"What's wrong?" Ryan sat down opposite Jack and prepared himself for bad news. "Has something happened?"

"You! That's what's wrong. I'm tired of pussy-footing around you and tired of looking at your scowling face."

"Yet here you are!" Ryan pointed out. He relaxed. It wasn't bad news. Jack was angry about something, but Jack's anger didn't usually last long. "Get to the point before I throw you out!"

Jack pulled a napkin from the holder on the table and placed it beneath his cup of coffee. He paused and looked around the cabin. "I don't see the four guys you'll need to assist you in throwing me out, my friend. But let's get serious. I'm here to do an intervention. As Cass pointed out, we've all been coddling you and helping you dig the hole you're living in. But I'm done with that!"

"Cass again!" Ryan said. "She kicked a hornets' nest and went on her merry way, and now, I'm the one getting stung. Forget your sermon. My mother already beat you to it." Ryan got up, refreshed his cup of coffee, then returned to the table.

"If Margaret agrees with Cass, then I know I'm right."

"What's it about Cass that's turned all of you into believers in the Gospel of Cass? She's only been here for a short time. Don't put any stock in what she says."

"Well, Cass just said out loud what we've all been thinking silently for a long time. I guess she thinks saving your ugly face is worth spouting off before a table of strangers."

"Hmph!" Ryan snorted. "Maybe Cass just likes messing with people's lives. Interfering where she doesn't belong. That's likely the real reason she got fired from her last job." Ryan was instantly sorry for his remark. His comment was wrong. He'd seen visual evidence of the true cause, thanks to the ugly threats painted on the clinic door.

"You know that's not true!" Jack angrily threw up his hands. "You know what your trouble is, Golden Boy?"

"I imagine you're going to tell me," Ryan replied. "I'm surprised it's taken you this long."

"You're attracted to Cass. I know you are," Jack said. "You're fighting it and afraid to admit it. You enjoy wearing your hair shirt and won't give it up for any reason. The shine has worn off your Golden Boy image, and you're now reveling in the glow of sympathy from everyone around you. Poor, poor Ryan!"

"I know you were shooting for a metaphor, but that one was pathetic!" Ryan couldn't help but laugh. Jack always added levity to a situation, even when he made a ham-handed attempt at being serious.

"Agreed. I should have just called you an *idiot* and left it at that."

"I'm on to you, too! You're insulting me, hoping you'll jolt me into agreeing with you." Ryan took a drink of his coffee, his mouth turned up in a sneer. "'Get on with your life, Ryan!' 'Forget the past!' 'Find love and happiness.' 'How hard can it be?' 'Just listen to Jack!'"

"Well, are my insults working? I've got many more in my arsenal."

"Cass and my mother kicked my ass all over the farm yesterday. Your insults pale in comparison."

Ryan hadn't figured out anything about Cass. Jack accused him of being attracted to her. Maybe he was, but a person couldn't actually ignore someone like Cass. She inserted herself into your business until eventually, you missed having her around, even if just as a sparring partner.

Cass had given him something else to think about during his sleepless night. Did she have an angle similar to Cheryl's? She had certainly lived a different lifestyle. She couldn't possibly want to trade an easy life in Philly for life in the mountains of North Carolina. But she was already here, his inner monologue—and his mother—argued back. Maybe he was just scared that he wouldn't spot a hidden agenda if she was playing him. He refused to walk into another trap.

"I can imagine your mom throwing down some unique Margaret-isms. You need to listen. We all care for you and just want to help. But admit it, you like Cass. I think she likes you, too."

"Should I ask her to the prom? Or pass a note to her in class?" Ryan tried another sneer at Jack's comment, but it turned into a chuckle. "Your dating calendar isn't exactly full, either, is it?"

"Well, I have a fix for that. Do you mind if I ask Cass out, since you're not interested?"

"I... well... sure. I'm not her father, screening her dates."

"You're not? I don't need your permission to ask for her hand in marriage?"

"You're certifiable!"

Jack, with all his craziness, had always been like a brother when they were younger. When Ryan went off to college and med school, then got involved with Cheryl, he'd neglected his best friend. But Jack never seemed to hold it against him. Ryan could always count on Jack to be around, even when he withdrew from everyone else.

His friendship with Jack was something else he needed to repair.

"Your reaction to the idea of me dating Cass is exactly what I expected: showing interest without admitting interest," Jack said. "When *I* set my eyes on someone, I'm not afraid to jump into the pool. That's the difference between you and me. You're scared. I get it, but it's time you got back on the horse."

"That metaphor is a little better, but still awful." Ryan laughed, got up from his seat, and slapped Jack on the back before checking his wristwatch. "I know you're just trying to help. I'll take all your comments and assumptions under advisement. But right now, I need to finish getting dressed and check on the injured hawk at the farm. Come back again soon—when you're not frothing at the mouth."

"Of course. I'll be back whether I'm invited or not. But I can't promise I won't have more insults. You'll think about Cass?" Jack asked as he got up from the table and gave Ryan a fist bump.

"Probably—way more than I should."

◆

In hindsight, Cass's outburst yesterday at dinner seemed more outrageous than when she first threw the hand grenade into the midst of the dinner party. It was done, though, so she might as well stop obsessing over why she did it. She would send a nice flower arrangement to Margaret, thanking her for the invitation to dinner and apologizing again for her thoughtless behavior.

A large stack of unopened mail was piled on the credenza, prompting Cass to come into her office this Friday morning. Due to the short work week, Cass hadn't had time to review the mail. It gave her something to do as she waited for Kelsey and someone from Scott Construction to join her for the walk-through while the clinic was closed to patients.

Raj and Mandy were still asleep when she left the house. Once the walk-through was finished, Cass would have plenty of time to visit with Mandy before she returned to Charlotte on Sunday.

The building was eerily quiet without the chatter of patients or staff or the sounds of construction activity. Like background music, the muffled voices, loud bumps, and banging of hammers from the other end of the building had become a normal part of her day. She would miss them when the construction was done and the crews left for good.

A musty smell hung in the air when Cass unlocked her office door. She pushed the door open as far as it would go, hoping the air from the hallway would circulate and freshen the stale office. It was funny how a closed-up building quickly took on a different atmosphere, and lost the sounds, smells, and imprints of its inhabitants.

As Cass moved the stack of mail to her desk and sat down, her thoughts turned to Ryan. Would he be the one who came from the construction company to do the walk-through? She wouldn't mind seeing him again, but she seriously doubted he'd be very anxious to see her—not after the way she had disrupted dinner yesterday.

The story Ryan had shared about the death of his fiancée cleared up many things, including why he'd retreated from the world and gave up his profession. But knowledge of what happened didn't mean she wouldn't again point out how Mason Valley needed his talents as a doctor.

The shock of finding out Ryan's secret—that he was a licensed medical doctor—had worn off. Cass's new goal was to convince him to practice again—and at her clinic. Ryan's self-imposed martyrdom might slow her in reaching that goal, but it wouldn't stop her. Ryan needed to get back into the profession he loved and stop hiding—and it wasn't solely because she needed a doctor for the clinic. She cared about him. He was wasting away as the world moved on without him.

A talk with Dr. Blankenship might help Ryan understand how Cheryl's death wasn't his fault. But Cass had meddled enough, and she wouldn't be the one to suggest he make an appointment.

When Cass and Ryan returned from their walk yesterday, their reception by the other dinner guests had surprised her. Mike and Jack had surrounded her immediately, pulling out their repertoire of stale jokes, each one trying to get the biggest laugh out of her. Mandy and Karen have given her sympathetic smiles.

"You get extra whipped cream for courage," Margaret had said without further explanation as she handed Cass a large piece of pumpkin pie topped with a two-inch-high cap of whipped cream.

Bill had poured her a glass of wine and whispered as he handed it to her, "Atta girl."

Lanie and Raj had invited her to sit beside them. The only one who didn't rhetorically high-five her was Ryan. He stayed as far away from her as possible.

But she hadn't expected their talk to change Hawk Man into a join-the-party kind of guy. And she was right. Ryan had retreated into a shadowed nook at the edge of the room—probably stewing and plotting his revenge. He left immediately after dessert. She assumed it was to attend to the injured hawk, but maybe he just wanted to get away from her.

Forcing thoughts of Ryan from of her mind, Cass began opening envelopes and sorting the mail into piles: bills she needed to approve before passing them on to Betsy to process for payment, a referral for a veteran who wanted to enroll in a four-week course of equestrian therapy—a program Kelsey had started because Jason used riding to help him get over his injuries and PTSD from serving in Afghanistan—and a letter from a veteran in Asheville, asking if he would be eligible for treatment if he moved to Mason Valley.

Cass quickly finished opening the envelopes; the only thing left was a postal mailing box. The label affixed to the top of the box indicated the contents were packed in dry ice.

Hmmm… must be some type of medication that needs to be kept cool, Cass thought. But who had ordered medication without her approval? And she wasn't aware of any medication used by their therapists that needed refrigeration.

Cass picked up a pair of scissors and cut the tape holding each end of the lid. She removed the lid and pulled out the dry ice packets, which were flat now that most of the dry ice had evaporated. A horrible smell wafted out of the box and hit Cass squarely in the face. She gagged, then swallowed as bitter bile rose in her throat.

"Oh my God!" Cass let out a muffled scream as she pulled back a sheet of brown packing paper, exposing the box's contents. She recoiled backward, landing hard in her chair. In disbelief that what she had seen was real, Cass sat up and peeked into the box again.

It was real! On a bed of bloody straw lay the rotting carcass of a large rattlesnake, its shriveled brown and gold body coiled as if to strike. A hunting knife, covered in congealed blood, and stuck between lifeless eyes, pinned the snake's severed head to the bottom of the box. A note was taped to the knife. "This is what happens to snakes!!" Read the ominous threat scrawled on the note.

Cass bolted from her desk, ran from the office, and dashed into the hallway. She had to get out and away from the stench and the bloody scene. Her knees shook as she leaned weakly against the wall and sobbed. Whoever wanted her dead wasn't going to stop until he was successful. He had managed to invade her office.

Breathing in short gulps, Cass slid slowly down the wall and buried her face in her hands.

A hand suddenly touched her shoulder. "Get away from me!" Cass screamed. Blinded by fear, she kicked out with both feet, her shoe connecting with something. Peeking through her fingers, she spotted two feet standing just in front of her. Ready to fight off an assailant, she sprang to a hunkered position and raised her fists.

"Cass! Cass! Stop! Stop fighting! What's wrong?"

Cass dropped her fists and looked up when she recognized Ryan's voice. He grasped her by the arms and helped her stand upright. Relief flooded through Cass as she sagged weakly against Ryan. "In… there…" Cass spoke between sobs, pointing toward her open door. "Don't leave me!" She grabbed Ryan's shirt when she felt him move.

"Shush! I won't leave you. I promise." Ryan folded his arms tightly around her and pressed her head to his shoulder. He turned toward Kelsey as she entered the hallway and walked toward them. "Kelsey, can you see what's going on in Cass's office?"

Kelsey nodded and entered the room, but emerged immediately, gagging and holding her hand over her nose. "We need to get the sheriff out here. Now!"

Sheriff Ferguson, along with Jason, arrived at the clinic within minutes.

"I've always hated snakes, but this one terrified me!" Cass shuddered as she described the discovery of the snake while opening the mail. "Who would do this to me?"

"Only a sick mind would do this—and take the time to stage it this way," Sherriff Ferguson said. He had already dispatched one of his deputies to take the box and the snake to the FBI office in Charlotte. A forensic examination might uncover DNA or other clues from the packaging material. "Whoever the perp turns out to be," Sheriff Ferguson informed the group, "he's now added another charge to his ever-growing list. He sent a death threat through the US mail."

"Sheriff Ferguson and I were just getting ready to go over the information Kelsey obtained from Ryan's photos of last week," Jason said. "Why don't we all get out of here and go to the sheriff's office? We can review the information together and get our minds on something less gruesome."

"Are you up for that?" Ryan raised Cass's chin and looked closely at her face. She still clung to him, unable to force herself to leave the safety of his arms. At her nod, he added, "I'll call Dad and ask him to send someone over today to disinfect your office."

"But the final building inspection!" Cass reminded them.

"We can do the walk-through whenever you feel like it," Kelsey said. "It's not that important, especially after all this."

At Cass's nodded agreement, they all left the building.

"You'll ride with me," Ryan said as he opened the door to his pickup.

Cass didn't object. She couldn't muster an argument against Ryan's suggestion, nor did she want to. She climbed into his truck.

When they entered the sheriff's office, Kelsey and Jason, along with Ben Wilder, were waiting with the sheriff, ready to discuss the photos of the van.

"We were going over Kelsey's analysis of the white van," Sheriff Ferguson explained as Cass and Ryan took seats at the table. Jason loaded a written report onto the video screen along-side Ryan's photos.

"The report, done by Jeff Collins, the forensic analysist at Barrett Security, indicates that the shadows in the photos are packing boxes. Beneath them are other boxes. Only a few inches of these other boxes are visible, but they appear to contain beer," Kelsey explained.

"Was Jeff able to determine what's in the top boxes?" Ben asked.

"Yes, he was able to read the label. The boxes contain a local brand of sweet potato chips called Sweet-Thins," Kelsey said.

"I did some research and found that they're produced at a small establishment in Greensboro," Jason added. "There's a wholesale warehouse in High Point that distributes them. If we can get a list of retailers who stock them, that might narrow our search as to the company that delivers them. We can first concentrate on stores in Mason Valley and nearby communities. As a start-up brand, they're probably sold in convenience stores, rather than grocery stores. As you know, there are a lot of convenience stores around here, ranging from chain stores to mom-and-pop operations."

"What's the brand of beer?" Ryan asked. "Is it from a local microbrewery?"

"I wish," Jason replied. "No, it's a national brand that's widely distributed."

"Sounds like the distribution of the sweet potato chips is our best lead," Ben acknowledged. "That might help identify the van driver, but we still don't know if he's our perp or involved in any of this. Let's not make assumptions that knock us off-track. I suggest we identify him, see if he's connected to Cass in anyway, and then bring him in for questioning."

"If we're correct about his timeline, he passes through Mason Valley each Wednesday," Ryan said. "The question is, is he making a delivery in town or just passing through?"

"We don't know," Sheriff Ferguson said. "My deputies are canvasing the area where the temporary tag was stolen to see if his van with the original plate shows up on someone's security camera."

"Wasn't the tag stolen from a convenience store?" Kelsey asked. "Maybe he delivers to that store, too."

"Yes, it was a convenience store. We're checking there, too. And now, we have to find an idiot that sends dead snakes through the mail and see if he's also tied to the Wednesday stalker." Sheriff Ferguson turned to Cass. "Cass, do you know when the box you found this morning was delivered?"

"I'm not sure, but I think maybe on Monday. Betsy, the office manager, delivers any mail she doesn't recognize as standard correspondence or anything that needs my approval and stacks it on my office credenza. I've been tied up with HR paperwork for new staff members, and I wasn't in any rush to sort through that stack since the office would be closed for two days this week. I decided to go through it this morning while I waited for Kelsey."

"Didn't you notice that smell?" the sheriff asked.

"Not until I entered my office today. And I assumed it was because the office had been closed up without the usual traffic in and out that would let fresh air in. The construction crews were all gone on Wednesday, and my office staff left early after seeing the last patient. I worked for a while after they all left."

"Don't do that!" Ryan said.

"Don't do what?" Cass turned toward Ryan. He was frowning at her. "Do my job?"

"Stay in that empty building when no one else is there," Ryan replied. "It's not safe until we catch this guy."

"You don't need to tell me that. This guy has more ways of terrorizing me than a jihadist." His weapon now was a butchered snake. "By the way, a couple weeks ago, I noticed that the back door lock had been scratched, like someone tried to open it without a key."

"Cass... you're just now bringing this up?" Ryan was getting exasperated with her.

"How was I to know it was important?" Cass asked. "It's just scratches around the key mechanism."

"Anything out of the ordinary is important," Ryan said. "Are there any other unusual things you've failed to mention?"

"You want a play-by-play description of my life?" Cass was getting irritated at Ryan, too.

"Just if it concerns anything unusual at home, on the road, or at the clinic," Ryan replied.

"Uh… I got locked in the maintenance shed not long ago. It wasn't a big deal, though. A gust of wind blew the door shut and jarred the latch back in place. I couldn't open the door from the inside. I managed to get out. No harm done."

"How'd you do that?" Ryan wasn't satisfied with her half answer.

"I dismantled the lock, and voila, the door opened." Cass waited for another explosion from Ryan, but all he did was sigh heavily.

"Why didn't you call me—or someone?" Ryan drummed his fingers on the table in agitation.

"Uh… I left my phone inside the clinic," Cass said meekly. In hindsight, what happened that day now seemed like an episode from a badly written comedy show. Cass was sorry she'd even mentioned it

"Cass! What—"

Cass was certain Ryan was winding up for a good scolding, but the sheriff interrupted, "Did you see anyone around? Hear anything?"

"No, I didn't see anyone when I went into the shed. I thought I heard a noise after I entered the shed, but later figured it was just the wind." Cass wasn't about to confess to Ryan that the whole incident occurred after the clinic was closed for the day—or mention that an ant invasion was what prompted her to go to the shed.

"Did you see any suspicious vehicles in the area?" Ben asked. "A white van, maybe?"

"No... wait! I did see a white van behind me earlier. But surely, there's more than one white van in Mason Valley. And this happened on a Friday, not a Wednesday," Cass replied. "That doesn't match the stalker's timeline."

"Wednesday is just an assumption. One piece of the puzzle. We don't know anything for sure. Cass, you need to take this more seriously," Ryan barked at her.

"Trust me, I'm taking *all* of this seriously." She was being pursued by a sicko who was extremely serious about harming her. But what did he expect to gain by all this? She didn't have any of her father's stolen money. If the perp followed the news, he'd know that. But sickos didn't always live in a rational world.

"The package was postmarked in Greensboro last Thursday, so it most likely reached your building on Monday, like you said." Jason was reviewing pictures of the box on his phone, getting their focus back onto the latest incident. "The dry ice lasted long enough to get through the postal system without the smell being detected. If my calculations are correct, it was in your office by the time the ice started to dissipate. And that's when the carcass started to deteriorate, too."

"Cass," Sheriff Ferguson said, "until we catch this guy, I want you to call us if you receive any mail that looks odd or that comes from an unfamiliar sender. We'll pick it up and check out the contents, then return it to you. He might try sending poison next. This person thinks of everything."

"Stop assuming things, and leave work before dark," Ryan ordered. "I know you think you can handle everything by yourself, but you're no match for this psychopath."

"Thanks for the vote of confidence." Ryan was right, though. After today, Cass didn't intend to make herself an easy target if she could avoid it. "So, I'm basically this man's prisoner."

"This case moves to our number-one priority. All resources will be used to catch this person," Sheriff Ferguson explained. "Jason and Kelsey are staying in Mason Valley next week to help. Jason knows the area, and we can use his expertise right now. The Charlotte bureau of the FBI has also joined the case. You'll probably be seeing them around the clinic. I'll bring in the Postal Inspectors on Monday. This person's days of freedom are numbered."

The meeting broke up, and Cass waited at the door for Ryan, her ride back to get her car. He, Kelsey, and Jason talked to the sheriff for a few minutes before he joined her.

"What was that about?" Cass asked as Ryan opened the door and motioned for her to precede him.

"Your safety, mostly," Ryan replied. "When Raj or the clinic guard can't be with you, someone else will be. Get used to it."

Cass nodded, lacking the will to disagree with Ryan. The ugly image of the coiled snake, the severed head, and the threatening message had scared her silent. Cass's fondness for arguing with Ryan was temporarily on hold.

Ryan drove Cass back to the clinic and walked her to her car. As they approached the car, an FBI agent with a leashed German shepherd dog stopped them. The dog responded to the agent's command and made a trip around the car, sniffing the trunk, tires, and undercarriage of her vehicle.

"Unlock the door, please," the agent said to Cass.

She complied, and the German shepherd made a thorough inspection of the interior's front and back seats.

"It's clean," the agent said once the dog had finished its inspection. "You can go now."

"Thank you," Cass said to the agent, then turned to Ryan. "Raj just texted that he's fixing pizza for a late lunch—a recipe he picked up during his travels in Italy. Can you join us?"

"I'd like to but can't. I'll follow you home and see you safely inside, but then, I have some other things to take care of," Ryan replied.

"I see... A date? An afternoon delight, as the song goes?" With bomb-sniffing dogs and FBI agents patrolling the parking lot, this was an odd time for Cass to inject romance into a conversation, especially with a man who had clearly sworn off romance. But after what she'd been through this morning, she was in a risk-taking "push the envelope" kind of mood.

"A date? It's the middle of the day. Not my style. I prefer to wait and plan a special evening, just for two." Ryan moved closer to Cass and lowered his voice. "Soft music. A nice bottle of wine. Whispers of love and of how we've missed each other since we were last together. Kisses that go on forever as anticipation builds for the next act."

"I see." Cass swallowed as the picture Ryan painted made her heart race. "You're just... Who...?" Cass stuttered. She should rethink *her* style and stop saying whatever popped into her head. Ryan was calling her bluff and had turned her brain into mush.

"Remember, the mourning dove may preen, flaunt, and tease, but the mighty hawk only takes it for so long before he strikes back." Ryan reached out and gently touched her cheek. He trailed his finger down to her mouth, paused, and then ran his thumb over her lips. "I'll follow you home."

He abruptly dropped his hand, turned, and walked to his truck. He climbed in and waited to follow her home.

Cass drew in a sharp breath, fumbled her first shaky attempt at opening her car door, and finally climbed in and started the motor. *Whew! What a day! Scared out of my wits by a dead snake, then ambushed by a few romantic words from Ryan.*

When Cass reached her house, the driveway was practically full of vehicles. Jack's truck was there, along with Raj's and

Mandy's cars. Cass parked behind Raj and walked back to meet Ryan as he exited his truck.

"I see that, as usual, Jack manages to go where the beautiful women are." Ryan nodded to Jack's truck.

"Mandy doesn't seem to mind having Jack around. Maybe I can use him as an inducement for her to come and work at the clinic. But since she's a nurse practitioner, she'll need to work under the supervision of an MD. Do you know anyone like that?"

"You've forgotten already—the fate of the meddling dove?"

"No, I'm just ignoring it. The little dove is tough for her size, even against the mighty hawk. Are you sure you can't come in for lunch?"

"No. I wish I could," Ryan replied. "Mr. Gleason called a while ago. He found a couple of injured birds this morning. His life's work seems to be searching the woods for injured wildlife, just to keep me busy. It's hunting season, and apparently, not all hunters are good shots. Lots of doves get caught in the cross-fire."

"Okay! Drop the dove analogies. I get your point. I interfere where I don't belong."

"That's putting it mildly, and one thing we agree on." Ryan bent down and placed a quick kiss on her cheek. "Try to relax and don't go anywhere alone. Make sure Raj sticks around. I'll see you tomorrow night at the Eagle's Nest."

"I'll be there." Cass turned and walked toward the house.

What was happening here? Had Ryan's hard heart suddenly softened? Where was the stone-cold, brooding, sullen man she usually saw? Maybe some of their talk yesterday had broken through after all. Or maybe he was just distracted by the stalker case—the one thing that seemed to hold his interest.

As Cass entered the house, her thoughts lingered on Ryan. Someone was stalking her and apparently wanted her dead, but her thoughts were elsewhere. Even after the frightening events of this morning, Cass felt light and happy, protected and un-afraid.

CHAPTER SIXTEEN

My dear friend, you're living a very interesting life here in Mason Valley," Mandy said. "All these tough, good-looking guys working overtime to keep you safe. But that aside, it's scary to see what you've been going through and that you even need protection."

Cass and Mandy were seated on the living room sofa, enjoying a glass of wine and some girl talk before retiring for the night. Raj and Jack had left the house after a pleasant evening. But Raj and Jack's guard duties weren't over yet.

Jack was driving the route back and forth in front of Cass's house a few times, looking for the suspicious white van—or anything unusual on the road—before heading home for the night. Raj was walking the perimeter of the property, checking for intruders who might be hiding in the trees. Raj now kept a loaded gun by his bed and monitored the security cameras day and night through his phone app. He was not taking any chances. Cass was finally convinced that all the security was necessary to keep her safe.

"I'd settle for less interesting." Cass shivered. "I see that dead, bloody snake and threatening note every time I close my eyes. I've always been afraid of snakes—dead or alive. That image is worse than any threat I received in Philly."

"But now, you have Dr. McDreamy running after you. *And* you don't seem to mind."

"Ha! Any running Ryan does is *away* from me," Cass replied. "I'm not chasing Ryan, per se. I'm chasing a doctor for the clinic."

"You think he'll start practicing medicine again? He was pretty devastated by what happened to his fiancée." Mandy picked up her wine glass and took a drink. "That was a horrible time. Everyone—the other doctors and nurses—loved and respected Dr. Scott. When he left, it was like one of our own had died. Cheryl's parents didn't help the situation. They were constantly in the media, accusing Ryan of murdering their daughter. They were out to ruin him professionally, if not personally. No wonder he ran for the mountains."

"He shared some details with me yesterday. I agree that what he went through was terrible, but I'd like to see him back doing what he loves: medicine. I know that's easy to say, but hard to do."

"I'm glad you've settled in here, too. You seem happy."

"Happy? With a stalker on my tail, I'm not sure I'd call what I feel *happy*, but I find the job satisfying. Want to share some of my happiness?" Cass prepared to make her pitch. "Have you given further consideration to joining me at the clinic? You'd have more autonomy in treating patients than you do now—just coordinate the hard cases with an MD."

"I… yes, I'm thinking about it. Truthfully, I'm getting a little burned out where I am. And sometimes, I feel like I'm just an errand girl for the MDs."

"And there's Jack. He'd be part of the deal. He's not someone I can guarantee in your contract, but from what I've noticed, I don't think he'd mind having you around."

"You're right. There *is* Jack." Mandy smiled. "What's his deal? Why hasn't someone grabbed him up before now? Does he have serious flaws I'm not seeing?"

"Jack's flaws are all part of his personality."

"Agreed. He's definitely not dull!"

"According to Jack, he stayed here in Mason Valley to help his dad and took over the family business when his father retired. He didn't move to the city after high school like a lot of young people in this area. I asked him the same question about love and marriage. Jack said that if he romanced or married someone from Mason Valley, they would most likely be one of his cousins." Cass laughed. "Lots of people here are related. I just don't think he's met the right person yet. He's a great guy, though, once you get past his dancing."

"What's wrong with his dancing?"

Cass recounted the night at the Eagle's Nest when Jack tossed her around the dance floor like a sack of potatoes. She shared how Ryan had insisted on driving her home, thinking her stumbling was from having too much to drink. Mandy was holding her stomach with laughter by the time Cass finished the story.

"Jack knew I was able to drive myself home but didn't say a thing," Cass added. "You'll see what I mean by his dancing tomorrow night. He's a great person, though—kind, funny, and would help anyone who needs it."

"Your safety was Ryan's major concern when he drove you home. The death of his fiancée was probably on his mind when he saw you bouncing off tables."

"I get that," Cass replied. "But he wouldn't let me explain. He just bulldozed in and took charge. Ryan's brother, Mike, calls him 'Cave Man,' and he acted like one that night. My objections were greeted with barely more than a grunt. If he'd pulled out a cudgel, hit me over the head, and slung me over his shoulder, it wouldn't have been out of character."

"Ooh, Cave Man! I like that. So… you're *both* hard-headed. Sounds like a match made in heaven."

"One of us is hard-headed, that's for sure! But not me."

"Sure, honey. Whatever you say," Mandy chuckled. "But let me think about your offer for a few days. I might surprise you and take you up on it."

"Good! Tomorrow morning, we'll drive into town. You'll see what a quaint, beautiful place it is and meet some very nice people."

The next morning after breakfast, Cass and Mandy prepared to drive into Mason Valley.

"Where do you think you're going?" Raj asked from behind them as they walked toward the front door. He stood in the hall outside his bedroom, dressed only in a pair of jeans, his hands crossed defiantly over his bare chest. Raj's bed-head hair stood on end as he frowned in displeasure.

"I'm taking Mandy on a tour of Mason Valley," Cass replied. "I plan—"

"No, you're not!" Raj held up one hand, cutting her off. "Don't you remember Ryan's instructions? You can only go out with me, Jack, or him. You're not going anywhere alone."

"Ryan overreacts. It's just into town. It's daylight, and it's a Saturday, not a Wednesday."

"You're not that dense, Cass," Raj said. "This creep managed to penetrate your office. He could be anywhere, at any time. Let me get dressed, and I'll drive you."

"But—"

"Stop! Don't argue. Do you want me to lock you in a closet, like the time you stole my baseball glove and wouldn't give it back?"

Raj's threat stopped Cass's objections. "I still plan to get you back for that," she muttered. He had only opened the closet door when Cass started crying. "I'm not six anymore and can howl even louder now."

"Whatever… Give me ten for shoes and shirt, and I'll be ready to go."

Within ten minutes, Raj was escorting them out the door and to his car.

They first drove by the medical clinic complex, showing Mandy where she'd be working if she accepted Cass's job offer. They slowed down as they passed but didn't enter the parking lot. The agent with the bomb-sniffing dog was gone, but two security guards patrolled the perimeter of the building.

Next on the tour was a drive past the city government building, the sheriff's office, and the retail district.

"I know you've had breakfast, but I haven't. I need to eat or at least have coffee," Raj said as he parked in front of Rita's Café.

"This is a good place to meet people and get a feel for the atmosphere of the town," Cass explained as she and Mandy entered the café, followed by Raj. After an introduction to Rita, they were seated at a table near the window. The patrons seated nearby greeted them with smiles.

"Have you heard about the legend of Love Vine Mountain?" Cass asked Mandy. She nodded toward the mountain, which was visible through the café window. The morning sun highlighted thick stands of mostly bare trees mixed with swaths of evergreens. The blaze of red, gold, and orange had now faded, along with the leaf peepers who visited the valley each fall to enjoy the beautiful foliage. "It has magical powers that can bring you love."

"No way! Magically find love? Tell me more," Mandy replied.

"According to Anna Wise, a member of my staff, you have to go up on the mountain and find the love vine, which grows prolifically there. Break off a section, wrap the vine into a ball, and then make a wish for love. You're free to specify someone you know or wish for a stranger you haven't yet met. Then, you toss the balled-up vine over your left shoulder, across your heart. And just like that, you'll meet your true love soon after."

"Sounds very scientific," Mandy chuckled. "I must try that. My field of love has suffered a drought recently."

"Anyone in mind?" Raj asked, quirking an eyebrow. "Jack, maybe?"

"I'd rather not depend on a vine to find my soulmate. Jack's nice, but doesn't your true love need to throw the vine, too?" Mandy asked. "The legend seems a little one-sided. Unrequited love? That's no fun!"

"According to Anna, that part of the legend is vague," Cass acknowledged. "But if you move here, you can use any method you think will work. I don't think Jack would object."

"How about you?" Mandy asked Cass. "Would you climb the mountain for… say, Doctor McDreamy?"

"Cass doesn't climb mountains. She just pisses men off and scares them away." Raj finished his last bite of scrambled eggs and sausage, then pushed his plate aside. "Like at Thanksgiving dinner. She can't control herself. Magic wouldn't come near her."

"As an older brother, you're a total failure." Cass aimed a jab for Raj's ribs but hit his elbow just as he raised his arm to take a drink. Coffee sloshed over his hand and onto the table. "And look at the mess you just made." Cass threw a napkin at Raj.

"You asked for it, Sis! I'm going to tell Ryan about that time at one of Mom's dinner parties when Lord What's-His-Name said he was 'knackered,' meaning he was tired, and you thought he said 'cracker.' You chirped, 'Polly wants a cracker?'"

"That did not happen!" Cass frowned at Raj. "Not that version, anyway. And he wasn't a lord. He wasn't anything other than the grandson of one of Grandfather's friends. I politely asked if he wanted the server to bring him some crackers. I didn't hear him clearly because of his soft voice and unintelligible British accent."

"To answer your question, Mandy? Yes, my sister has the hots for Ryan Scott." This time, Raj was ready for the shot to his ribs. He deflected Cass's fist with his arm.

CHAPTER SEVENTEEN

The days marched closer to December. Soon, Cass will have lived in Mason Valley for three months. The time had passed quickly, tied up as she was in formulating and executing plans for the medical clinic, finding staff, and tending to a myriad of other administrative duties. In some ways, she felt as if she'd always lived here.

The citizens of Mason Valley accepted her presence and now viewed her as just another Mason Valley resident. They must've all heard something about her father's arrest by now, but no one mentioned it or appeared to hold her responsible for her father's troubles. In the coffee shops, sidewalk kiosks, and retail stores, they all knew her and greeted her by name. Mayor Landry called her occasionally to ask if she needed anything and to check on the progress of the clinic.

In October, the city council had invited her to speak and share her vision for the clinic and the benefits and services it would bring to the area. Cass gladly accepted, always happy to discuss the topic that meant as much to her as it did to the local citizens.

Cass was thoroughly entrenched in Mason Valley society now. If the stalker's goal was to send her fleeing, he'd failed miserably.

Today was Wednesday, the stalker's day of choice to strike, but Cass was more determined than ever to go about her life, focusing on her job as the clinic's director. Whatever evil drove him to threaten her life would be exposed in time. She personally couldn't do anything about him, but law enforcement could, and several agencies were now fully engaged in catching him.

When she'd returned to work following Thanksgiving break, Cass had gingerly eased through her office door. Filled with dread, she entered the room where the contents of a postal box had sent her running, practically screaming, into the hallway. But Bill Scott had, as promised, sent someone to fumigate the room. The putrid stench of the rotting snake was gone. A pleasant odor still hung in the air this morning.

Spending time with Mandy and reminiscing about their college days had replaced the horror of snakes, stalkers, and threats. Gathering with the happy crowd on Saturday night for dancing and live music at the Eagle's Nest made life seem almost normal again. Ryan even asked her to dance, having been converted to the benefits of said activity since the debacle with Jack. And miracles do happen—Cave Man came out of his shell long enough to apologize for his behavior that night.

Cass's self-appointed protectors took their job even more seriously after the snake incident. Raj tailed her to and from work each day, ran all the errands, and did all the grocery shopping. The night they went to the Eagle's Nest, all that was missing from the VIP treatment to and from the bar and grill was a police escort.

Cass settled herself behind her desk, forcing her mind off the reason she needed protection and back onto the job at hand. She opened her computer to the patient logs and clicked on the monthly statistical report. Updated daily, the columns on the report listed all upcoming appointments and highlighted patients that were scheduled for a follow-up from previous visits.

Last week, Dr. Blankenship had voiced frustration that some of her patients came for a visit, maybe two, but then didn't return to continue their treatment as she advised. Often, some people viewed the need for mental health services as a sign of weakness. The people of Mason Valley seemed unusually stoic and liked to handle their problems on their own—an admirable trait, but not always a practical one.

Cass had devised a remedy for Dr. Blankenship's concern: an outreach program. Therapists could visit the homes of patients who needed additional therapy, see how they were coping, and if possible, encourage them to return for more counseling. Some patients might be doing well after just one visit, but others may have stopped coming for personal reasons, became even more discouraged, and sank further into depression. Cass planned to ask the Sullivans if they might be interested in running such a program.

As Cass was scrolling through the names of the upcoming appointments, one entry caught her eye: "R. Scott, 7 p.m." Hmmm… could that be *the* Ryan Scott? An evening appointment, after everyone left for the day? Dr. Blankenship did occasionally stay late to accommodate a patient's work schedule.

If this was *the* Ryan, it was a very good sign. Maybe he'd come to realize he needed help in dealing with the implosion of his life following his fiancée's death. Dr. Blankenship could help him sort through his confusion and maybe give him a different perspective on the tragedy and its aftermath. But Cass wouldn't snoop and try to identify "R. Scott." Whoever he was, he was making the right move.

Cass was sorting the list to isolate the no-shows on the follow-up appointment log when someone stopped at her office

door. She looked up, and Clayton Thomas stood in the doorway.

"Clayton! Please come in." Cass stood up and crossed the
room to welcome him. "I didn't know you were going to be in
town today."

"I drove up from Atlanta this morning. A spur-of-the-moment decision. I just wanted to check things out and see how
everything was going."

"Have a seat," Cass said as she walked back to her desk and
sat down. Clayton paused for a moment before the chair she
pointed to. Did he think she should offer him her seat behind
the desk? That wasn't going to happen. But maybe she should
stop assuming the worst about him. Clayton was here and interested in the clinic, and that was a good thing. "Things are going
great. The new wing is practically done. It mostly just needs the
soft furnishings and some pieces of equipment. I'll give you a
tour before you leave."

They chatted for a few minutes about the view of Love Vine
Mountain seen through the office window and what a beautiful
fall day it was. Cass fully participated in the conversation, but
her suspicions about his reason for the visit were increasing.
Instinct told her that the scenery and weather were not why he
was here.

"I'd like to look over your expense reports while I'm here,"
Clayton said, switching to business.

"No problem, but they're exactly like the ones I send you
each month. No hidden purchases or add-ons after I compile
them. I pride myself on being audit-ready at any time—always
with a clean audit in mind." Cass had a hard time not letting her
annoyance show in her comment. Clayton was basically accusing her of keeping two sets of books.

"I'm not accusing you of distorting the numbers. I just want
to make sure that the tools you're using are sufficient and that

you're capturing all expenditures."

"Clayton," Cass said, finally unable to hide her irritation. "This isn't my first job. I've been a clinic director for six years and passed numerous audits without a single problem. And that was at a large for-profit organization. Running this facility is simple in comparison."

"Okay! Okay!" Clayton held up his hands to stop her. "I'm just checking. I heard about your problems in Philadelphia. Just wanted to make sure things are on the up-and-up. But I'll take your word for it."

"Fudging numbers on the expense reports was *not* why I left Philadelphia." Cass gritted her teeth, then turned her angry response into a calmer, more conversational tone. She also didn't believe that the expense reports were Clayton's main reason for coming to Mason Valley this morning. "You don't have to take my word. Everything is included in the reports I send you."

"How are you coming along with hiring staff?" Clayton switched topics, clearly not wanting to raise Cass's ire further by questioning the financial statements.

"I've hired the administrative and medical techs. They're ready to start as soon as we open. I'm planning a week of training before the opening date."

"So, no physicians hired yet?" Clayton asked. "You know, I have a friend who just finished her medical residency, and I think she might be willing to relocate here. Yes, I do think she would. She mentioned she'd like to live somewhere quiet. This town is nothing but quiet. Hiring her would relieve you of that search."

So, this was his *real* reason for dropping in unexpectedly. Did he want to plant a spy inside that could keep him informed of what Cass might be up to behind his back? Cass's earlier resolution to not aways think the worst of Clayton just flew out the window.

"No, that won't be necessary. I'm in talks with a nurse prac-titioner and a medical doctor about coming to work here." She had no idea if either Mandy or Ryan would agree to work at the clinic, but she *was* in talks with them. Nagging Ryan was more accurate, but to Cass, that was semantics; nagging and talking meant the same thing.

"Do I know them?" Clayton asked. "Would they be a good fit for living here in the mountains?"

"No, you don't know them." Clayton wouldn't get any more information than she was forced to give. The people she hired would be her decision, and she didn't plan to turn that decision over to Clayton. "But yes, they would be a good fit. They're actually from nearby—just outside of town."

"Well, we don't want some broken-down, worn-out country doctor who hasn't kept up with modern medicine's practices and procedures. I really hope that's not your plan."

"Nope! Young, modern, experienced graduates of the best medical schools. They're the complete package." Cass almost laughed out loud at the thought of Ryan being described as a "broken-down, worn-out country doctor."

"I hope you're right." Clayton didn't sound convinced that her candidates were the best choices. He rose from his seat. "Keep me updated. Let's take that tour you were talking about earlier. I want to be back in Atlanta before rush hour."

After they toured the new medical wing and the existing mental health wing, Cass and Clayton paused in front of her office.

"Everything looks good and seems to be on track," Clay-ton said. "I feel better now that we've met face-to-face and I've inspected everything for myself. Let me know if you need help finding a physician. I'm sure my friend would be interested if your plans fall through"

"I'll do that." Cass eyed Clayton as he walked down the hallway toward the front door.

Cass entered her office and stopped to look out the window that faced the parking lot. Clayton climbed into his car and drove away. Cass felt a moment of sympathy for him. He wanted to micromanage every aspect of a business and didn't trust the people who'd been hired to run it.

Clayton couldn't be much older than his late thirties, maybe forty. Yet somewhere in his career, he had probably trusted someone and got burned in the process. Since her father's arrest, Cass could relate to how a broken trust might affect a person's attitude toward others. As the CEO of several companies, Clayton's constant distrust of managers' decisions must be a stressful way to do his job.

But making excuses for Clayton and trying to rationalize his abrasive attitude could be way off the mark. He might simply believe a woman was incapable of handling the responsibilities demanded by the director's job.

Cass wouldn't allow Clayton's constant criticism to change her management philosophy: cross every T, dot every I, and do it honestly and legally, all while providing a healthy environment in which her staff could work and grow and give them the tools they needed to serve the patients.

If Clayton thought he could micromanage her, too bad. He'd have to adapt and accept her management style. Right was on her side—as were the Wilders.

CHAPTER EIGHTEEN

J ason neared the city limits of Mason Valley on his way back
from a meeting with the manager of the distribution warehouse in High Point. He'd had a long day, and it wasn't over
yet. Sheriff Ferguson waited for him at his office.

A manila folder containing a list of names and addresses of
stores that regularly purchased Sweet-Thin chips from the High
Point warehouse rested on the seat beside Jason. There was also
a list of companies who picked up the orders and made the deliveries to the stores. These lists could be the break they'd been
looking for or at least a clue as to the identity of the person who
was stalking Cass. Or they could lead to a dead end. But even a
dead end would narrow the search. A big part of an investigation was eliminating theories that were wrong.

Yesterday had been a bust. Jason spent the entire day reviewing security camera footage from outside the convenience
store where the stalker had stolen and later returned the temporary tag. Jason had scoured the footage until his eyes blurred
but came up empty—no leads to help identify the driver of the
van.

Jason had spotted the new truck with its temporary tag in the parking lot and a white van driving by the convenience store, but none of the footage showed when or how the tag was stolen, nor did it show the license plate currently on the van. The stalker had managed to avoid detection on both stealing and returning the tag.

This guy was devious, smart, and driven by hatred for Cass. Jason's years of law enforcement experience had taught him that crimes fueled by hatred were usually personal. And many times, that same hatred caused the criminal to get sloppy and make a fatal mistake.

The FBI was working the Philadelphia angle. Their current premise was that one of Kenneth Jordan's victims wanted their pound of flesh. What better way to get back at Jordan than through his daughter, Cass?

Jason wasn't so sure about that theory. Terrorizing Cass didn't have an endgame. Even if the stalker managed to hurt Cass—or worse—where was the connection between the crime and the retribution? How would hurting Cass get back the money they'd lost?

The stalker also seemed familiar with the area around Mason Valley. He'd managed to find a diamondback rattlesnake; most likely, he had captured it while it was hibernating up in the mountains. But as the FBI pointed out, someone from Philadelphia could've hired a local to do their dirty business. That was true. Criminals weren't always logical or sane individuals. But that theory still didn't have an endgame.

Jason was doing the grunt work for Sheriff Ferguson. Grunt work was nothing new to him. As the former sheriff of Mason Valley in charge of a miniscule staff, he had frequently done the most tedious jobs himself. Sometimes, it was trivial clues that solved the cases that landed on his desk. His Army motto, "Whatever it takes," was still the rule he followed and practiced routinely in his current job at the Atlanta Police Department.

Jason punched in Ryan's number on his cell phone.

"Hey," Ryan answered immediately. "Any luck on your search?"

"Not yet. The security camera footage was a bust. But I'm on my way to the sheriff's office with a list of company names from the distribution warehouse in High Point."

"You mind if I join you? I can be there in about twenty minutes."

"Sure. Come join us. It was your photo that gave us this clue, so your help on the next step would be welcome. My ETA at the sheriff's office is about fifteen minutes."

"Okay. See you there." Ryan disconnected the call.

When Jason walked into the sheriff's office, Sheriff Ferguson was seated in his usual place at the head of the conference table, waiting for him.

"How many companies are we talking about?" Sheriff Ferguson asked, dispensing with any greetings.

"Twelve." Jason opened the folder on the table. "They don't keep a record of the individual drivers or their routes. The companies with the contracts to deliver assign the routes and drivers. By the way, Ryan is going to join us in a few minutes."

"Good. We can always use an extra hand." Sheriff Ferguson nodded toward the glass door. "I think he just drove up."

"Hey, Ryan," Jason greeted Ryan as he came through the door. "Glad you had time to join us. Have a seat."

"Twelve companies, huh? That's a lot of companies and employee names to research. Let's divide the list between the three of us." Sheriff Ferguson pointed to the two empty desks on the other side of the room. "You can use the deputies' computers. I'll log you into the databases we need."

"Good plan." Jason walked to the copier and made two additional copies of the lists. He returned to the table, marked off a section for each of them, and handed one to Ryan and one to the sheriff. "Just look for anything unusual or suspicious in the employees' background—anything that pops out and you think might need further investigation."

Jason and Ryan moved to the deputies' desks, sat down, and began searching for suspicious activities or crimes in the companies' histories or in the individual drivers' backgrounds.

Over the next two hours, Jason, Ryan, and the sheriff worked in silence as they scoured online records, searching for connections to Philadelphia or to Cass's family, anyone with a criminal history, or someone with a profile that might suggest they could be behind the threats against Cass. The silence was occasionally broken by groans and sighs as a potential lead fell apart.

"You said that some of the companies hire ex-cons?" Ryan asked Jason.

"Yes. The manager said they like to give people who've committed minor offenses a second chance."

"Who does the background checks on them?"

"The delivery companies do," Jason said. "The warehouse just requires the companies to sign a statement that they've completed a full background check."

"No holes in that system!" Ryan looked back at his computer screen, flipped through a couple tabs, and peered closer at the data on the screen. He turned back toward Jason. "Here's a company called Black Panther Deliveries that has only one employee—the owner. I'm not a detective, but the owner certifying his own criminal record sounds like a major flaw in their background checks."

"Yeah, I imagine some of the companies just go through the motions. Such a system absolves the warehouse of any responsibility. That's basically all they want—a 'cover your ass' piece of paper." Jason got up from his desk and walked over to stand by

Ryan. "What's the owner's name?"

"Owner and driver, Simon Mitchell," Ryan replied. "Age fifty-two. Shows an address in Salisbury."

"Check him out." Jason started to walk back to his computer station but paused as a sudden thought came to him. He turned to address the sheriff. "Hmm… Mitchell… Simon Mitchell… Denny, do you still have the records on the Coeburn case?"

"Yes," the sheriff replied. "We won't retire those for a few more years. They're still in the active case file. A couple of the men haven't gone to trial yet. They're represented by big, expensive lawyers who're just dragging out the case, hoping we'll forget."

"Open the active investigations files," Jason instructed Ryan. "Search for the Coeburn case. Now, search for Mitchell."

"Yep! Here he is," Ryan said as the data pulled up on his screen.

"I'll be damned." Jason peered over Ryan's shoulder and began reading the details on the screen. "He *was* part of that case. I thought his name sounded familiar."

"Looks that way," Ryan said.

Sheriff Ferguson came to stand behind Ryan and Jason.

"It seems Simon Mitchell took a cooperating plea deal." Jason read the report over Ryan's shoulder. "The authorities couldn't prove he offered money for an underage girl, though they suspected that was the reason for his association with Coeburn. They just didn't have hard evidence. The scumbag gave up minimal evidence, paid a large fine, and received a lighter sentence."

"Let me check something." The sheriff returned to his desk and entered a search into his   computer. "Well, it looks like Mitchell served just eighteen months of his two-year sentence. Got released for good behavior four months ago."

"So…" Ryan got up from his desk, stretched, and flexed his

shoulders. He grabbed a bottle of water from the refrigerator in the corner before returning to the desk. "What does this mean? Is this our suspect? We all agree he's a pervert, but why the vendetta against Cass? Was Mitchell an investor with her father? How does Cass fit into this?"

"Good question. I believe his attorney was from Philadelphia. That's the only connection I know of off the top of my head, but criminals seem to find each other easily. It's as if they have a network," the sheriff replied. He leaned back in his chair and placed his hands behind his head, deep in thought. He suddenly sat up straight and swiveled to face Jason and Ryan. "Maybe we need to change our focus and look at Cass's stalker from a different angle. Maybe Mitchell's connection to Coeburn is the important link."

"I don't remember many details of Mitchell's involvement," Jason said. "Since he pleaded guilty, there wasn't a trial, so my testimony wasn't needed. His case paled in comparison to Coeburn's, so it didn't receive much publicity."

"You had moved to Atlanta by the time of Mitchell's arrest. As I recall, he was a very angry man and not shy about letting everyone know it. I remember him screaming, 'I'll fight this! Someone will pay!' as they handcuffed him and led him away."

"What was his background?" Ryan asked. "Other than being a sleazebag."

"He was a businessman. Owned a delivery business," the sheriff said. "I'd say it was medium-size and apparently successful. He had several drivers who delivered across the North Carolina area and into neighboring states. But he was forced to sell the business to raise money for his lawyers and to pay his fine. His wife divorced him, and her settlement took the rest of his money."

"He gave up all that just to satisfy his sick obsession with abusing teenage girls?" Ryan threw his pen down on the desk in disgust. "I've treated abuse victims in the ER. The physical and mental damage inflicted on the victims is something one never forgets. Mitchell should've been locked up for life."

"Yep! You're preaching to the choir. Makes no sense," the sheriff agreed. "At the time of his arrest, Mitchell made some very incendiary remarks. According to him, everyone else had ruined his life, not his perversion."

"Yeah," Jason agreed. "Maybe his anger still drives him to lash out. Maybe anyone can serve that purpose."

"But Cass is the target," Ryan reminded them. "We shouldn't get offtrack and lose sight of that. If Mitchell is the stalker, why choose Cass to threaten and harass?"

"You're right. We don't know anything for sure," the sheriff said. "It's hard to read a sick mind. But he's at least a lead. We'll bring him in for questioning. Also, check out that lawyer of his and look for ties to Kenneth Jordan."

"Let's not forget Cass's protection, either," Ryan said. "Jack, Raj, and I can continue what we're doing."

"Why don't you take her up to that mountain cabin of yours? She'd be safe there. A stalker would need a bloodhound to find her." Jason smiled and winked at the sheriff.

"I know you're trying to be funny," Ryan replied, "but have you met Cass? She does what she wants. And she has a job. No one is keeping her from that."

"Maybe you could get creative. Do something to sweep her off her feet, then whisk her away to your mountain hideaway," Jason persisted. "What happened to that basketball star who dazzled all the girls every time he stepped onto the hardwood?"

"Says the man who knew Kelsey for over a year in Afghanistan and didn't make a move," Sheriff Ferguson reminded Jason.

"Things were different in a war zone," Jason responded. "And I thought she was engaged." It wasn't because he didn't want to know Kelsey better or was nursing a broken heart, as

Ryan was. Admittedly, the results were the same, and he had missed out on too many years with Kelsey—just as he suspected Ryan was doing with Cass. Based on his observations, Ryan was *very* interested in Cass. He just needed a push.

"With Cass, even a conversation makes one feel like they're in a war zone." Ryan smiled. "You take care of your own women, and I'll take care of mine."

"Sadly, we don't believe you. And Ryan, you don't have a woman. That's your problem," Sheriff Ferguson pointed out. "But we're going to catch this stalker, and once we do, I plan to lock you in the detox cell and hold you there until you get over that broken heart you're still nursing. It's time you left the past behind and got on with your life."

"No joke," Jason added. "I lost several years with Kelsey that we'll never get back. But I don't let a day go by that I don't try to make it up to her."

"Amen," Sheriff Ferguson agreed.

"The situation between me and Cass isn't simple. And my past is… complicated," Ryan insisted.

"Uh-huh. Of course. It always is!" Jason commented as he sat back down at his computer. "Situations get even more complicated when you avoid them."

"I'm working on the things I can control," Ryan said. "Cass is stubborn and has her own ideas—about everything."

"He's got it bad, Jason," Sheriff Ferguson chuckled.

"Stubborn? Ah… I see! But think of the reward once you convince her to join your side," Jason laughed.

"My 'woman' problem—or lack thereof—will get solved in due time," Ryan said. "But right now, we need to focus on who's terrorizing said woman. You both are better at that than advising me on romance."

"Agreed." Jason turned his attention back to the computer screen and pulled up a list of convenience stores in the area.

It was getting late, but convenience stores were usually open around the clock. Jason picked up the phone and dialed the number of a store on his list. They would now concentrate on the stores served by Black Panther Deliveries. Once they'd identified those, they could focus on the stores closest to Mason Valley, working outward from there.

The first two stores he called didn't have any connection to Black Panther Deliveries. Jason started to dial a third number, paused, then put down the phone.

"Sheriff." Jason swiveled his chair around to look at Sheriff Ferguson. "Tomorrow is Wednesday, potentially our stalker's day to visit Mason Valley. Let's sic your deputies on Mitchell and see if they can locate his sorry ass by scouring the area."

"Good idea! I'll put both shifts to work around the clock," Sheriff Ferguson agreed. "If Mitchell is our stalker, let's put him away for good this time."

CHAPTER NINETEEN

Another Wednesday! Cass shivered at the thought of what might happen later today. Her stalker had been silent since he sent the snake. Probably busy, out looking for a bigger snake—maybe a boa constrictor this time.

The authorities didn't believe he'd given up. He was lying low, most likely plotting his next move.

To keep her mind occupied, Cass started putting together a compensation package for Mandy. She hadn't yet given Cass a final answer on taking the job at the clinic, but she seemed open to the idea. When Mandy returned to Charlotte after her Thanksgiving visit, she'd promised Cass a decision very soon. Cass would be ready to submit the benefits package to Clayton as soon as that happened.

Jason and Kelsey had returned to Mason Valley. Jason was taking more vacation time to help the sheriff with the stalker investigation. Kelsey had completed the rescheduled walkthrough of the medical clinic and signed off on the construction. Only a delivery of furniture was left to make it ready to accept patients.

Well, there was still the pesky problem of hiring two doc-tors.

Clayton had quickly approved the salaries and benefits packages for the admin and medical technicians, no questions asked. Of course, Kelsey had been on the line when Cass pre-sented the figures to Clayton. He was very complimentary during the call. Since he'd accepted those packages, there shouldn't be any problem with the compensation offer she was creating for Mandy.

And if Clayton did object, she'd tattle to Kelsey like a third-grader caught up in a playground dispute.

"What are you smiling about?" Ryan asked from the door-way.

"Oh!" Cass looked up, surprised to see him. His normal scowl was gone but his eyes held a look of concern. "Well… uh, I was thinking about you. Want to go to the supply closet? You know, like you did in medical school?"

"Ha! What kind of school did *you* go to?

"Not me! But I've heard lots of stories about med students sneaking around and hooking up."

"You've heard stories from TV dramas, not real life. Or my life, anyway. Thirty-six-hour days didn't leave any time for sup-ply-closet hanky-panky."

"Ahh, now you've destroyed one of my fantasies." Cass logged off her computer, closed it, and clasped her hands in front of her. "I'm just trying to put a smile on that grumpy face of yours. Since that's not going to happen, what else can I do for you?"

"I don't usually smile when I'm being propositioned," Ryan said, ignoring her last question. He sat down in the chair facing Cass's desk. "I'm deadly serious when I weigh such offers! But with you, I take your flirting with a grain of salt. You're all talk and no action."

"Gee, thanks. There you go again, bursting my bubble! You have me all figured out, don't you? But you're right. I was only kidding… this time."

"See? You're already backing away from your proposition, like a crawfish in a dry creek bed."

Ryan was right. She was mostly talk, but she did enjoy the back-and-forth of their arguments. But teasing Ryan sometimes got results she didn't expect.

"You make outrageous comments just to shock," he continued. "One day, I might take you up on the offer of a trip to the supply closet. What will you do then?"

"It's best to keep you guessing." Cass wanted to throw out another tease but thought she'd better not push him further. He might act on his threat and expose her flirting as more real than she was ready to admit, even to herself. The tiniest hint of a smile turned Ryan's eyes a bright blue. He was the one teasing now. Maybe he did have her figured out.

"But let's get serious. I don't like this." Ryan leaned forward and frowned.

"I said I won't do it again, okay? It'd take someone more shocking than me to crack that hard shell of yours."

"Don't sell yourself short. But I was talking about the plan for tonight: to use you as a bait."

"Oh! Well, I'm ready to turn *victim* into *bait* if it will help catch this guy!"

"Whatever you call it, you need to take it seriously. I don't like the plan."

The plan Ryan referred to was one hatched by Jason, Ben Wilder, the FBI, and Sheriff Ferguson. Today was Wednesday, the stalker's preferred day to spread his mayhem, and Cass had agreed to be used as bait tonight, hoping to draw the stalker out and into a trap. He had been quiet recently, but the authorities figured he wasn't done and was just waiting for the perfect opportunity. Cass was going to give him that opportunity.

Over the last two days, the security personnel assigned to the clinic—one of which was an FBI agent—had moved inside, but they still kept vigil through the windows that looked out onto the building's perimeter. Raj had stopped following Cass to the clinic but instead parked a short distance away and waited for Cass's text that she was safely inside.

The staff had been briefed by the FBI agent and advised to remain alert but to continue business as usual. To anyone not in on the plan, it looked as though the clinic was seeing patients as usual and without any security guards patrolling the grounds.

Kelsey had dropped Jason and Ben off early this morning before daylight, while Mike, Jack, Raj, and Ryan had arrived disguised in delivery uniforms and hidden in two truckloads of furniture. After the chairs, sofas, tables, and other pieces of furniture were unloaded, the trucks left without them. When darkness came, Sheriff Ferguson and a deputy would be cruising the vicinity only a few minutes away, waiting to respond to any calls for assistance.

Cass had agreed to do her part. She was nervous about baiting the trap, but it was time to rid herself of this nightmare she'd been caught up in for several weeks. No one claimed that this was a fail-proof plan or that it would come off as planned. But being on the offensive was better than letting the stalker continue to set the agenda.

The sheriff had a possible suspect, but thus far, they'd been unable to locate him. Sheriff Ferguson thought the man was probably hiding out in the mountains, and he returned there to lie low after each attack. Rather than spending weeks scouring the mountainous terrain looking for the suspect, they hoped to draw him out and catch him in the act. The suspect, a delivery company driver, had missed his pickup at the warehouse last week. The FBI believed the man's hatred was escalating; his desire to harm Cass now took precedence over doing his job.

Everything about tonight's plan was based on speculation, but Cass trusted the authorities who devised the plan. They delt with criminals every day, and these situations were not new to them.

"I'll be fine," Cass assured Ryan. "With so many strong men looking out for me, what could go wrong?"

"I can think of a lot of things, but it's best not to go there. Did Jack tinker with your car?"

"Yes, he came earlier this morning in his wrecker and raised the hood, as if I had car trouble—which I now do, since he disconnected a battery cable."

"Promise me you'll be careful." Ryan stood to leave.

"Always. This Philly girl can take care of herself. I have my pepper spray ready. But you know, he may not show," Cass replied.

"Stalkers have patterns," Ryan said. "They're similar to arsonists who can't stay away from the scene of a fire. Stalkers can't stay away from their victims. They're thrilled by the chase, but their greatest fulfillment comes from the terror they create. They like to see their victim's fear up close. Something tells me he'll be here."

"Thanks for the comforting words, Doctor Ryan! I'll be careful!" Cold chills ran down Cass's spine as Ryan's words reminded her of her part in the plan. She was the bait for the stalker.

Just past 7:30 p.m.—the agreed-upon time for Cass to leave work—she turned out the lights in her office and left the building. The rest of the staff had left at their usual time.

The time for action had arrived, which was in many ways a relief. Cass's eyes had been glued to the clock for the last two hours, watching the minutes slowly tick away, unable to focus on anything other than the man who might be waiting for her outside in the dark.

Cass's car was parked in one of the darkest corners of the parking lot, the perfect place to lure a stealth attacker. She pulled her coat tighter around her, took a deep breath, and stepped out into the night. A cold wind blew across the parking lot, scattering leaves in its wake.

Cass felt eyes staring at her as she crossed the darkened pavement toward her car. Did the eyes belong to Raj, who hid in the shrubs on the east side of the building? Or Ryan who stood like a statue behind an evergreen bush in a dark corner? Or the FBI agents and the other men who stood just inside the darkened building, their eyes searching for any movement in the parking lot? Or was it her stalker waiting nearby and glee-fully eyeing his prey as she walked toward him?

Cass opened her car door, got in, and pressed the car's starter. A grinding sound came as the engine searched for the battery connection. Cass tried again but with the same results.

Showtime! Now, she had to draw her attacker out from the shadows.

"*Oh, faff!*" Cass slapped the steering wheel in frustration. She took a deep breath, pressed the hood release, and picked up her car keys. With her finger firmly on the trigger of the can-nister of peppery spray, she slid from the seat and walked to the front of the car. She raised the hood, bent forward, and peered closely at the engine.

Cass smelled him before she even sensed his presence behind her. She had worked in the medical field long enough to identify the smell of chloroform. Before she could react, someone lunged at her from behind. A hand holding a chlo-roform-soaked rag slapped across her face as another hand grabbed her around the neck.

Cass reacted instinctively. Punching back and up with all her strength, she slammed her elbow into the attacker's Adam's apple. Surprised and knocked off-balance by her response, the man staggered backward. The chloroform-soaked rag fell to the ground.

Cass whipped around to face the man. Using a maneuver taught in most self-defense classes, she kicked out with her foot, aiming for the man's groin. She missed her target and hit his thigh with a glancing blow. Before Cass could right herself, the attacker grabbed her foot and flipped her to the ground. She landed on her back with a thud. As the man lunged toward her, Cass pointed the pepper spray at his face and pressed the trigger.

"You bitch! I'll kill you!" the attacker screamed as the pepper spray made contact with his eyes. He fell to his knees, clawing his face as he tried to wipe his burning eyes.

Bright lights suddenly illuminated the parking lot, and shouts came from all directions. Cass scrambled backward on the ground, away from her assailant. Ryan and Raj raced toward her as the other men poured from the building.

Ryan was the first to reach Cass. As the attacker lunged at her again, Ryan's fist connected with his chin. A second blow landed just as the assailant started to rise and sent him reeling backward.

"You scumbag," Raj yelled as he fell on top of the man, pinning him to the pavement.

"It's okay, Raj. We have him." Jason grabbed Raj's arm as he pulled back his fist to land a blow to the man's face.

The stalker cowered on the ground, defeated. Jason yanked him to his feet and twisted his arms behind him. The FBI agent locked handcuffs on his wrists just as the sheriff's cruiser came screaming into the parking lot.

"Are you okay?" Ryan pulled Cass to her feet and looked at her for signs of injury. He gently touched the bright-red marks on her neck.

"I'm okay. Tough Philly girl, remember?" Cass's voice shook from adrenaline and the memory of the cold, wet cloth slipping over her face as a hand squeezed her neck. She began to tremble. "He was going to strangle me! The jerk was going to strangle me!"

"Shh, it's alright. You're safe now." Jack handed Ryan a blanket. He placed it around her shoulders, then pulled her against him to warm her shaking body.

"We got it all on video," the FBI agent said to the group. He walked to the trees in front of Cass's car and removed the camera equipment from a tree limb. The agent smiled at Cass and nodded to the group of men surrounding her. "I'm going to head out. You appear to be in good hands. Many, many good hands, I might add. We'll get your statement later, Ms. Jordan."

"Thank you," Cass said, "for helping end this nightmare."

"Another criminal is going away for a long time and we have you to thank, Ms. Jordan. Our job now will be to answer the question you and everyone else wants to know: why this man chose you to terrorize. I promise you'll get that answer."

Sheriff Ferguson and the FBI agent loaded the man into the sheriff's cruiser, climbed in, and with a short burst of the siren, left the parking lot on their way to lock up Cass's assailant and begin the interrogation.

"I'll take you home in your car. Jack or someone can bring my truck," Ryan said as Jack reconnected the battery cables and closed the hood.

Cass nodded in agreement. A sheriff's deputy arrived to shuttle the other men to their personal vehicles, which were parked at Jack's auto repair shop.

◆

"Sit." Ryan nodded toward the sofa as they entered Cass's living room. Cass sat down, then drew the blanket Jack had given her even closer around her shoulders. She felt cold in the deepest parts of her body.

Ryan poured Cass a glass of wine from the bottle on the counter, then returned to the kitchen and looked into the refrigerator. "There's not a lot in here that I can whip into an edible dish. So, how about some cheesy scrambled eggs and toast? It's quick and easy—one of my specialties." Ryan took a carton of eggs and a block of cheese from the refrigerator and got to work.

"One? How many specialties do you have?" The wine had begun to spread warmth throughout Cass's body. The shaking had stopped. Back in the safety of her home, she'd begun to feel slightly more normal.

"I have lots!" Ryan deadpanned as he cracked eggs in a bowl. "'Show, don't tell'—isn't that the saying? Oh! You mean cooking? I was thinking of my other skills."

"Uh-huh! So, you *can* joke after all!" Cass got up from the sofa. Still clutching the blanket, she walked to the bar that separated the kitchen from the living room.

"'Ripping out pages. Going through phases...'" Ryan began singing the song he'd debuted at the Eagle's Nest the last time they were all there. "'Rewriting my story, not looking for glory.'" He ended with, "'I'm turning the pages. That's one for the ages. But won't ask you to wait, until I make sense of it all.'"

One line in his debuted version had referenced a "heart in pieces and the pain never ceases." The song started out hopeful but ended on a sad note; it was a song of heartbreak and longing for what could have been. The pain reflected in Ryan's song caused Cass's heart to squeeze.

"I doubt there's glory in scrambling eggs." Cass smiled, trying to make light of the lyrics. Were the words directed at someone in particular? Or was this simply Ryan's way of lyrically telling her to "bugger off," as her grandfather would say, and not expect anything from him? To think the words might be for her at all was reading way too much into them. Their history didn't support that theory. Most likely, the song was just an artistic arrangement of words without any hidden message. "Is cooking one of your new phases?" Cass sat down on a stool and placed her drink on the bar.

"Nah. I'd never be able to compete with someone like Raj, but I won't starve—as long as there are eggs. I found sliced ham in the fridge and took two slices. I hope that's alright." Ryan set two plates of eggs with slices of ham and toast on the bar, then walked around and sat down beside Cass.

"It's fine. Raj and I have this long-standing rule: if there's not a name on something in the fridge, it belongs to whoever gets to it first. Although, I used to get mad at him when he found my stash of chocolate bars and ate all of them without asking."

"Siblings can be a pain. Mike goes out of his way to needle me. He loves to argue—similar to you."

"And I've noticed you don't disappoint him." Cass smiled, ignoring his accusation. "Did you ever sing professionally?"

"No, it's just a hobby for me. Lanie could have gone professional, though. She's that good. She thought about a singing career for a while, then decided to study photography instead. I started joining her onstage when she was about eight years old and I was fifteen. She was afraid to go before an audience by herself. When Mike opened the bar, he asked if we'd perform until his business was established and he found some other acts. We're still there, performing when we're both available."

"How did you learn to play guitar? You're very good at that, too."

"What? You're giving me a compliment? Come on! Out with the punch line."

"You're nuts! How's that?"

"Better… more like the Cass I've come to know and lo… Uh, more like yourself. The wine must be working." Ryan didn't look at her. He took a bite of his eggs before continuing, "My grandfather taught me. He could play all types of instruments in different styles and sounds. I've stuck with the acoustic guitar, but I've added my personal contemporary twist."

"It's a very nice sound. By the way, where's my brother?" Cass hadn't seen Raj since he'd pinned the stalker to the asphalt in the parking lot.

"At the sheriff's office, I believe. He and Jack promised to bring my truck over here. I also heard Raj ask Denny if he could sit in on the interrogation. He really wants to know why this stranger targeted you."

"I'd like to know that, too. I might rub people the wrong way sometimes, but no one has wanted to kill me before."

"Might? Did you say *might*?"

"Only when I'm right," Cass insisted.

"Hmph," Ryan snorted as he picked up their plates, took them to the sink, rinsed them, and loaded them into the dishwasher. He returned to the bar and held out his hand to Cass. "Come!"

"'Sit!' 'Come!'" Cass echoed. "Mike's right: you speak in caveman grunts. Or maybe you're a wannabe dog trainer."

"Quite!" Ryan held up a forefinger, then grabbed her hand and led her to the living room sofa. "Sit!"

Cass laughed but did as Ryan instructed, sitting down on the sofa.

"Are you staying?" Cass anxiously waited for Ryan's answer.

"Do you want me to?"

"Yes, please. The assault tonight hasn't completely left my head yet."

"I'll stay. You're a very brave person, Cass Jordan, to offer yourself up like that, knowing what might happen." Ryan removed his heavy outer shirt, slipped out of his shoes, then sat down beside her. "Are you going to cling to that blanket from now on?" He nodded at the blanket she'd had a death grip on since Ryan wrapped it around her after the attack.

"Yes, it's my security blanket," Cass replied, tightly grasping its ends.

"Not a problem." Ryan tucked the blanket tighter around her, then pulled her into the crook of his arm. He leaned back into the sofa cushions and turned on the TV. He scrolled through the channels until he found a movie channel.

Cass snuggled deeper into Ryan's arms, laid her head on his shoulder, and sighed deeply. She was safe, and soon, she relaxed into sleep.

Cass heard a noise and cracked open one eye. Raj was in the kitchen getting a snack from the refrigerator. He placed a sandwich and apple on a plate, filled a glass with water, took a drink, and then quietly left the room, heading to his bedroom.

Cass glanced up at Ryan. He was asleep, his arms still wrapped tightly around her. She was warm and unafraid for the first time since the stalker had jumped her from behind.

Cass tried not to read more into the current situation than was warranted. But she couldn't ignore how she felt at this moment: safe and protected by a man she liked and admired. If she let her mind wander off into "what if" territory, her feelings might prove to be deeper than simple admiration.

As she relaxed against Ryan's warm body, practical Cassandra argued with impulsive Cass. Ryan was a caring man and a trained doctor. He would see it as his duty to take care of her tonight. He'd do the same for anyone subjected to the situation she'd just lived through.

But would he kiss just anyone the way he'd kissed her? Paint a romantic scene with words that took her breath away? Their one kiss may have started out as a contest—or a power play between a city girl and a country boy—but just for a moment, Cass let her mind consider other possibilities—namely, that tonight they were not rivals and that she was more than just a duty to Ryan.

Cass acknowledged that her thoughts were crazy. Tomorrow, Ryan could easily go back to being the scowling, stone-faced man who was still haunted by his former fiancée. Competing with a ghost was next to impossible.

Ryan had made it clear more than once that Cass was nothing more than a nagging thorn in his side. Every time she thought she saw a crack in his facade, it froze over like an Alaskan pond in the middle of winter. "Running hot and cold" aptly described Ryan.

But tonight, impulsive Cass won the argument with practical Cassandra. Cass stretched upward and placed a light, but lingering kiss on Ryan's lips. His lips moved slightly in response, and his eyelids fluttered, but he didn't wake up.

Cass snuggled closer to Ryan, and his arms tightened around her. She'd make the most of this night and worry about ghosts tomorrow. Cass fell back to sleep, a contented smile on her lips.

CHAPTER TWENTY

Ryan was awakened by a loud clatter. He instinctively reached toward the space beside him where Cass had spent the night. She was gone. Ryan got up, ready to search the house, to find her, to make sure she was alright. He relaxed when he spotted Cass in the kitchen near the stove.

"Sorry, I didn't mean to wake you. I dropped a pan in the sink." Cass turned back to the stove and took something from the oven. "You want some coffee? I just brewed a pot."

Cass had recently showered and was dressed in jeans and a long-sleeved T-shirt. A ponytail held her wet blonde hair high on the crown of her head. Each time Cass moved her head, the ponytail swished back and forth.

For some reason, the motion of the ponytail reminded Ryan of the golden stands of wild wheat that grew around the stock pond on his parents' farm. He and Mike used to spend hours fishing there each summer. They hardly ever caught any fish and rarely spoke, but the comradery and bonding between brothers during those lazy, warm summer days was the thing he remembered most.

Ryan closed his eyes for a moment and again felt the warm sunshine on his shirtless back. He could almost hear the plopping of the fishing line as the bobber hit the water and the sparrows and blackbirds providing background noise as they sang in the thickets. Like a symphony, the musical rhythm of a magical country summer played across Ryan's memory—simple, but fun-filled days, accompanied by swaying stands of wild wheat, tall grasses and warm breezes that rippled the water in the pond.

Then, adulthood intruded, thought Ryan as he leaned forward, rubbed the sleep out of his eyes, and finger-combed his hair. He yawned. *Responsibility ruins everything. Maybe all this sudden angst should go into the next song I write.* At least then, wishing for a simpler time would be good for something.

"Coffee sounds good—to-go. If you have a paper cup, that is." Ryan stood up and stretched his long arms over his head, then neatly folded the blanket and placed it on the back of the sofa. "I need to be going." He nodded to the clock on the microwave that showed 6:45 a.m. "Dad expected me at the jobsite fifteen minutes ago."

"I'm sure he'll understand if you take a moment to eat." Cass picked up a plate of warmed croissants and carried them to the table, along with a carafe of freshly brewed coffee, cream, sugar, and two coffee cups. After filling the cups with dark, steaming coffee, she returned to the kitchen and opened the refrigerator door. Her voice was muffled as she leaned in. "Do you like blackberry or strawberry preserves?"

"Either one is fine. But first, come here." Ryan walked toward the kitchen and met Cass near the table.

"Why?"

"I want to check the bruises on your neck." Ryan tipped her chin first to the right, then to the left. He gently ran his fingertips down both sides. "Not too deep. The right side is more scratched than bruised. Put an ice pack on the bruises. They should start to fade in a week. Apply antibacterial ointment to the scratch."

"Yes, Doctor." Cass caught Ryan's hand and held it against her neck. She closed her eyes and purred. "That feels so good. The healing hands of a Dr. McDreamy."

"You're impossible." Ryan rubbed his thumb over her cheek, then reluctantly turned away and sat down at the table. He added cream to his coffee and took a sip, followed by a bite of the croissant. "Umm… this is good!" Ryan said.

"I'd like to take credit, but you can thank Mountain Makins' Pastry Shop for the croissants. I can't cook as well as Raj, but like you, I don't starve. I'm actually more than a pretty face." Cass sat down in the chair opposite Ryan at the table.

"Hmph," Ryan grunted as he gazed at Cass across the table. "Pretty face" was an understatement. With her wet hair piled on top of her head and her face scrubbed clean, she was a beautiful woman—an all-natural woman.

As Ryan slathered a croissant with blackberry jam, he let his mind toy with the idea of having Cass across the table from him every morning. He quickly sidelined the far-fetched idea. He still didn't know Cass all that well. And she was the daughter of wealthy socialites—though one was going to prison. She was used to a different lifestyle than his.

Cheryl had so easily fooled him. What he thought was love just turned out to be infatuation on his part. A mirage. And Cheryl's attraction to him was only a means to an end. She'd caught herself a naïve country boy; all that was left to do was reel him in. And as a result, both their lives disintegrated and scattered like damage following a violent North Carolina thunderstorm.

Ryan was older and more experienced now. Since Cheryl, he'd avoided similar traps. His method? Close himself off and not let thoughts of loving someone enter his mind. That method had served him well thus far—until Cass arrived and took up residence in his head.

There was a genuine openness about Cass—no insincere phoniness, even when she was deliberately pushing his buttons and looking for an argument. Her flirting was all an act, too. If he made a serious pass at her, she'd run for the mountains.

Since he lived on the mountain, that might work out in his favor.

Ryan quashed his crazy, idiotic thoughts. After spending the night with Cass curled up beside him, it was probably just his libido talking. But why was he suddenly remembering when happier times were the norm? And longing to feel that way again?

"I really should be going." Ryan drained the last of his coffee and finished his second croissant. He pushed back from the table. "It's after 7:30 a.m. Dad's going to fire me."

"I doubt that. Not after what happened last night. One more cup of coffee before you go." Cass refilled his coffee cup. As she set the pot down, the doorbell rang. She turned and started toward the door.

"No, wait! Let me get it!" Ryan jumped up from the table and stopped her. "Are you expecting anyone?"

"No." Cass shook her head.

"Our perp could have an accomplice," Ryan cautioned as he pushed Cass behind him. He walked to the door and pulled back the curtain that covered the window in the door. Two strangers—an older woman and a younger man—stood on the porch. They appeared harmless, so Ryan opened the door. "May I help you?" he asked.

"I… ah… I'm looking for Cassandra Jordan," the woman replied. She glanced over to double-check the house number placard by the door. "This is the address I was given. I thought she lived here."

"Mom? What… what in the world are you doing here?" Cass's eyes widened as she peered around Ryan's shoulder, surprised to find her mother standing on her porch. "It's okay, Ryan. This is my mother—my other stalker."

Ryan opened the door wide and stepped back. An older version of Cass and a tall, thin man entered the house.

"How did you find me? And what are you doing here?" Cass asked.

"Raj gave me your address," Cecilia explained, her cultured British accent apparent. "When he called, he mentioned that some strange things have been happening to you since you moved here. Snakes in your office. Vile threats scrawled on the door. John and I flew into Charlotte early this morning and rented a car. And here we are. We came to see for ourselves that you're alright." She turned to the man who accompanied her. "You remember John, Sandra Redford's grandson?"

"It's been a while since I last saw you." John Redford embraced Cass and kissed her cheek. "I've missed you, and I was worried, too."

"No need for either of you to worry. I'm fine." Cass returned John's hug, then stepped away and introduced Ryan. "This is Ryan Scott. We just finished breakfast. There's coffee and croissants left if you're hungry." Cass pointed to the kitchen table.

"Nice to meet you both," Ryan greeted the visitors.

Cecilia looked Ryan up and down. Was that confusion or displeasure in her gaze? "Scott? So, you belong to the Scott Construction truck in the driveway?"

"Yes, ma'am, that would be me." Ryan turned to Cass. "I need to be going."

"Put you boots and shirt on first," Cass replied, pointing to his T-shirt and stockinged feet. "I think you left them by the sofa."

"Right." Ryan walked into the living room to get his shoes and shirt. Cecilia's eyes, filled with speculation, followed Ryan to the sofa. He sat down and quickly slipped into his work boots, then shrugged into his shirt, buttoned up the front, and pocketed his truck keys and wallet.

By the look in Cass's mother's eyes as she assessed Ryan, his pedigree fell short in her estimation. He wasn't the class of person she wanted sharing an early-morning breakfast with her daughter. Sharing breakfast was okay, while partially un-dressed—no!

Cecilia continued watching Ryan, inspecting him like a butterfly trapped under glass. No need for her to say it out loud: Ryan the construction worker wasn't good enough for her daughter. He didn't measure up to the properly bred En-glishman she'd dragged from Philly to the wild and uncivilized mountains of North Carolina.

Ryan wasn't about to correct Cecilia's misreading of this morning's situation between him and Cass. Let the socialite be horrified that her daughter had spent the night with an unso-phisticated construction worker from Mason Valley. He might even throw in a hillbilly accent if she continued to frown at him.

Cass led her mother and John into the breakfast nook, cleared away her and Ryan's dishes, and poured each of them a cup of coffee. She placed another plate of croissants on the table before returning to the front door where Ryan waited to say goodbye.

"Kiss me," Cass whispered as she approached Ryan.

A request like that in front of her guests? Why? What was Cass up to?

Ryan's first thought was to refuse. Cass planned to use him to shock her mother—or maybe to make John jealous? Maybe his earlier assessment that Cass was *genuine* was wrong.

"Just a pretend kiss goodbye to rile up my bloodhound

mother—you know, throw her off the scent. She'll badger me about John all day if I don't give her something else to chew on."

"Isn't he your boyfriend? He's looking this way. My guess is he thinks he is."

"Oh, yeah. He's one among many." Cass rose up on her tip-toes and softly brushed Ryan's lips in a friendly kiss goodbye.

Ryan wasn't about to be used. Been there, done that! Cass wanted to put on a show for her mother? He could help with that. But they'd do it his way. "A con job? Is that what you want, City Girl?" he whispered as he pulled Cass tightly against him. "Half measures don't work—in construction or in medicine. A pretend kiss won't fool your mother—or make your boyfriend jealous. If it's worth doing, it's worth doing right! Go all in! Can you handle that?"

Ryan didn't wait for an answer. He gently pulled Cass to him and cupped her face in his hands. His long fingers slid into her hair as he covered her lips in a long, slow kiss. As heat rose between them, Cass parted her lips, allowing Ryan to deepen the kiss. He was first demanding, then barely touching, then demanding, then gentle again. Fire and ice! Ice and fire!

What started out as a pretense had quickly blazed fast and hot into a fire. Cass's eager response threw more fuel on the fire. They were both breathless when the kiss ended.

"You handled that well, City Girl." Ryan reluctantly broke away. He swallowed, hoping the effort would help slow his racing heart. Cass didn't back away; instead, she gave a contented sigh and laid her head on his chest. Ryan raised her chin and smiled. "Is that a purr I hear coming from you?"

"My brain is mush. It's all I can muster," Cass said as she lifted her head.

"I have to go. And you have visitors. Have Raj call me if he has any new information about Mitchell." At Cass's nod, Ryan kissed her forehead, opened the front door, and walked toward his truck. Cecilia's rental car was parked behind him, but with a little jockeying, Ryan managed to squeak by. Without looking Cass's way, he backed onto the road.

As Ryan drove to the jobsite—a new day care center located on the north side of Mason Valley—his mind remained on Cass. What just happened? So much for his initial goal of teaching Cass the art of the con. That was no con job! Clearly, neither had brought their A game during their previous encounter.

"You're the con!" he whispered to himself. True! He'd wanted to kiss Cass even before her mother showed up, and their kiss revealed just how badly he'd wanted to. Cass's willingness to participate had only encouraged him.

The "all-in" Country Boy had met his match on the kissing Richter scale. And as if he hadn't learned a lesson previously, it was with another City Girl.

Ryan's thoughts soon turned to John Redford, a British stick-in-the-mud if there ever was one. John was obviously interested in Cass; otherwise, he wouldn't have traveled to North Carolina to see her. Also obvious was that Cass's mother approved of him. A handpicked future son-in-law? Most likely, she was already planning the wedding—if not on paper, then in her head.

John, the stiff, stodgy Englishman, didn't seem like an appropriate match for fun-loving, inappropriate Cass. A smile would probably break his face. Ryan quickly noted the irony in that thought. As Cass frequently pointed out, he wasn't a barrel of laughs himself.

And Ryan Scott, self-imposed recluse, was not an authority on the dynamics between couples or what made them compatible. Ryan had mucked up his last two relationships—first, his engagement with Cheryl, and then, his short-lived fling with his high-school sweetheart, Stephanie. Too much gloom surrounding the first one had doomed the second one.

Ryan pulled into the parking lot of the day care construction site and grabbed his tool belt from his truck. He whistled softly as he walked toward the building and the millwork awaiting installation.

Ryan was happy, the happiest he'd felt in some time. Although he wished Cass had never endured Mitchell's stalking, Ryan's assistance in the investigation and in Mitchell's capture made him feel as if he was doing something important again. Doing something more than hammering a nail through a piece of wood had awakened his brain. Sprouts of optimism about a future had taken root despite his best efforts to kill them.

Cass's bravery and refusal to adapt her routine because of her stalker had forced Ryan to question why he was hiding out in the mountains with only regrets and nightmares for company. But lately, memories of mornings before his life collapsed had begun to surface—mornings when he'd woken up excited and looking eagerly to the day ahead.

As Ryan picked up a length of molding and climbed the ladder to affix it in place, the feel of Cass's warm body pressed against his in sleep last night, the vision of her face and her swishy golden ponytail this morning intruded on his thoughts.

"Ouch!" Distracted by his wondering mind, Ryan missed the finishing nail and instead hit his finger with the hammer—a not-so-gentle reminder that even a mundane job like his required concentration. He'd best not revisit that scorching-hot goodbye kiss with Cass, because there was a good chance he'd send a nail straight through his hand.

CHAPTER TWENTY-ONE

Cass watched until Ryan's truck drove around the bend in the road and out of sight. Their little show for her mother's benefit had turned into something much more than what she'd suggested. Ryan hadn't meekly gone along and let her dictate the execution of her proposal. He'd taken complete control of the situation, and gave much more than she asked for. That kiss was not done with half measures!

Maybe Raj was right: Ryan challenged her, and that was what was missing in the men like John that her mother tried to fix her up with. Cass touched her lips that were still warm from Ryan's kiss. Mutual give-and-take definitely made things interesting.

Cass walked slowly back to the kitchen-dining area, dreading the lecture she knew was coming from her mother once they found time alone. Cecilia would surely go on one of her usual tirades. The first topic would be why Ryan, "the construction worker," was in her house this morning. That would be followed by what John, the English nobleman—although a low-ranking one as noblemen went—might think of such conduct.

An argument over Cecilia's interference in Cass's life had been building since she deliberately caused Cass's breakup with Stephen. Cass had suppressed her anger at the time, but since then, she'd ignored Cecilia's matchmaking schemes and any comments she made regarding the men Cass dated. There'd never be a perfect time to bluntly tell her mother to stop meddling. But Cecilia's own problems were bigger now than her disappointment in Cass's marital status. Cecilia's life was the one in turmoil; she should concentrate on that.

Raj was in the kitchen when Cass entered. He pulled a frying pan out of a lower cupboard. "I'm going to make some Florentine omelets," he said as he took a carton of eggs, spinach, and cheese from the refrigerator.

"None for me, thanks. But I'll make another pot of coffee." Cass avoided her mother's eyes as she picked up the carafe and walked to the coffee maker. "Ryan and I had croissants earlier."

"That was very thoughtless, Sis! Sending your lover off to work with only pastries to eat."

Cass gave Raj's ribs a sharp jab with her elbow.

"Ouch!" Raj exclaimed, then muttered quietly, "Your post-coital glow is showing. And I saw that scene at the door. Sparks shot into the air like a New Year's Eve celebration in Times Square."

"Don't you dare bring up last night!" Cass narrowed her eyes at Raj, daring further comment. She added ground coffee to the coffee maker and pressed the 'Brew' button.

"Mum's the word," Raj whispered back. "But don't you think that by seeing Ryan here, Mom's figured it out? But don't worry! I won't mention your sex life." Raj dodged the dish towel Cass threw at him. "Oh, you meant what happened with Mitchell's capture!"

"Cassandra, this blackberry jam is superb." Cecilia slathered a second spoonful of jam on her croissant and took a bite. "Such rich flavor and texture! What's the brand?"

"No brand. It's homemade. According to Carolyn, the lady who gave it to me, the blackberries grow wild on her property here in Mason Valley."

"I think they could market and sell this. I'm sure any source of income would be welcomed," Cecilia replied.

Cass didn't respond to Cecilia's condescending comment. She carried the carafe to the table and refreshed her mother's coffee, then John's. The temporary diversion of a discussion about homemade preserves, despite her mother's insensitive comments, was welcome. As Raj pointed out, Cecilia had digested the situation she barged in on—a partially dressed Ryan in Cass's home in the early morning—and had come to the wrong conclusion. She was bursting with questions—and probably criticisms.

Staying silent this time wasn't an option. Cass wouldn't listen to Cecilia disparage Ryan. He'd put Cass's safety above his personal responsibilities and obligations. Ryan had spent the night holding her and asking nothing in return, because he instinctively knew she didn't want to be left alone.

Cass had hoped to use the goodbye scene at the door to throw her mother off the scent, but she knew even that wouldn't make Cecilia back off and accept that Ryan and Cass could be in a relationship. Rather than being deterred, Cecilia would now be even more determined to nip this "unsuitable" romance between Cass and Ryan in the bud.

"It's good that they have wild fruits to preserve and supplement their diets. At least they won't starve." Cecilia took another bite of the croissant. "It's good, though."

"It is. And Mom, stop it! You're not so out of touch that you actually think you're in the backwoods where they hunt game for food, eat only homemade preserves, or wear homespun clothing." Always mindful of Cecilia's teachings, Cass didn't want to argue in front of John, but she wouldn't stand by and listen to her mother criticize the people who had welcomed Cass, rallied around her, and protected her when she was being stalked and threatened.

"I suppose you're right," Cecilia grudgingly admitted. "But this place is quite different from the life you're accustomed to. You could have that life again if you'd just come home with me and John. You don't have to work, much less live, in a hostile place where someone is threatening you. Plus, you're not getting any younger. It's time you got married and started a family. That's what Winslow women do."

Cecilia's timeworn argument: find a man who's financially able to take care of you. Your biological clock is creeping closer to midnight. What Cecilia really meant was for Cass to have kids, turn them over to a nanny, go shopping at expensive boutiques, and spend her days at a spa. The most important decision she'd have to make was approve the menu and table settings for her next dinner party. In Cecilia's mind, that constituted women's work. She was happy with that life, but it wasn't for Cass.

"It's the twenty-first century, Mom, remember? And I'm also a Jordan. Jordan women always had careers. Grandma and Grandpa Jordan believed that marriage is a partnership. I agree, and I like—" Cass stopped herself from defending the choices she'd made. She'd been poised to point out the many ways her mother was out of step with the modern woman, but that wouldn't change her mother's views. Convincing her mother that she was wrong about anything was always difficult. But this was the first time Cecilia had traveled six hundred miles to badger Cass about her life and career choices.

"Here's your omelets," Raj interrupted, setting plates in front of Cecilia and John. "And a plate of toast. More coffee?"

At John's nod, Raj filled his cup, returned to pick up his plate in the kitchen, and then took a seat beside Cass. "So, John, after we eat, would you like to take a drive and see the town?"

"Yes, that sounds great," John replied. "That is, if Cecilia doesn't need me here."

"Mom, you can come with us if you like," Raj suggested.

"No, but thanks. I imagine we saw all there was to see as we drove through town on our way here," Cecilia replied. "The town's very small. You and John go."

"Ryan wants you to call him if you learned anything last night," Cass said to Raj.

"I didn't find out much. The man's name, according to the sheriff, is Mitchell. That's about it. They didn't interrogate him last night," Raj replied. "He complained that he didn't feel well, and the sheriff took him to an urgent care clinic near Asheville. Mitchell was asleep when they returned. I came home at that point."

"Who's Mitchell?" Cecilia asked, looking first at Raj and then at Cass.

"Cass's stalker," Raj replied.

"Raj," Cass warned before giving up on trying to stop Raj from talking. Raj was like a human tornado; he wouldn't stop until he blew himself out and spilled everything he knew about Mitchell. Besides, Cecilia would hear about it sooner or later.

"It was a major takedown! Ryan was on Mitchell within seconds after he jumped Cass from behind." Raj ignored Cass's "you're not helping" glare and continued his recitation, championing Ryan. "The way Ryan punched Mitchell, it's a wonder his head didn't fly off. I was closer, but Ryan beat us all across the parking lot. The lover rushes in and saves the fair maiden—like something from a made-for-TV movie!"

"Raj, would you stop it?" Cass kicked his foot under the table.

"Oh, my goodness!" Cecilia clasped her hands over her heart. "What… what in the world is going on in this place?"

"That was an excellent plan, using you as bait. Your kick to his groin was genius. And who knows what he would've done if you hadn't blasted him with pepper spray!" Raj ignored Cass's plea to stop talking. His embellished tale of Mitchell's capture made Cass's part sound even more dangerous than it had been. But Raj apparently had a plan: use the incident to draw their mother's attention away from questions about Ryan. Cass grudgingly admitted it was a good strategy, and so far it was working.

"Bait? Cass? How did you get mixed up with these people? Who would put you at such risk?" Cecilia's voice ranged from surprise, to outrage, then demanding. "Cass, you need to leave this town right now! Leave this violent place and come home."

"I agree with Cecilia," John said, nodding. He had remained quiet until now, listening to the conversation while eating his omelet. "This Ryan person put you in danger? As bait? Bloody hell, what kind of man would do that to a woman?"

"Calm down!" Cass looked from Cecilia to John. "Ryan didn't devise the plan. Sheriff Ferguson and the FBI planned it, and I agreed to do my part. I wasn't in as much danger as Raj makes it sound. Ryan and all the other men had the place surrounded. No one was hurt, so it worked out well. And now, it's over. Let's drop it!"

"Your life is being threatened by criminals, and you tell me to calm down? To drop it?" Cecilia's voice raised, horrified. "Cassandra, this is not how I raised you—to associate with rogues and criminals. Ryan, the sheriff, and whomever else carelessly put your life in danger! And all because of a local small-town criminal they couldn't arrest on their own."

"For the last time, Ryan had nothing to do with this—not that you're listening to anything I say. And as far as we know, this 'local' criminal may well be one of Dad's victims from Philadelphia. Maybe I do 'associate' with criminals—my own family."

"Cassandra, watch your tongue! This isn't about…" Cecilia sputtered to a halt, and Cass felt sudden sympathy for her mother. For so long, Cecilia had played the part of the high-society priestess, floating above all the troubles of lowly commoners. She didn't know how to handle shame in her own family.

"Well," Raj said as he picked up his plate and rose from the table. "John, let me get my keys and wallet from my room, and we'll take that drive into town." He placed his plate in the dishwasher, left the room, and quickly returned, shrugging into his jacket. "Ready?" he asked.

John nodded and stood up to join him, apparently happy to escape the shouting match that was brewing between Cass and her mother.

"Coward," Cass muttered as she passed Raj on her way to the kitchen. "Remember, payback is hell, and yours is coming."

Cass puttered in the kitchen for a few minutes, loading the dishwasher and wiping down the appliances and countertops. When she couldn't find anything else that needed her attention, she reluctantly returned to the table. Her mother sat staring out the window.

"Let's move into the living room where it's more comfortable," Cass said. "But first, I need to call my office manager and let her know I won't be in today. Then, we can talk."

Cecilia nodded, got up from the table, walked to the sofa, and sat down. She leaned back into the cushions, her hands tightly clasped in her lap. What the set of her mouth indicated wasn't clear—pain over her personal situation, or disappointment over Cass's intention to stay in Mason Valley?

Cass usually closed her ears and nodded without comment until Cecilia finished one of her sermons about Cass's unmar-

ried status, her career, and her general behavior. But not standing up to Cecilia had only encouraged more interference.

Cass called Carolyn, who assured her that no one expected
her to come into the office after last night's events. Things were
pretty quiet at the clinic, and if Clayton called, they'd direct him
to call her cell.

Immediately after hanging up with Carolyn, Cass's phone
rang with a call from Kelsey.

"I'm doing fine," Cass assured her. "Just trying to put it out
of my mind."

"Glad to hear it," Kelsey said. "If you need anything, don't
hesitate to call."

"I'll do that, and thanks for calling." Cass disconnected the
call and walked into the living room. She took a seat on the
other end of the sofa, pulled up her knees, and turned to face
her mother.

"This man, Ryan, that you spent the night with—he's a construction worker?"

This was not what Cass expected to discuss, but Cecilia
always got right to the point of what was most important to her.
Cass could tell her that Ryan was a trained medical doctor. That
might raise Cecilia's opinion of him somewhat, but it shouldn't
matter what his occupation was if he and Cass were in a relationship.

A relationship between her and Ryan? That was laughable.
Mostly what she got from Ryan were scowls—and a few hot
kisses—not a commitment to love her forever. Still, last night
was special.

"We didn't spend the night together. At least, not in the way
your tone suggests."

"A half-dressed man sharing breakfast with you?" Cecilia
countered. "I'm not blind."

"We're friends. Ryan didn't want to leave me alone after

what happened, and I didn't want to be alone, either. And yes, Ryan works for his father in construction. But what does that have to do with anything?"

"I know you think that love is all that matters. But a construction worker can never support you in the way you're accustomed to," Cecilia stated. "You'd never be able to afford the things we do together—our shopping trips, for instance."

Cass inhaled, halting her initial harsh response. Cecilia weighed the acceptability of Cass's suitors by their bank accounts. Her impression of Ryan was nothing new. "Ryan is a good man. Isn't that enough if we love each other and he makes me happy? And the shopping trips are your idea, not mine," Cass countered. "I don't pay for the shopping trips now—you do. I go because we're spending time together and doing something *you* love. Yes, I like pretty clothes, but if you never bought me another pair of expensive shoes, my life wouldn't change. I'm used to taking care of my financial needs. I'm paid a good salary as clinic director. I don't need a husband or my parents to support me."

"That's what you say now, but you don't miss something until you don't have it any longer. There's more to marriage than love. Marriage to a common... *laborer* can't provide you with the life I want for you."

"What *you* want? Not what *I* want?" Cass was certain Cecilia had been about to say "marriage to a commoner." Cass's grandfather hadn't even been the British ambassador; he'd just served as the ambassador's chief of staff and was also a "commoner." Cecilia had misrepresented her father's position for so long, it seemed she now believed her own hype.

"I had such high hopes for you. John could give you the status you deserve."

Cass suppressed a groan. Cecilia would never change. What a stressful way to live! Maintaining a fake status must be extremely tiring—always on guard, afraid one small slip would give you away.

"Mom, did you ever love Dad?" Cass directed the conversation away from Cecilia's dreams for her and back to real-life issues.

"Cassandra! How can you ask such a thing?" Cecilia scolded. "Of course I did. I still do." Cecilia looked away from Cass, her eyes focused on a picture on the opposite wall. "We fell madly in love the moment we met." Temporarily lost in the past, with her guard down, Cecilia's eyes took on a faraway look as she remembered the day when she met Kenneth Jordan.

"How did you meet? Wasn't it at a diplomatic function?"

"Yes. At a Christmas party for the British embassy staff." Cecilia looked over at Cass, and a smile touched her lips. "Your father came as a guest of one of the staff. You know that wonderful laugh he has? It was even more infectious back then. I first heard it from across the room. I knew the man he came with, so I walked over to speak with George and inserted myself into their conversation. I was inveigling for an introduction to his friend. And it worked."

"Ah… Cecilia Winslow, a woman on the prowl," Cass commented quietly, not wanting to distract her mother from the story about her parents' first meeting.

Cecilia had never shared details of her first meeting with Kenneth Jordan before. His current legal troubles must have opened a door to the past. Perhaps Cecilia was searching for a time with pleasant memories, when she was happy.

"Your father had the most gorgeous smile I'd ever seen." Cecilia continued her narrative. "His whole face lit up when we were introduced. He was very handsome—tall with broad shoulders—and quite dashing. I think we fell in love the first evening we met."

Cecilia as a young woman, meeting and falling in love with

the man she wanted to spend her life with—and knowing it the first time they met—was not the mother Cass knew. Which raised the question of why she was always pushing Cass to marry men Cass didn't even like very much. What happened to that starry-eyed couple? Somewhere along the line, their love had wandered offtrack and lost its magic.

"Was he a stockbroker at the time you met?"

"Yes, but at a very low level," Cecilia replied. "We went through some rough times, but I had a small trust fund that we used to get by. But soon, Kenneth was established and very successful. When the last market crash occurred, I thought we were surely done for, but your father did miraculously well, while everyone else lost everything. I was so proud of him at the time. Only now have I realized how he managed that." Cecilia's mouth thinned to a straight line. She turned to face Cass. Anger replaced the starry-eyed look of a moment ago. "Your grandmother Winslow warned me against marrying Kenneth. Just as I've warned you about the importance of choosing the right man. But I wouldn't listen. What did she know about love? I thought she didn't understand how being with Kenneth made me feel. At the time, I thought she was meddling and overreacting."

"That does sound like meddling to me," Cass commented sarcastically.

"No, her advice was spot-on. She regularly pointed out that a strong financial foundation would endure long after love cooled and burned out. She was right. Just look where we are now. I never want this to happen to you."

"Grandma not only meddled; she did it cynically."

"You can poke fun at her advice all you want, but she's been proven correct. I want you to have a marriage that lasts. A strong financial foundation is necessary to make it last. I honestly don't think this Ryan person can give you that."

"First of all, Ryan and I haven't known each other very long. We're not even dating, so we're certainly not discussing marriage. Second, he's working through a failed relationship that he's still not over. Third, *you* can't pick the person I fall in love with. That's *my* choice."

"I'm just warning you of the pitfalls and trying to help you avoid the mistakes I've made. I don't want you to end up married to a… a criminal…" Cecilia's voice broke as she acknowledged out loud that her husband was a criminal.

"Dad says he did all this for you—that your spending kept escalating and that this was the only way he could give you the lifestyle you enjoyed and expected."

"Huh! He did this for himself. He never once asked me to cut back."

"That's what I told him, but based on what you just said, I suspect he didn't want to be seen as a failure by you or by your family. Didn't you wonder why he and his clients were doing so well when everyone else you knew was going broke or was forced to sell all or most of their assets to stay afloat?"

"I… well… I guess I didn't want to think something like that could happen to us. I thought he was smarter than the others and very good at his job. I was never involved in his business. And for once, my mother was very proud of Kenneth. He was a genius, while everyone else were losers. I waited years for her to approve of my marriage."

"And now, we're back to the point I'm trying to make," Cass said. "I'm self-sufficient and can take care of myself. I don't need a husband's bank account to fall back on. What I need is love and support. Stop pushing me the way your mother pushed you." Cass moved closer to her mother and hugged her. Cecilia felt fragile in her arms, her shoulders tense and bony. "I love you, but you can't manage my life. If I make a mess of it, it's all on me—my mess."

"I know, and I'm sorry. I apologize for what I did to you and Stephen. I thought that by interfering, I was doing the right thing for you. But this incident with your father has made me question everything I ever thought was right. I'll try to stay out of your life."

"Not out of my life, just out of my career choices and my love life," Cass corrected her. "If Stephen had been *the* one, I would've probably ignored you and did as I wanted."

"Probably. You were always headstrong—a Jordan trait." Cecilia paused, then gave Cass a self-deprecating smile. "Bollocks! So, I dragged John down here for no reason? He's not a marriage candidate in your eyes? I thought you liked him, and he's very well-off."

"No. You can cancel the wedding venue and caterers." Cass shook her mother's shoulder playfully. "I like John as a friend, but he has the personality of a wet noodle."

"He is rather bland. A wet noodle might be more interesting," Cecilia laughed.

"True. John's money doesn't interest me. I want someone who's fiery and passionately in love with me—a man who respects me and listens to my opinions, but isn't afraid to tell me when he disagrees. Many of the milquetoast men you've trotted out for me are the ones who need taking care of."

"You exaggerate, but I get your point. So, does Ryan fit your description of your ideal man? I saw that passionate and *fiery* display at the door," Cecilia added. "I'm surprised the buttons on his shirt didn't melt."

"Just between us girls," Cass leaned closer to her mother and smiled broadly, "oh yes! Exactly like that!"

CHAPTER TWENTY-TWO

As soon as breakfast was over on Friday morning, Cass said goodbye to her mother and John on the front porch. Cecilia had spent the night in the extra bedroom, while Raj gave up his room to John and slept on the living room sofa.

Cecilia hadn't planned a long visit to begin with—just long enough to convince Cass to return to Philadelphia with her. Since Cass had made it clear she wasn't leaving Mason Valley, Cecilia and John were returning to Philadelphia today.

Cass and Cecilia had continued their discussion the day before until Raj and John returned from their tour of the town.

"You have to stop interfering with my life and stop playing matchmaker," Cass had reiterated. "If you continue, don't be surprised if I go full Grandpa on you and tell you to sod off.'"

Cecilia had promised she'd stop trying to marry her daughter off to every eligible bachelor she met. Recent events with her husband may have finally shown Cecilia just how limited her ability was to control other people.

"The job before me is to rehabilitate my own life," Cecilia

acknowledged at one point. "From now on, Cass, do as you see fit. I have my hands full with your father right now."

After they agreed to a truce, the mother-daughter discussion had progressed from Cass's lack of a marriage to her father's legal problems.

"When we get back to Philadelphia, I plan to visit Kenneth," Cecilia promised. "I want to apologize for leaving him when he needed me. I just didn't know how to handle all the public condemnation, the humiliation, and the bad press following his arrest. I'm not sure I'll handle it any better now, but I'll try. My friends will shun me over what Kenneth did, but I'll deal with that when it comes."

"Remember in junior high, when Katrina Lowery started the rumor that I made disparaging remarks about the dress Belinda Moreno wore to the ninth-grade dance? It wasn't true, but Katrina convinced my friends that it was, and they turned against me. Do you remember what you told me? 'If my friends didn't believe my side of the story and stand with me, then they weren't true friends.'"

"I remember, but this is a bit more serious than a spat in school," Cecilia said.

"Not to a ninth-grader. As soon as I made the varsity basketball squad and we started winning, those friends all came crawling back. But by then, I had new friends and didn't need my old flock."

"You've carried that grudge this long?"

"Of course not! I'm just saying that any friends who turn against you because of this are not the people you thought they were. You'll make new friends."

"I hope you're right. I'm embarrassed to face any of them."

"You'll be fine. Starting over can be exciting," Cass said. "Dad needs support from all of us, but mostly from you. That's about all we can do for him right now."

Cecilia appeared genuinely sympathetic to her husband's problems and truthful about her desire to support him—a sea change from her recent behavior. How long this would last once she returned to life in Philadelphia was anyone's guess.

"I guess you're staying here and not coming home?" John asked as he hugged Cass goodbye. "I think I know why. It's this guy, Ryan, isn't it?"

"I'm here because of my job. Ryan is just a friend." Cass returned his hug. John sounded like her mother; he assumed Cass's whole life centered around finding a husband.

"Friends it is, then. I surmised this would be the outcome of this trip, but Cecilia's like a reckless lorry driver, and you best not get in her way," John chuckled, showing an unusual humorous side.

"My mother doesn't understand the word 'no,'" Cass agreed. "Go and be happy. There's lots of available women waiting for you in Philly—and probably even more in London."

As soon as Cecilia and John said goodbye, Cass dressed for work. But before she left for the clinic, she called her father. She'd convinced Cecilia that she needed to support him; now, Cass needed to as well. After they exchanged greetings, Cass got to the main reason for her call.

"Dad, I'm sorry for what I said the last time I saw you. I know I hurt you," Cass said.

"You don't need to apologize, Sweetheart. You didn't say anything I didn't already know. I brought this on myself, and it's time to stop blaming others. I'm sorry for involving you and causing you to lose your job and, well, I'm sorry for everything."

"I know. I'm actually happy here in North Carolina, but I'm worried about you."

"I'll take my punishment. Don't you worry."

Cass's eyes filled with tears. Her father was trying to sound brave, but a shakiness underlaid his words. "Have you received a trial date?"

"Sometime in February. I don't dwell on it. I just show up when my lawyer tells me to."

"I'll be there to support you. Raj, too. We won't let you go through this alone."

"I don't deserve your support."

This time, Cass's eyes overflowed. The resignation and defeat in his voice hurt. His lawyers didn't have any miracles that could save him from prison, so Kenneth Jordan had come to terms with what he'd done. He no longer hoped for a way out or was blaming others.

Cass's father had always been a steady, calming presence in her life. With a booming laugh, he was larger than life and fun-loving—Cass's hero. He never got wound up over Cass's behavior like Cecilia did. While Cecilia was busy correcting Cass on her manners or posture, Kenneth was slipping her chocolates, gum, or some other treat.

There wasn't much left for father and daughter to say to each other. Kenneth insisted she didn't have to come to his trial, and she insisted she did. What they both wanted was for this to never have happened. Since it had, they would all muddle through and hope for the best.

Cass arrived at work and parked as far away from the spot of the stalker's attack as she could. The memory of his hands closing around her neck would remain front and center for some time to come.

The question she hadn't been able to shake was what she had done to this stranger to make him hate her so much. He'd tried to render her unconscious with chloroform, likely with the ultimate goal of strangling her to death.

Cass had found a moment alone with Raj before breakfast this morning, and he'd expanded on what he'd told Cecilia and John. Still, Raj had very little new information.

Once Sheriff Ferguson had booked Mitchell, he clammed up and refused to speak. He didn't even ask for a lawyer. He was placed in a cell, but about an hour later, Mitchell complained that he was ill. Sheriff Ferguson and FBI Agent Boyd took him to an urgent care clinic in east Asheville. The doctor on duty couldn't find anything wrong with Mitchell except for an extreme case of agitation. The doctor administered an injection of medication for anxiety. It was after midnight by the time the sheriff returned Mitchell to his cell. By then, Mitchell was sleeping off the effects of the medication. It was obvious to all that Mitchell was still playing the system, using a feigned illness to stall the interrogation.

Cass spent the day working in her office as if nothing unusual had happened. The clinic staff didn't deluge her with questions. They showed their concern and support in other ways. Coffee and blueberry muffins from Rita's Café were waiting for her when she arrived. A meal of fried chicken and mashed potatoes mysteriously arrived for her lunch. It wasn't the soul food that warmed Cass's heart, but rather the kindness and thoughtfulness of her staff at a time when she needed it most.

It was almost quitting time when Cass's phone rang with a call from the sheriff's office

"Do you want to join a meeting for an update on the investigation into Mitchell?" Sheriff Ferguson asked. "I believe you'll be interested in what we found."

"Absolutely," Cass responded. "I'll be there in about twenty minutes."

She left the building immediately after hanging up the phone.

Fear—or, as Cass liked to think of it, *preparation*—had become a habit when she felt exposed. As she crossed the parking lot, shadowy pockets of darkness near the building loomed like sinister black holes in the fading light. Cass took a wide berth around them, her finger fixed firmly on the trigger of her pepper spray canister. Just because Mitchell was in the hands of law enforcement, it didn't mean she was ready to change her habits.

Cass should have been turning cartwheels in celebration instead of furtively checking every nook and cranny around her. She had good news. Mandy had accepted the job offer from the Barrett Medical Center. She would be moving to Mason Valley once she completed her two-weeks'-notice period.

One NP hired, one doctor to go!

Cass entered the sheriff's office to find the usual group—Ryan, Jack, Jason, Ben, and Raj—seated around the conference table with Sheriff Ferguson. They had all been present for Mitchell's capture and arrest. Kelsey was at the table tonight, too, though her pregnancy had kept her from participating in the actual capture.

Cass avoided looking directly at Ryan as his gaze followed her approach. The memory of their parting kiss warmed her cheeks. She fought to control a blush.

"So, is Mitchell from Philadelphia and connected to my father in some way?" Cass asked as she sat down in the chair Ryan held for her between him and Kelsey. "Was he a victim of my father's scheme?"

"No." Sheriff Ferguson opened a folder in front of him. "That wasn't his motivation. His only connection to Philadelphia appears to be that the lawyer who represented him in a previous case was from there."

"However, we did find out that he's a real nutjob," Jason said.

"He is," the sheriff agreed. "We searched his van and found a rifle, a handgun, and thirty rounds of ammo. He claimed those were for protection since he travels a lot, but that's a lot of firepower just for protection. If we hadn't captured him, I believe he would've escalated to something even more violent than assault."

"Oh, my goodness! But I don't understand." Cass's voice wobbled at the implication of the sheriff's words. "I never met this man. Why did he target me?"

Ryan placed a reassuring hand on her arm.

"Actually, you were his target, but only indirectly," Sherriff Ferguson replied. "The clinic and Kelsey and Jason were his real targets. In his warped and hate-filled mind, Mitchell thought that if he got rid of you—ran you off or something worse—the clinic would shut down. He assumed no one else would be willing to take the director's job, and if they did, he'd go after them, too."

"Michell thought he was so clever that he'd never get caught. Another miscalculation," Ben added. "He couldn't physically get to Kelsey and Jason in Atlanta, so you were his target by default."

"I still don't understand. Why would he care if Mason Valley opened a medical clinic?" The puzzle pieces didn't fit together. She *and* the clinic had to go?

"No doubt you've heard about the Coeburn case from a few years ago—the pedophile who set up camp on Love Vine Mountain?" Jason asked. At Cass's nod, he continued, "Mitchell was a customer of Coeburn's. He was caught and pled guilty in exchange for a lesser sentence. He spent almost two years in federal prison. He was released a few months ago."

"He blamed Jason and me for his downfall," Kelsey said, picking up the story. "Because of his arrest, Mitchell lost his business, his wife, and his status as a local businessman. No one wanted to be connected or do business with a convicted pedophile. When he went to prison, the clinic was under construction but hadn't opened. When he was released, he learned that the clinic was my project. He wanted to destroy it to get back at me."

"His goal was a simple tit for tat," the sheriff further explained. "Running you—and any subsequent director—off would shut down the clinic, taking away something important from Kelsey and Jason. It was retribution for what they took from him. You were just the means to an end."

"Oh, my goodness," Cass said again. "That's crazy! I guess I should be happy that it wasn't one of the disturbed individuals from Philly trying to get back at me for what my father did. But this seems almost worse. I don't have any personal connection to Mitchell, yet he still wanted to kill me."

"A deranged mind can contort any situation to fit his narrative," Ben explained. "I think it's safe to say that this man won't be bothering you again."

"I hope you can put this behind you," Kelsey said. "You're doing an amazing job as the clinic's director. I don't want to lose you."

"Quitting hasn't once crossed my mind," Cass replied. "It would take more than slashed tires, death threats, a stinky dead snake, and a near-strangulation to run me off." Cass visibly shivered as she listed the stalker's attempts to harm and intimidate her.

"You forgot being locked in the maintenance shed," Ryan added.

"He was behind that, too?" Cass asked. "That was a Friday, not his usual Wednesday. The wind didn't blow the door shut?"

"No, it was Mitchell. When he realized that we knew everything else about him, he bragged about that, too," Sheriff Ferguson replied. "Wednesdays were his normal delivery days, but he was in town that Friday to make a special delivery. He saw you drive to the clinic, so he didn't want to miss an opportunity to terrorize you a little more."

"You made it easy for him by going into the shed," Ryan said with a frown.

"I *was* scared when I couldn't open the door, but I was absolutely certain I wasn't staying in there for the weekend. By locking me in a shed with so many tools, indicates just how little thought he put into his plan, or how well he knew me. I'd have cut a hole in the door or dismantled it completely to get out."

"Locked in the maintenance shed? What were you doing in there?" Raj asked. He had remained quiet until now. Leave it to her brother to bring up a topic she wanted to avoid. "You've never mentioned this to me."

"I forgot a book I planned to read over the weekend, so I went back to the office to get it."

Her partial answer didn't satisfy Ryan. He was like a bloodhound, alerted to the fact that she was hiding something. "The book was in the maintenance shed." Ryan commented. It wasn't a question but a statement. His fingers drummed quietly on the table as he waited for further explanation.

"No, I... uh... there were ants in the hallway outside my office door." Cass tried to stop the heat that rose in her face. After what happened, saying aloud her reason for going to the maintenance shed made it seem like a lame idea. "I had to get rid of them somehow."

"Ants?" Raj asked. "And you went to the shed, why? To get a hammer to beat the little buggers to death?"

Raj and Jack were trying not to laugh but weren't succeeding very well. This was exactly why she hadn't mentioned the ants before. The incident would live long in Raj's memory—and Jack's. They would bring up the story at every opportunity and of course embellish it until it was nothing like what really happened—Cass had been terrorized by some tiny ants, along with Mitchell, the stalker.

"You went out in the dark while a criminal was stalking you and risked your life over a few ants? *Ants?*" Ryan asked in disbelief. "What were you thinking?"

"It wasn't dark when I went in there. I was looking for a pesticide or ant bait," Cass explained. "And you don't understand. There were a million of them on the hunt for dinner, marching straight toward the computer and electrical connections."

"An ant-mageddon," Jack chuckled.

"Good one!" Raj gave Jack a fist bump.

"Why didn't you call someone to take care of the ants? I would've come to help." Ryan's frown deepened.

"That's why." Cass pointed at Raj and Jack. "The grade-school boys won't ever let this go."

"She's right, Ryan," Ben interrupted. "She needed to stop the ants someway and do it quickly. Ants can destroy a power source. I've seen it happen."

"Thank you, Ben. At least someone knows I'm not crazy." Cass looked at Ryan and added, "I didn't call anyone because I felt confident that I could handle the situation. That is, until the door locked me in. But I managed that, too." Cass searched for another subject to get them off the topic of ants. She turned to the sheriff. "So, where is Mitchell now?"

"The FBI took him to Charlotte. He violated a variety of federal as well as state laws. Trying to strangle you adds attempted murder. I'm sure there are other offenses we haven't discovered yet."

"I wasn't going to let him run me off, so add 'bad judge of character' to his rap sheet." Cass shivered as the sheriff mentioned again Mitchell's attempt to strangle her. Still, what she said was true; she hadn't once thought of giving up.

"We're very grateful that you didn't quit," Kelsey said. "And relieved that it's over and that you're safe. I'm sorry it was because of Jason and me that you were in danger."

"If I had been right and someone from Philly had followed me here, where would I have run to if I quit?" Cass's voice quivered. She'd been strong throughout the ordeal with Mitchell, but now that he'd been arrested, she was finally acknowledging just how dangerous her situation had been. Cass sagged in her chair with relief. "The mobs in Philadelphia at least had a reason—a misplaced reason—for striking out at me. But Mitchell's deranged mind focused on me, a random person, as the target for his hatred. That seems almost worse than the Philly mobs."

Ryan covered her hand with his. His touch was comforting and reassuring.

Cass straightened in her chair and addressed everyone seated at the table. "I'd like to thank all of you for helping catch Mitchell. I don't know what I would have done without each of you." Then, she turned to Ryan. "With this mystery solved, I'm hoping to open the clinic soon. I've just hired a nurse practitioner, and I'm chasing a licensed medical doctor. I've heard one lives in the mountains nearby. I've recently picked up a hot trail." The others gathered around the table nodded their approval.

"You mean you're chasing a hot doctor," Raj joked.

Cass glared at Raj but ignored his comment.

"You sound pretty confident." Ryan ignored Raj's comment, too. "This person could be hard to find, given the rough terrain on Love Vine Mountain."

"Confident? Well, yes, I am!" Cass nodded. "It's only a matter of time before I track him down and bring him back to civilization. He can't hide forever."

"Maybe he wants to be left alone, and that's why he lives on the mountain," Ryan countered without smiling.

With Mitchell locked up, Ryan's work with the sheriff and his efforts to protect her were over. Construction at the clinic was complete. Both developments meant she wouldn't see him as often and Ryan would retreat back behind his wall—something she couldn't let happen. "Well, he has a choice." Cass nodded firmly. "He can come peacefully, or, if necessary, I'll harass him into submission. I won't let up until he agrees."

"Bring it on, City Girl," Ryan challenged.

CHAPTER TWENTY-THREE

Ryan carried his cup of coffee to the cabin's porch and sat down in a rocking chair. A December moon hung over the valley, lighting the sky, but it didn't penetrate the canopy of trees sheltering the cabin. The porch was dark, but Ryan had left the porch light off, preferring to sit in the darkness. The only sounds disturbing the silence were a few rustling leaves—hardy stragglers that still clung to the tree branches—and the mourning doves stirring in the thicket east of the cabin, awakened by Ryan's presence on the porch. This time of day—just before dawn, when the night was quiet and peaceful—was the perfect time to reflect on the wreck he'd made of his life and how he planned to fix it.

Ryan's cabin was located just south of the infamous Coeburn property. His two-acre parcel ran almost straight up the mountainside but had enough flat land for a cabin. The land went up for sale about the time Ryan had returned home from Charlotte. The absent owner chose to sell the land and avoid all risks associated with ownership of that plot, since he wasn't around to keep pedophiles and squatters away. Ryan had purchased the acreage immediately after returning to Mason Valley.

There, he built the cabin as a comfortable hideaway. It was the perfect place to isolate, lick his wounds, and avoid all outside interference. In his retreat on the mountain, he could brood all he wanted without distractions—except for Mr. Gleason, of course, who stopped by almost daily with wounded birds and animals, seeking Hawk Man's medical assistance.

Ryan took a sip of coffee, stretched out his legs, leaned back, and stilled the rocking chair's motion. He closed his eyes, drew in several deep breaths, and focused, trying to retrieve fragments of a dream he'd had last night. This dream was different from his usual one filled with squealing brakes, tearing metal, and explosions. The images from last night's dream were fuzzy, but Ryan felt certain that a sassy woman with sparkling brown eyes and a swishy blonde ponytail stood beside him at the fishing pond on his parents' farm. And neither one of them was interested in fishing.

For two years, hope and optimism had been missing from his life, but this morning, a stirring of *something* he couldn't yet identified pulsed through him. How much did Cass, annoying as she was, have to do with his new feeling?

Her outburst at Thanksgiving dinner had unleashed a torrent of advice aimed squarely at him. His mother's and Jack's lectures had followed Cass's, and both basically echoed her words. Three people sharing the same view couldn't all be wrong, especially when one of them was his mother.

Ryan had never intended to hurt his family or his friends. He'd sunk into depression, and before he knew it, it had become a way of life. He'd lost track of who he was. His parents had patiently waited for him to get over his grief and climb out of the hole he'd dug for himself.

Cass wasn't that patient.

All of them—friends and family alike—deserved better than

the way he'd been treating them. His newest revelation was that he, Ryan Scott, also deserved better than a detached, isolated existence. Ryan's first step in climbing out of that hole was booking an appointment with Dr. Blankenship.

When he'd stopped by her office, Dr. Blankenship had quickly accommodated his request for an appointment after work. If needing an after-hours appointment was his way of hoping to weasel out of talking to her, Doctor B. had knocked that right off his list of excuses.

Dr. Blankenship was a calm, middle-aged woman who immediately put him at ease. She began their first session by quietly asking questions as he told the story of Cheryl's death. More importantly, she just let Ryan talk, break down the situation as he saw it, and sort through the events leading to the accident and the way he handled its aftermath.

When he'd finished his story, Dr. Blankenship pointed out something that should have been obvious to Ryan, but wasn't: he kept mentioning his decision to end the engagement, seeing it as the catalyst responsible for the horrible chain of events that followed. He was at fault, and Cheryl had died because of him.

"Ryan, you're a very caring man," Dr. Blankenship said. "That's why you became a doctor in the first place. But you're not at fault for being who you are or for resisting Cheryl's efforts to change you into a man designed to her specifications."

"But I didn't resist at first. I was infatuated with Cheryl's carefree lifestyle. It was all new to me. She always had something exciting and entertaining on the agenda. But I soon started to question the point of so much self-absorption. Now, I feel stupid and shallow to admit it, but I fell for the lifestyle, not the person."

"That's a story as old as mankind. What young man hasn't longed for the unattainable—movie stars, glitz, glamor, wealth? Isn't that a rite of passage? You just got closer to achieving it than most young men do." Dr. Blankenship got up from her desk. "How about a glass of sweet tea?" At Ryan's nod, she walked to the coffee bar, filled two glasses with ice cubes, then poured the tea. She handed a glass to Ryan.

"But I led her on." Ryan stubbornly stuck to his belief that he was responsible for Cheryl's accident. He took a drink, then set the glass of tea on a napkin on the corner of the desk. "If I hadn't asked her to marry me, I wouldn't have needed to break it off. I'm not sure why it took the engagement for me to finally wise up."

"Your engagement was a commitment for life. *Forever* is a long time. It's a huge leap."

"Almost immediately after I gave her the ring, I knew it wouldn't work out. We weren't right for each other. By then, I felt trapped but lacked the guts to tell her until she found us an apartment in New York and set up a job interview for me. She didn't even run it by me first."

"Being hesitant to hurt her doesn't mean you led her on. Sounds more like she tricked *you*. Courtship is about getting to know each other. Some people—not all, but some—hide certain character traits early in a relationship—jealousy, manipulation, lying, cheating, whatever. Only after they feel secure in the relationship—such as after an engagement—will they drop their guard. Often, by this time, we don't want to admit to ourselves that we've made a gigantic mistake. We postpone changing the situation ourselves, hoping the decision will somehow be made for us."

"But in my profession, I'm an observer of people. I search for the truth, even when a patient can't tell me or is evasive about what's wrong. I always thought distinguishing truth from fiction was one of my strengths."

"I'm sure you're very good at diagnosing an ailment, but your heart isn't one of your patients," Dr. Blankenship said.

"You were infatuated, then realized that the luster of an exciting life with Cheryl had worn off. You were forced into making the decision."

"Which was cowardly of me, don't you think? Waiting until I was forced to be honest with her?"

"No, it was the honest and honorable thing to do, even if a little late. You've taken on an unnecessary burden of guilt. Is that why you stopped practicing medicine?"

"I'm not completely sure why I stopped," Ryan said. "Medicine, Cheryl's death, our argument, my inability to save her—everything got all tangled up into one tragic mess. I just had to get away from it all."

"I see. In your eyes, you were a failure as a person because you couldn't do what Cheryl asked of you—force yourself to love her and change who you are to suit her. Then, you put off telling her the truth until you were forced to, and that makes you a coward. Then, you failed as a doctor because you couldn't save her after an accident that you believe you caused."

"You make it sound so simple," Ryan said.

"The human mind is anything but simple. We're adept at twisting ourselves into all sorts of mental disorders. Don't be hard on yourself. PTSD is extremely hard to diagnose in oneself. You've been unable to separate yourself from a traumatic event you think you caused. In your mind, breaking the engagement triggered tragic events. Survivors often ignore the part others played in a tragedy. They survived, so they must bear the full burden."

"That actually makes sense."

"You're surprised?" Dr. Blankenship smiled and pointed to a row of framed degrees on the office wall. "Trying to remake yourself to fit someone else's portrait of you is what's dishonest. It's a charade and not good for you or Cheryl. A marriage like that would never last. A pretense can only go on for so long."

"I stopped pretending and wanted out. But I never expected Cheryl to react the way she did."

"As I see it, Ryan, you've confused *your action* with Cheryl's *angry reaction*. They're not the same. You assumed total responsibility for her death while failing to give yourself credit for being honest. By being truthful, you hoped to save both of you from an intolerable situation. But she died, and you gave up medicine and a normal life to punish yourself."

"I was always confident in my abilities as a doctor. I powered through any trauma I faced without falling apart," Ryan said. "I thought of myself as a strong person. Shouldn't I have been able to handle Cheryl's death without causing my family and friends so much pain?"

"You're only human. We can all lose sight when a problem involves us personally. But Ryan, 'grin and bear it' won't be found in any psychiatry manuals."

After his session with Dr. Blankenship and a great deal of self-examination, Ryan's brain fog started to lift. Doctor B. was right: he'd denied himself a normal life as punishment for Cheryl's death, even though nothing he sacrificed could ever change the outcome.

Ryan drained the last of the coffee in his cup and stood up from the rocking chair. That was all the time he had for soul-searching this morning. He needed to get a move on. The birds and animals in cages out back needed to be fed before he got on the road. He had a long drive ahead of him this morning.

♦

That was fun, but I'm still not finished, Cass thought as she stopped at a sidewalk bench to consolidate her packages into one shopping bag. Ryan and her father were the two still unfilled gifts on her Christmas list; both men were unusual cases, and that made it hard to shop for them.

With Ryan, what did one buy for a hermit? If he didn't have it already, he most likely didn't want it or need it. And as for her father, he was going to prison and had minimal needs.

Poor Dad! This might be the last Christmas he's free.

Thus far, Cecilia was standing by him, as she'd promised during her visit with Cass. She was still in Philadelphia and had hired an expert legal team with a history of defending white-collar criminals. Cecilia hoped the lawyers could somehow shorten Kenneth's sentence. Time would tell if that worked, but the prospect of a shorter sentence seemed iffy at best.

On this mid-December morning, Mason Valley's Main Street was filled with holiday shoppers. A buzz of chatter and laughter filled this normally quiet street, thanks to the noisy tourists who had come in from all over the region. The friendly mountain town was known for going all-out for the holiday season. Every corner of Main Street was decorated. Businesses rolled out the welcome mat to all who visited, encouraging them to relax and enjoy their time in Mason Valley.

The holiday spirit had grabbed Cass, too, and she'd set out on this spur-of-the-moment Christmas shopping spree to purchase gifts for her staff and friends. She'd browsed the small shops and kiosks along Main Street, purchasing handmade Christmas ornaments for the office staff, a cornhusk angel for Ryan's mother, a silk scarf for Mandy, and a picture frame for Lanie. Cecilia's gift, a cashmere sweater, would be delivered from one of her favorite stores in New York City a few days before Christmas.

Raj was getting a heavy denim shirt lined with flannel. He'd mentioned a possible trip to the northernmost part of Alaska sometime in the new year following their father's trial. Raj had asked Lanie to go with him, since she would graduate from college at the end of the semester and would be free to travel. Alaska was a photographer's dream.

Jack's gift was dance lessons at a new studio that had just opened up in town. He would get a kick out of that. Cass had already warned the instructor what to expect from Jack.

Cass decided to stop and shop as she drove home from the clinic, where she had finished up some administrative duties left over from the past week. Without an assistant, picking up the slack on a Saturday was becoming a normal part of her job. Squeezing funds out of Clayton for clinic expenses took up more of her work hours than it should. If she asked for it, Clayton was against it. Cass hadn't yet figured out if he distrusted her or if that was just Clayton's normal way of operating. Whoever said, "Fear of losing control, controls the man," must have known Clayton Thomas. But after Mitchell's take-down, Clayton's bluster didn't scare Cass. She now saw him more as a house cat than a tiger.

As Cass walked to her parked car, she gazed up at Love Vine Mountain, wondering what Ryan was doing today up there in his lair. She spent a lot of time thinking about him lately, trying to categorize their relationship. The "pretend" kiss they'd shared had surely moved their relationship to a different level—at least, it had for her. And the night he'd stayed with her after Mitchell's attack had carved out a spot in her heart that would always belong to Ryan, regardless of what happened to them in the future.

As Cass started her car and pulled out of her parking space, the immediate and most important question concerning Ryan was whether she could convince him to practice medicine again and do it at the Barrett Medical Center. Cass needed an answer soon; the clinic would open at the beginning of the new year. She didn't want to, but she'd have to look elsewhere if Ryan flatly declined. But he hadn't shut her down completely the last time she broached the subject.

Cass planned to bring the subject up again tonight. She and Raj had accepted Jack's invitation to join him for dinner and dancing at the Eagle's Nest. Going to the Eagle's Nest on Saturday nights had become almost a weekly ritual. Mike's establishment was the best venue Mason Valley offered—good food and drink, great entertainment, and lots of friendly people.

Mandy also planned to join them. She would be arriving later today, bringing a carload of personal items—her first step in permanently moving to Mason Valley.

As Cass drove toward the supermarket to pick up the items Raj needed for the lunch he was preparing, shoppers on the street recognized her, smiled, and waved. Despite the problems she'd faced lately—if one could call near-strangulation by a stalker a "problem"—Cass was satisfied with her life in the mountain town.

The decision to move to Mason Valley had been the right one.

♦

Ryan removed his green scrubs, hung them on the bathroom hook, and stepped into the shower. As the warm water flowed over his tired body, he reflected on the day he'd just completed. He was tired but deeply satisfied, his inner self stimulated by a job he loved and believed he did well—even if the job was only for one day.

His friend Gregg was a doctor at a free clinic in Charlotte, and he routinely requested Ryan's assistance in treating patients there. Seeing Gregg's requests for what they were—an effort to coax Ryan back into practicing medicine—Ryan always refused. But this time, Gregg had sounded more urgent. It was Saturday,

normally a half day at the clinic, but Gregg had so many patients that appointments filled the schedule for the entire day.
Gregg and his partner couldn't possibly give that many patients
the attention they needed. Ryan had relented, agreed to help
him out, and drove in from Mason Valley early this morning.

Ryan stepped from the shower, dried off, and dressed in a
fresh set of clothes he'd brought with him. Since he was in Charlotte, there was another stop he wanted to make before driving
back home. Ryan dreaded facing the Rhineharts, but it was
something he had to do to face down another ghost.

Ryan thanked Gregg for the use of his shower, declined his
invitation to spend the night, and drove to the suburbs on the
northern side of Charlotte. He had borrowed his mother's car,
a late-model SUV, so it wouldn't stick out like his truck would
when parked in the Rhineharts' upscale neighborhood.

Two years ago, he'd left town immediately after Cheryl's fu-
neral. He'd sat in the last pew, avoiding all contact with Cheryl's
parents during the service. Once the service ended, he slipped
out of the church and out of town. They hadn't spoken since.

William Rhinehart had agreed to meet with Ryan today but
cautioned that Marilyn's anger toward Ryan hadn't abated even
a little bit. She still blamed him for their daughter's death.

Marilyn's anger was apparent when both she and William
answered the door. "What are you doing here?" she snapped.
Marilyn was the one who yanked the door open. Ready for a
fight, she was primed to slam the door in Ryan's face. Only William's hand on the door kept her from following through. "Haven't you caused enough pain? If you're here to ask for forgive-
ness for murdering our daughter, that's not going to happen."

"Marilyn, stop," William said. "I invited him over. Come in,
Ryan. We'll listen to what you have to say."

Ryan took a deep breath and stepped inside. This wasn't going to be easy. He hadn't expected a friendly meeting, but Mar-

ilyn was out to make this as hard as possible on him. Rubbing
salt into his wounds with hurtful accusations couldn't make him
feel any worse than he already did, but Marilyn's anger wouldn't
keep him from explaining what led to Cheryl's accident. That
was something he had to do for them and for himself.

Ryan followed William and Marilyn into the sitting room.

"You should be in jail!" Marilyn, her face twisted with pain
and anger, stalked to the sofa and sat down. William sat beside
her, with Ryan seated across from them. "Our lawyers are still
planning to sue you for Cheryl's death."

"Marilyn, that's not true." William patted her hand gently.
He shook his head sadly at her. "Our lawyers told you there isn't
a case. Ryan wasn't driving or even near the car. You know that.
You've got to accept facts. This hatred is eating you alive."

"I understand how you feel, Mrs. Rhinehart. I really do. I'm
deeply sorry for your loss." Ryan would take responsibility for
his actions prior to the accident, but Cheryl's parents needed to
know the part Cheryl had played in the accident.

"Get it all out in the open," Dr. B. had advised him.

"Cheryl and I broke up that night because I didn't want to
move to New York City and start my medical career over," Ryan
said. "I'm not a trained cardiologist, but she thought I could just
walk into a new practice and immediately become the star on
the surgical team. That's not how medicine works. She wouldn't
accept my explanation. She thought I was making excuses just
to get out of our engagement."

"We always thought you two had something special," William said, surprised. "Did you want out of the engagement?"

"Our fight started when I told her that I didn't want to
move to New York. She got angry. Truthfully, we hadn't been
seeing eye-to-eye for quite some time. She didn't understand
my responsibilities as a doctor and thought I could just call the
ER and say I was taking the day off if there was something she

wanted to do. At first, I tried to fit my schedule into hers, but in time, it became impossible. And soon, I didn't even try. Nothing I did pleased her."

"She seemed so happy when you announced the engagement," Marilyn objected. "She never mentioned any problems between the two of you. You're just trying to blame her now that she can't defend herself."

"That's not true. And yes, she was happy. I was too, at first. But then, she began planning our lives without consulting me. My mistake was in humoring her for as long as I did and not telling her how I really felt. That was cowardly, I know. I hoped she'd come to realize on her own that I wasn't the person she wanted."

"What happened that night?" William asked.

"Cheryl drank too much. When she couldn't convince me to change my mind about moving, she got angry. The angrier she got, the more she drank. I tried to stop her, but she never listened to anyone—especially me—if there was something she wanted to do. I asked her not to leave in her condition and said we'd talk the next morning. She refused. I regret that I wasn't able to convince her to stay, but I couldn't force her."

"Once Cheryl decided something, it was hard to change her mind. That part's on us," William said.

"Cheryl sped out of the driveway, and well, you know what happened next. Her injuries were severe. I tried my best to save her. But I failed. That will live with me for the rest of my life."

"I don't believe that! You went on with your life," Marilyn snapped, her voice making it a harsh accusation. "You moved on with your professional *and* personal life. You're probably married with children now. You're happy. Nothing changed for you. Our daughter is dead, and the finality of that is something I can't accept."

"I gave up practicing medicine that night." Ryan grimaced

at Marilyn's assumption. The hell he'd lived through the last two years could hardly be described as "going on with your life." "I loved practicing medicine, but I lost all desire to do it. I guess that was my penance for Cheryl's death. A personal life doesn't exist for me."

"I didn't know you gave up medicine…" Marilyn's voice was barely above a whisper.

"But now, you're starting to rethink that decision? Your penance is done?" William was very insightful, but he wasn't entirely right or entirely wrong. Ryan's feelings were more nuanced—or more confused.

"I'm taking responsibility for not breaking the engagement off sooner, but I'm also absolving myself of guilt over things that were beyond my control. Cheryl's behavior caused the accident. She drove recklessly, too fast, and under the influence. No doctor alive could have saved her. It's taken me a long time to accept that fact."

"Oh yes, I see. Blame the victim!" Marilyn's accusation stung, but Ryan had heard those words before—from himself. Marilyn only echoed thoughts he'd mulled over many times. As Doctor B. had pointed out, Cheryl had paid the highest price by losing her life; Ryan was alive, so it was easier to blame himself than his dead fiancée.

"Marilyn, please stop." William took her hand and squeezed it. "Ryan is not to blame for our daughter's death. You need to accept that something terrible happened and that Cheryl was at fault."

"I can't accept that she's gone. I just can't," Marilyn sobbed quietly, wiping her eyes with a crumpled-up tissue.

"You must." William put his arm around her and pulled her closer. "Your grief has you locked in a prison, much like Ryan. Both your lives are ticking away while you cling to what might have been. It's time for you both to move forward." William stood and held out his hand to Ryan. "Thank you for coming by, Ryan. I think getting this out into the open will do us all some good." He shook Ryan's hand, then turned to his wife. "Isn't that right, Marilyn?"

"Maybe." Marilyn's voice broke. "But I miss my daughter every day." She didn't stand up but sat with her hands clasped in her lap, staring blankly across the room. She avoided looking at William or Ryan.

"I'm sorry. If I could change the outcome of that night, I would." Ryan addressed Marilyn before following William out of the room.

"Thanks for coming by. I know it wasn't easy. Give Marilyn time. She's wrestling with her own guilt. She never denied Cheryl anything. She wants to blame you instead of admitting that we both spoiled Cheryl."

"I understand," Ryan said. "It's hard to judge your own behavior objectively. It's taken me two years to figure that out."

"Marilyn and I both are responsible for the way Cheryl grew up." William nodded, discovering the truth in his words. "I see that now. Cheryl's demands grew bigger and bigger as we became more financially successful. She was the center of our world and came to believe that her needs far outweighed everyone else's. We erred by never telling her any different." William shook Ryan's hand again. "I hope this will be a new beginning for all of us. Life goes on—maybe not the way we want it to, but it does go on. I wish nothing but the best for you, Ryan."

When Ryan reached his car, he sat for a moment, thinking. The meeting with Cheryl's parents had lifted a weight off of him. Facing them and "getting it all out" was two years late, but he'd give himself credit for meeting them today rather than focusing on any past shortcomings.

Ryan looked at his watch; it was after eight p.m. He'd promised Mike that he'd be back in time to perform at the Eagle's

Nest tonight, but he'd been up since four a.m. The emotional meeting with the Rhineharts had completely drained him, and he still faced a two-hour drive back to Mason Valley.

Before starting the car, Ryan texted Mike and Lanie to let them know he wouldn't be performing tonight. Lanie didn't need him. She was capable of entertaining the crowd all by herself. He just wanted to get home, open a cold beer, put his feet up, and watch a winter moon rise over the mountains.

♦

Jack picked Cass and Mandy up and drove them to the Eagle's Nest. Jack hadn't given up his job as one of Cass's protectors, even though her stalker was in jail. Or maybe the real reason Jack insisted on picking them up was Mandy. Jack didn't hide his pleasure when Cass told him that Mandy had accepted the job at Barrett Medical Center.

Raj had taken his own car tonight and would meet them at the bar and grill. Raj was another smitten man—smitten with Lanie. Apparently, Raj had something planned with Lanie after the bar closed and didn't want his sister tagging along.

As Cass climbed into the back seat, she looked at the empty seat beside her. She was disappointed Ryan wasn't there, but not surprised. Double-dating didn't sound like a "Ryan thing." "Is Ryan already at the Eagle's Nest?" Cass asked.

"I don't know," Jack said as he backed out of the driveway. "He went to Charlotte early this morning. He didn't say why he was going. But he's supposed to sing with Lanie later tonight."

"Charlotte?" Cass's mind began sifting through the possible reasons why Ryan might take an unscheduled trip to Charlotte. Was he ready to practice medicine again and was interviewing for a position? Or was he meeting an old flame? Cass didn't like either of those reasons. She was powerless if he was seeing an ex-girlfriend, but her recruitment effort to hire him as a doctor needed a more aggressive approach. Time was her enemy if someone was trying to poach her prospective candidate for the job.

As soon as they entered the Eagle's Nest and found a table, Cass began searching the room, looking for Ryan.

Mike approached their table. "He's not here," he said by way of greeting.

"Oh." Cass didn't deny who she was looking for.

"Ryan got delayed in Charlotte and won't be back until late tonight," Mike added.

Cass started to ask why Ryan went to Charlotte but held back her intrusive question.

"I'm guessing he's there on business." Apparently, Mike was a mind reader, too.

"You're guessing? So, you don't know for sure?"

"Cave Man doesn't venture down from his mountain lair unless it's for business." Mike started to walk away, then turned back. "Order some dinner, have a drink, relax, and enjoy the evening. Ryan will be home tomorrow. I'm guessing he'll miss seeing you the same way you're missing him."

"You're guessing again, so you don't know for sure?"

"I'm good at reading my little brother's hard head. Cave Man is evolving." Mike put his hand on her shoulder and shook it gently. "Enjoy yourself. Have patience. My brother will give up his nonsense eventually. And yes, that's also a guess."

Cass did relax, and she enjoyed the evening. She danced once with Jack—who didn't try any frenetic dance moves this time—and with a couple men she didn't know. But as she laughed and danced, Cass's thoughts were on Ryan and her conversation with Mike. He could read Ryan? Cass certainly couldn't read him. Ryan was complicated. Try as she might, she hadn't found a consistent way to lure him out of his sullen and brooding ways. But he had stopped insulting her as he did when they first met, so that was progress.

Mike hinted that Ryan was changing. Whether that was true or not, if she saw him tomorrow, she planned to give him her best sales pitch. She needed a doctor for the clinic, and Ryan was a natural fit for the job. The status of their relationship wouldn't change that.

CHAPTER TWENTY-FOUR

Rough terrain?" Cass muttered as she turned off the main road, entered the woods, and took the narrow, graded road that began at the base of Love Vine Mountain and wound upward. "A cattle trail would be easier to navigate than this road."

Mike had said Ryan was coming back from Charlotte last night. Since it was Sunday and still early, Cass was counting on finding him at home this morning.

Bare tree limbs overhung the mountain road and brushed the top of her car. A screen of dead vines and brush lined both sides of the road. The cold winds of winter had now descended over the region, turning the mountain into a muted version of itself from just a month ago.

Ryan wasn't kidding when he said she'd have a hard time finding him. But she had dressed appropriately for hiking over mountainous trails, if it came to that. Cecilia would have a case of the vapers if she even knew Cass had purchased her hiking boots, sweatshirt, and fleece-lined windbreaker at the Mason Valley Feed Store from right next to a display of hammers, saws, and ladders. But Cass still wore her designer jeans; a girl couldn't give up everything, and the denim was soft, comfy, and stretched into the perfect fit.

Cass's SUV crawled slowly upward along the twisting road. Steep and narrow, it was only wide enough in most places for one vehicle. *What's the protocol if I meet a car coming from the other direction?* Protocol be damned! Driving in reverse and tumbling down the mountainside wasn't on her agenda today.

Ryan's disappearance yesterday had created a new urgency in convincing him to take the open MD position at Barrett Medical Center. Plus, she just wanted to see him. Last night, she'd felt odd without Ryan at the table. She'd been a single amidst many happy couples. And she missed their usual repartee—or arguments, depending on how you looked at it—which she found stimulating and enjoyable.

Jack had given her directions to Ryan's home, the cabin he'd built after he moved back from Charlotte. He'd chosen the perfect spot to retreat and hide from the world. Secluded and with few homesteads, it could pass for an unsettled wilderness—the perfect place to avoid all interaction with society.

Cass passed a couple of log cabins before she came to one that fit the description Jack gave her. Ryan's truck was parked in front of the cabin, further confirming that this was his place. She pulled to a stop just off the gravel driveway. She spotted Ryan in front of the carport, ripping a sheet of plywood with a table saw. With his back turned and ear protectors deadening the sound, he hadn't heard Cass's arrival.

Cass climbed the slight incline to the yard. A basketball hoop was installed on a concrete pad in front of the carport, and a basketball lay near the edge of the yard—an open invitation for Cass to take a shot. Ryan hadn't believed her when she said she'd played varsity basketball in high school. Could she still make a three-pointer? Or would she embarrass herself and hit the chimney or the opposite side of the house? Proving Ryan wrong made it worth a try.

Cass picked up the basketball, aimed at the net, and launched the ball toward the hoop.

"And the crowd goes wild!" she yelled as the ball cleared the rim and swooshed through the net.

Startled, Ryan turned around, surprised to find Cass behind him. He frowned, shut off the saw, and removed his ear protectors. Unshaven and with his dark hair longish and uncombed, he looked as if he had just rolled out of bed. The blue plaid flannel shirt under a fleece-lined vest finished the portrait of a rugged mountain man—and a handsome one, too.

"What are you doing here?" Ryan scowled.

"Making you eat crow for laughing at me and not believing that I too experienced basketball glory."

"Well, you've impressed me, but why are you here? I don't believe that you came all the way up the mountain to bag a three-pointer."

"I'm chasing a medical doctor, remember?" Cass walked closer. "I heard one lives on this mountain. The story goes, he's very reclusive and can be extremely unfriendly at times. You remind me of him. Although, he usually looks a little more refined than you."

"Huh! Maybe you don't know him after all. Maybe he likes the unrefined look."

"Maybe. Both looks have their... uh, shall we say good points." Cass straightened the collar of Ryan's vest. She let her hand linger on his chest.

"Hmph! I see you've also availed yourself of the valley's haute couture."

"Nice look, don't you think?" Placing her hands on her hips, Cass twirled around. "I didn't know how far I'd have to go to catch my quarry. I'm dressed for a foot-chase, if necessary. I desperately need a doctor."

"Why? You don't look sick." A tiny smile pulled at the corners of Ryan's mouth as he replaced his ear protectors, turned on the saw again, and finished ripping the board.

Cass waited until he turned off the saw again. "What are you building?" she asked. She would postpone her sales pitch, but she'd only let it slide for a little while. She wouldn't leave the mountain without getting an answer.

"Come. I'll show you." Ryan picked up the board and led Cass around to the back of the cabin.

In a clearing behind the cabin was a row of cages holding birds, a squirrel, a fox, and a couple of rabbits. Most had bandaged wounds on various parts of their bodies. Ryan walked to the cage located on the far end of the row.

"These two are Mr. Gleason's latest finds. I'm running out of cages and need to make a two-room suite." Ryan pointed to a red-tailed hawk, its wing in a splint and bandaged; a mourning dove with a white bandage around its middle squatted in one corner. "A bullet broke the hawk's wing, and it looks like a bullet also grazed the dove's chest."

"They can't coexist in the same cage?"

"No. The dove isn't hurt as badly as the hawk. She's a pesky little thing and won't leave him alone. She flits around cooing, preening, picking at him, stealing his food, and being just plain annoying. She's a distraction to the poor guy. He can't rest because of her."

"'She'? How do you know it's a female?" Cass asked.

"She's smaller and has fewer markings than the males. Plus, she's very annoying. Gotta be a female. I've named her Cass." Ryan smiled.

Ryan named the dove Cass? And she was a distraction? The hawk couldn't rest because of her? Hmm. She'd just pick out the good parts of Ryan's statement and ignore the rest. "Huh!

She hasn't moved since we've been standing here. You may have meant that as an insult, but try again. You missed your mark. All I heard was that the dove is very sweet."

"I'd never insult you!" Ryan objected. "They both need rest and less distraction." Ryan opened the cage, slipped the divider inside, then attached it to the sides of the cage. "I'll move one of them to another cage once I can discharge a patient."

"Home-wrecker," Cass said. "They might be in love by then."

"Different species rarely find anything in common. But they do look cute together."

"My! My! There's hope for you yet, Dr. Scott. Who would've thought you're actually a romantic?" Cass turned and looked over Ryan's setup for treating wild animals and birds. "This place looks like a hospital ER. Ryan, you obviously still love medicine. Otherwise, you wouldn't be treating a menagerie of injured wildlife. Why don't you come and work at the clinic? We need you."

"Let's go inside, and I'll show you around—since you drove all this way," Ryan said, ignoring Cass's suggestion.

"It wasn't *that* far, but yes, I'd love to see what a hermit calls home."

Cass followed Ryan up onto the back porch and into the cabin's interior. *This hermit lives very comfortably*, Cass thought as she looked around the room. The interior walls were a mixture of wood paneling and painted Sheetrock. Nicely framed pictures of scenes around Mason Valley adorned the walls. The first room was a kitchen-and-living-room combination with a fireplace on the back wall. He had all the niceties of a home: electricity, running water, even TV reception.

"This is very nice," Cass said. "Electric lines run up here, too, I see."

"Yes, it's part of the rural electrification program, but I keep a generator just in case storms knock out the power. But there's no city water or sewer. I have my own well and septic tank."

Ryan led her through the rest of the cabin: a comfortably sized master bedroom with an ensuite bath, another bedroom, and a guest bath. The loft was an office and music room.

"My mother did the decorating," Ryan explained. "Left to me, it would be bare and more cave-like. I imagine that's what you expected."

"Something like that. Hermits don't usually live in luxury like this! Your mother did a nice job."

"She did. Having a father who owns a construction business and a mother who's an interior designer helps hermits avoid austerity."

"Are those Lanie's photographs on the wall?"

"Yes. She's good, don't you think?"

"They're beautiful." Cass stopped in front of a scenic view of Love Vine Mountain decked out in springtime finery. The redbuds and dogwood trees were in full bloom and covered the mountain with splotches of red and white on a background of green.

Ryan led Cass back to the kitchen and poured two glasses of sweet tea. "Let's take our drinks out to the side porch, and I'll show you the most incredible view you've ever seen."

Cass followed Ryan to the porch and sat down beside him in the swing. "Wow! Look at that! I can see for miles from here—the whole valley, as well as the town! This view really is incredible."

"I like it. It's very calm and peaceful. I missed all of this when I lived in Charlotte." Ryan's usual brooding expression was missing. He appeared relaxed and content. "It's my window on the world, even if this world is small." He began pushing the swing slowly back and forth.

"You know, you're not such a bear when you're in your own habitat," Cass said as she accepted a blanket Ryan pulled from a nearby chair and tucked around her legs. She wasn't cold since she was dressed appropriately for the mountain chill. Ryan's thoughtful gesture warmed her more than the blanket.

"I might be loosening up. Or wising up. Either way, I'm still a work in progress."

"Did your session with Dr. Blankenship help?"

Ryan turned toward her, leaned back, and frowned at her. "What? You've been spying on me?

"Yes! Of course! I was hiding in an alcove and drooling over your handsome body as you walked by. My plan was to grab you, pull you into the supply room, and… well, I hadn't planned what would happen beyond that. I hoped you would know the next step and take the lead." Cass shook her head and frowned at him. "Your question is a bit conceited, don't you think? You really think I've nothing more important to do than sneak around and spy on you? Just so you know, I get statistical reports showing our patient load and data on patient visits."

"Oh… well, for what it's worth, between your two scenarios, I prefer the first one." Ryan wagged his eyebrows at her. "But yes, Dr. B. was very helpful. She cleared up some things for me—things I basically knew but couldn't accept. My other therapist was more blunt and less gentle with my feelings."

"You have a second therapist?"

"My mother. She ordered me to straighten up and turn my life around. She threatened to kick my ass if I didn't do as she said."

"Thank you, Margaret! I'd listen if I were you. I don't think Margaret makes idle threats."

"She never has… that I'm aware of. When Momma speaks, we all listen."

"Does this mean you'll consider coming to work at the clinic? We don't have an alcove, so you'll be safe from me." Cass should probably wait until Ryan was further along in developing his new life plan, but waiting was not something she was good at. And she was under pressure to hire a doctor. And she wanted *him*. "Working at the clinic and serving the town and the people you obviously love will be good for you. It'll help you do as Margaret suggested."

"You don't give up, do you? Don't push me," Ryan said, but the gruffness often in his voice when she pushed him was missing.

"I have to push you. I *need* you!" Encouraged that he hadn't pushed *her* off the porch, Cass continued, "And if I don't badger and push, you'll be like one of your hawks and continue to perch up here on the mountain, hiding away from everyone. Hawk Man will never get back to doing what he should be doing: 'doctoring,' to quote Mr. Gleason." Cass paused for a breath, then pushed further. "Helping others is strong medicine."

"You're the bossiest woman I've ever met—except for my mother. But you're right… in this one matter. I do miss practicing medicine," Ryan admitted. "I went to Charlotte yesterday to assist a friend at a free clinic he runs."

"You did what? Wow! How did that feel?" So, that was the reason for his long day in Charlotte.

"It was a lot of sick people. Some patients acted as if they were bothering me by asking for help."

"Patients are often uncomfortable accepting help for free. But it's very gratifying to be the one with the skills to help them—and give them hope."

"Okay, I'll work for you. I do miss 'doctoring.' You'll never leave me alone, otherwise."

"You will? Oh, happy days! Thank you! Thank you!" Cass grabbed Ryan and hugged him. That he'd agreed so easily surprised her. The aggressive hard-sell closing argument she'd prepared wouldn't be needed. "What made you change your mind?"

"My talk with Dr. B. helped, but mostly, it was you," Ryan replied. "I watched you go to work every day, face your fears, even as Mitchell was terrorizing and threating you. Meanwhile, I handled my situation by running away. At the time, I believed that would help, but my nightmares followed me wherever I went. But you? You faced your danger head-on and even participated in Mitchell's capture."

"I don't know about all that. I boast that Philly girls don't cut and run, but I let the mobs run me out of Philadelphia. When Mitchell began stalking me, I still had a job to do. Plus, there weren't many places left to run. Most times, I was scared to my core." Cass shivered at the memory of black diamond markings on a glistening yellow body. "That bloody, dead rattlesnake scared me more than Mitchell's hands wrapped around my neck."

"But even that didn't stop you. You went right back to work. You're a very brave person."

"My mother would call me reckless, not brave."

"Apparently, your mother doesn't know the real you. She sees a delicate, helpless female that needs to be coddled and protected—preferably by a wealthy, effete, cold, and rigid Englishman."

"You're right about that! My mother doesn't know me if she thinks 'cold and rigid' is what I want in a man."

"I noticed. There's nothing cold or rigid about you," Ryan acknowledged. "But you *are* an exasperating, brash, barb-throwing, take-no-prisoners, bossy woman—who is also warm and caring behind your brashness."

"Did any of my barbs pierce that hard heart of yours?"

"Umm…maybe. But I'm anxious to see what you might come up with next," Ryan said. "I did something else while in Charlotte yesterday."

"Oh?"

"I visited Cheryl's parents." Ryan described his meeting with the Rhineharts. "Cheryl's mother still blames me, but William seemed to understand. Regardless of how Marilyn feels, I'm through blaming myself for things beyond my control."

"That was very courageous of you, facing Cheryl's mother's wrath."

"Not brave, but the right thing to do. I hope Marilyn eventually accepts the truth. Wallowing in self-pity is crippling. I know firsthand."

"It is." Cass didn't know the depth of Ryan's internal struggles over Cheryl's death, but she had witnessed his withdrawal from his family and his profession. "I'm anxious to open the clinic and begin accepting patients. With you and Mandy onboard, we can do that. I'm so happy, I might kiss you, Ryan— uh, Dr. Scott! I need to be professional since we'll be working together."

"Not professional all the time, I hope!" Ryan turned to Cass and pulled her into his arms. "Don't threaten me, then stop." He slowly bent toward her, touched her mouth lightly, then pulled back.

"What's stopping *you*?" Cass strained toward him, willing him to finish what he'd started.

"Didn't we discuss the value of anticipation?" Ryan ran his hands over her shoulders and down her back. His mouth gently skimmed the spot under her ear, along her jaw, then back to hover over her lips. He whispered, "Wait a bit, City Girl. Savor the moment."

"I don't want to wait." Cass wrapped her arms around his neck, pulling him even closer. "You brag a lot, Country Boy. Time to live up to your boast."

Ryan tipped her chin upward, and his lips closed over hers in a long, sweet kiss. When they broke apart, an unusual feeling throbbed through Cass's body. She finally knew what loving someone was all about: two people bound together by passion, acceptance of differences, and a commitment to each other through good times and bad.

"Kiss me again?" she asked tentatively as she searched Ryan's face for any sign that he shared her feelings.

An answering light, much deeper and stronger than fleeting desire, shone in the depths of Ryan's blue eyes as he smiled at her. "That's a pretty timid request for someone who's bossed me around for months now," he said softly. "Surely, you can do better than that."

"Let me show you!" Cass locked her hands behind Ryan's neck. She kissed him the way she'd only imagined before while watching her favorite romantic movies, and picturing herself and Ryan in the starring roles. *Sorry, Newman, move over! Real life is so much better than the movies!*

When they broke apart again, Cass asked, "Does this mean you've turned a page?" She referenced the song he'd recently composed. Their relationship had changed, whether Ryan was ready to say it out loud or not.

"You turn all my pages, Cass Jordan—the whole book." Ryan tightened his arms around her, kissed her forehead, and straightened the blanket over them. "My story has taken a giant leap forward. I'm in love with you, City Girl."

"Good to hear, Country Boy! I'm in love with you, too." Cass sighed happily and snuggled deeper into Ryan's arms. *This* was where she belonged.

Life's turns and twist never failed to amaze. Adversity was often the first step toward good fortune. Cass Jordan, a city girl, hit rock-bottom and was forced to flee to a small town hidden in the mountains of North Carolina. By a stroke of luck, she met a country boy—someone she'd unknowingly waited for all her life as she continually discarded her mother's handpicked suitors one right after the other. The city girl and the country boy saved each other while also learning what it meant to truly love someone.

As Cass gazed into Ryan's blue eyes, a new light shone in their depths. Sadness was replaced by interest and curiosity about things outside his own head. The haunting images that had plagued him for the last two years were finally moving to where they belonged: the past.

As their relationship grew stronger and they built a life together, Cass would no doubt push, prod, badger, and generally annoy Ryan. That was her nature. And no doubt, Ryan would push back firmly whenever he disagreed with her. But rather than dreading the expected confrontations with Ryan, the prospect filled Cass with excitement.

Making up with Hawk Man would be incredible!